The
Last Vampire

by
Joe Black

To Auntie Kay,
We always enjoy having
you down on the farm! I'm
so glad you enjoyed this
book! ♡ Joe Black

The Last Vampire

by Joe Black

ISBN-13: 978-1729602782
ISBN-10: 1729602789

Disclaimer

The Last Vampire is a work of fiction. Although parts of the book may have been inspired by real-life events.

Acknowledgments

I would like to thank Terrill Boers for her support in life! You're the kindest and most loving person I know. Love you, Mom!

I would like to thank Molly Brog for her countless hours of hard work editing this book and making it the best it could be! You're a wonderful person that I will never forget.

I would like to thank Liz Cram for her help and hard work reviewing and editing this book! You're an inspiration to all of those around you!

I would like to thank Lauren Turpen for her never-ending ability to bring out the best in those around her. I owe many of my first starts in my careers to you! Love you, Aunt Lauren, aka "My favorite aunt".

I would like to thank Nadine Cram. She has put hours of work and has helped me very much in the editing and polishing of this book. Thanks love!

The Last Vampire

Chapter 1

In Seattle, it rains nine months of the year, or so they say. It seems that way when you live here. The frequent rain spells encourage people to take advantage of good weather when it finally arrives. A fact that is all too clear when hordes of people flood the streets coming out from their various hiding places as the sun finally breaks through the clouds. In the Emerald City, you never know when the weather will cooperate.

Few people know why Seattle was named after a story about munchkins and a wicked witch. To be named after a legendary tale such as the Wizard of Oz almost gives the city a magical impression. Seattle's resemblance to the city of OZ might be due to the numerous evergreens that glow a brilliant green on a bright sunny day. At times it is a magnificent region in which to live, especially in summer.

Tonight is not so beautiful though it is mid-May and a typical Northwest late night. The dark cloudy sky lurks above as street lights illuminate the trace amounts of drizzle that dance and swirl in the gentle breeze.

From the hilltop street in front of Bill's Bar and Grill, you can see the brilliant, almost mysterious luminescence of the lights of the city only a short distance away. The Space Needle stands tall and proud in clear view of the bar, a remnant from the 1962 World's Fair. One of the L's in Bill's neon sign went out last fall, and Bill has shown no indication of fixing it. Bill doesn't seem to care too much about the fact that his bar is falling into disrepair, or perhaps he does not have the cash to repair it.

The sign is not the only evidence the establishment has seen better times. The old, bare, wood siding does not look like it has seen new paint in ages. Although it gives the bar a rundown look, it also gives it some rustic personality. Most patrons like the rough rural appearance of this old tavern that acts as a quick retreat, as if it were somewhere deep in the country despite its suburb location.

Inside you will see the typical setting that you find in most pubs. Several flat screen TVs hang from key locations on the old walls, while a pungent odor of aged cedar fills the air. It is impossible not to notice the pool tables that sit in the far corner, guarded by a few electronic dart boards.

Bill's is dimly lit, mostly because Bill changed all the overhead lights to the lowest wattage he could find, he thought it might save on his electric bill. Red glass shaded pendant lights hang from the ceiling and dangle in each of the sitting booths.

The glow is offering just enough light to provide a cozy place to have an intimate conversation with someone who might be sitting across the table in the back to back bench style seating. It is getting late, and only three people remain in the bar. Tom is one of them. He is the bartender, Bill's son-in-law. Tom is in his early 40s and has a large belly draped with a dirty apron.

He started to gray early in life, and his salt and pepper, slicked back hair attest to that fact. The barkeep hasn't shaved in two days, and his stubble stands out on his light skin. Surprisingly enough he did not know how to make many drinks when he got the job. Everyone who knows him figured out he only got the job because of nepotism. He works hard, however, and is now getting much better at making drinks after two years of employment. His favorite drink to make is a Shirley Temple, which he finds a little embarrassing because it is not a manly drink.

A lone man in a dark brown hooded jacket, sits in one of the faintly lit booths with his hood down. He faces the bar with a glass in his hand that only has ice left in it. He peers up from time to time, and what distinguishes this shadowy figure from others is the fact that his eyes seem to glow in the dim gloom of the booth.

A striking, beautiful young woman with light brown hair and golden highlights is at the bar. She is wearing a dark, long jacket that would hang just above the floor if she were standing. Tom has tried on several occasions to strike up a conversation with her, but she isn't much for talking, so he leaves her to her full glass. A suitor had bought her the drink several hours before, but she still has not taken more than a sip from it as far as Tom can tell. She talked to the young, handsome man who bought it for her for about thirty minutes, but he had left an hour ago, disappointed.

Although she is a regular, she never does seem to drink much, so Tom sometimes wonders why she even comes in the first place. He does not mind though. Bartenders usually like having someone as attractive as her in his bar. She draws a crowd and men buy her drinks often.

The flat screen TV directly over the bar gives anyone sitting in the stools a great view of whatever game or broadcast that might be on. At this time of night, Tom prefers the news. The broadcaster is reporting on a local rapist who is terrorizing the city, and police seem to be clueless having no suspects.

Tom cleans glasses and gets the bar ready to close. He is halfway listening to the broadcast when he glances over and notices the attractive woman staring at her glass in deep contemplation. With as much time as he has spent in the bar, he can tell when someone is thirsty. He is a little confused because she looks thirsty, but appears to have little interest in her drink.

"Roslyn, is everything ok?" Tom asks, half expecting she will probably not respond.

She surprises him with a brief reply, "Yes, Tom, thank you." She flashes her dazzling smile in his direction.

It has been a long time since a woman that beautiful has smiled at him. He can not deny the fact it makes him feel warm inside. He can not help the feeling that he has inside, despite the fact he would never cheat on his wife and never has, even though he has had several opportunities.

"Can I call a cab for you?" he asks still a little shocked she answered, but encouraged at the same time.

"No thank you," she says in her sweet, tender, soft voice.

She almost looks like an angel sitting there, Tom thinks.

Her fair skin seems almost to be glowing.

"Are you sure? It's not safe these days," Tom insists.

"Yes, I'm sure. You're very thoughtful." She looks up from her glass with a smile that is so beautiful it nearly takes Tom's breath away. "I'll be fine. I do have to go now." She begins gathering herself.

"Have a great night, and thanks for coming in." Tom sheepishly waves with his towel still in his hand.

She half grins again and stands up from the bar, leaving her drink nearly untouched, and gracefully walks to the door opening it. After a short step, she pauses, looks up, notices the drizzle still dancing in the orange glow of the bright streetlights. She pulls her hood over her head and proceeds out the door. The lone man, as if awakened from a stupor, suddenly and without a word walks to the bar, pays his bill in cash, and hurries out the door also pulling his hood over his head.

Roslyn heads down the hill in the direction of the city. The world's fair with its brilliant lights fill the night sky with a faint mystical aura over the city. When Roslyn reaches the street corner, she stops and casually hits the crosswalk button with her fist and waits, turning her body slightly.

The movement is enough that she notices the man in the hood from the bar coming the same way she has. He is still a few hundred feet behind and walking unceremoniously towards the street corner where she is currently standing. The light changes and the well-recognized and slightly annoying audible signal to walk chirps, piercing the silence, letting anyone in the area know it is safe to cross the road.

Slightly startled, Roslyn quickly begins to cross the street trying to avoid the urge to look over her shoulder at the man who is getting closer. Once across the road, she notices the "walk" sign changes to "don't walk" and the man is still on the other side of the street. She lets out a sigh of relief as she notices he is not crossing after her and continues her path towards downtown. The man's now walking parallel with her on the other side of the street, peering from under his dark hood in her direction from time to time.

Roslyn increases her speed, trying to put some distance between her and the ominous man, but with each increase in her pace, he matches his pace to hers. She notices a sign up ahead that reads "Green Lake Park." The sign also has a map of the lake. The warning on the sign jumps out at her, "Stay on the Path." She can not help but think that this is good advice, she knows the park well and enters quickly in the hopes of eluding her sinister pursuer.

She glances behind her, noticing the shadowy figure of the man crossing the street towards the park and her. A startle reflex prompts her to run! She rationalizes the park has many dark walkways that are familiar to her and perfect for her escape.

From the entrance of the park, even in the dark, she can vaguely make out the wandering dark asphalt pathways encircling the small lake. The only real light in the area on a night like this comes from the streetlights bordering the beautifully manicured park. The eerie shadows of the rows of park trees jostle hauntingly.

Roslyn begins to have second thoughts. It might have been the worst place to go because she has heard there are lots of assaults that occur in the parks at night. Her loud, hard-soled shoes pound the asphalt track making her sound like a team of horses galloping as she speeds down the path, not bothering to look over her shoulder again.

She darts behind a large hedge and peers from the shadows, scanning for her stalker. Moments seem like hours as she impatiently waits for him to pass by but there is no trace of the shady man to be seen. After a couple of minutes, she creeps out from behind the hedge and gingerly begins to walk back the way she had come, looking over her shoulder as she does.

She pulls out an old, gold locket from around her neck and kisses it, a habit that she has gotten into since the man she loved gave it to her. It has always given her strength in stressful situations. She unconsciously releases the locket when a sudden noise comes from a nearby wood dock, causing her to jump. In the dim light, the dock appears to hover on the dark water. The locket dangles freely from her neck. Her nerves settle a little when she realizes it is only a tabby cat when it races past her, obviously more scared than she is. Clutching her chest, she continues again on her way.

"Where're you going?" A deep man's voice emanates from the shadows.

She jumps again and looks in the direction of the voice, but sees no one. She seems paralyzed with fear because she does not answer immediately.

"Where're you going?" the voice asks again, this time more aggressively.

"What do you want?" her voice trembles.

"I just want to know where you're going," the voice has an eerie tone.

A male leaves the shadows, slowly and cautiously like a giant spider moving in on a fly. The gloom of the street lights reveals it is the male from the bar. He is tall with slender shoulders and big hands that almost seem to slowly reach for her like the legs of a large arachnid. His light blue eyes appear to almost glow from his sunken narrow face as they linger under his dark hood. He has faded grey jeans and black, lace-up boots that give the impression that he might be ex-military.

"I don't see how that is any of your business," she replies, stepping away from him.

"Oh, don't be like that," he says sharply.

"Leave me alone." She begins to back away but does not take her eyes off him.

"Where do you think you're going?" He quickly pursues her, reaching out for her again with his spider-like hands.

She starts to run but is quickly stopped in her tracks when he grabs her shoulder from behind and turns her back around. Although he is slender, he is much larger than she is.

"I said leave me alone!" she yells.

He smirks with a light in his eyes that looks like dancing fire. "I don't think so, beautiful," his voice has a terrifying cackle.

Out of impulse and with a sudden burst of courage, she kicks him in the groin, causing the tall, sinister man to double over and fall to the ground with a painful groan. She stands above him triumphantly.

Suddenly, she regains her senses and is aware of the impending danger, so she bolts for the park entrance. The man looks up from the ground, still clutching his throbbing groin. He forces himself onto his feet despite the crippling pain. He hobbles after her and strains to a full sprint, fearing her escape. She can see the glow of the street lights ahead of her; freedom is near! She is almost out of the park when he grabs a handful of her hair; he has a hold of his fly. Her head whips back with violent force. Off balance, she turns to fight when he grabs her by the throat and pushes her up against a large tree.

"Please, stop!" she pleads despite the firm grip on her throat.

He cackles and rips opened her long overcoat with his free hand. As he begins to look her over he can not help but notice the old gold locket hanging just above her cleavage. He shows little interest in it; he has what he really wants. He can feel her firm, cool skin under his large hand which clutches her throat. He reaches down to the bottom of her skirt and violently pulls it up to her waist, she feebly kicks and struggles. Both her hands work frantically on his slender hand to free herself from the death grip now pinching off most of her air supply.

"Please . . . stop!" she pleads.

He notices her brilliant, blue eyes sparkling from the distant glow of the street lights like a couple of deep blue sapphires; they have a gem-like quality. He notices the unusual facets in the color of her eyes. It is something he has never seen before. The unusual appearance is very stunning. Her beauty only seems to encourage him.

He viciously rips her panties off and starts to unbuckle his pants. "You girls make it too easy.

What were you thinking coming into the park at night," he sneers.

He pulls out his male member and moves into position when she starts to laugh, her gem-like eyes twinkling sharply.

Shocked by her unusual behavior, he stops short of this goal. "What's so funny," he demands, squeezing her throat even tighter.

"Besides the fact you have the smallest penis I've ever seen?" she says boldly.

Curiosity changes to rage as his eyes fill with hate. "I was going to have a little fun with you. Now when I'm finished with you," his eyes harden, "I'm going to kill you, bitch!" The fire in his eyes burns brighter than ever.

She only laughs louder, which only enrages him further.

"You're dead, bitch!" he yells.

Suddenly, a sharp pain shoots through the man's hand like a bolt of lightning. The pain is so intense it instantly brings the black-hearted man to his knees. His hand once wrapped around the woman's throat is now clutched tightly in her small, solid hand. She is crushing the bones in his hand merely by squeezing it with hers.

"What the fuck?" he screams in tremendous pain and complete disbelief.

He watches as in the dim light; her eyes change from a brilliant blue to a ruby red! Her canine teeth protrude from her striking red lips like short daggers.

"What the hell are you?" he yells in absolute horror.

"Evildoers always taste better," she says in a powerful, terrifying voice as she attacks him.

She bites him on the neck and quickly drains his blood. His face turns to a sickly white as the life drains from his body. His eyes turn filmy, and his once strong body goes limp. In little time, the dark, dreadful man is no more.

Chapter 2

Later that morning, a few short miles away at the Bellevue branch of Children's Hospital, Dr. Michael Bauer is busy making his morning rounds. Michael finished his residency only three years ago and is very happy to be officially starting his practice. He never liked being supervised to do a job he felt he was born to do. He loves helping people get better, especially children. It is probably partially due to an intense need to feel in control.

When he was a child, he helplessly watched as his mother nearly died from a severe case of pneumonia. He can not forget the powerless feeling he had as he watched her lie in bed spiraling towards a slow and painful death. The quick response from a talented doctor saved her life and made a considerable impression on the young Michael Bauer. He felt like it was like magic how the doctor kept her from death's door.

The near loss of the only woman he loved in his life changed him forever. A never-ending fear of death haunted him from that day on. He has never run from a fight; he is determined to learn everything he could to defeat death itself. Unable to shake the powerless feelings he had felt back then, he has vowed not to feel that way again.

Now a full-grown man, he is taller than most of his colleagues. Nearly six foot two with a muscular build, dark neatly trimmed hair, and dreamy blue eyes. Most women find him very attractive, but they also have little tolerance for the heavy work schedule that consumes most of his time. He has been out to coffee with a couple of women recently but has not been on what he would call a real date since college.

He is constantly trying to convince himself it does not matter. He feels he should occupy his thoughts with more important matters, like saving lives. At least that is what he tells himself. He finds it much harder to sell himself on that story late at night when he comes home to an empty house and an empty bed. He misses the soft touch of a beautiful woman. Something at this point, he has almost forgotten, it has been so long.

For the most part, he does not have the time to think about the luxury of having a significant other. He drowns out those thoughts during the day by staying focused on taking care of his patients.

Michael grew up in the small town of Fall City in Washington. When he moved there with his parents at age seven, the largest and only real store in the town was an IGA. The small town seemed to suit him just fine. Even in his young mind he had felt crowded in the city in which he grew up. He felt much better in the calm, open air of a rural town. He can remember observing the immensity of the vast fields and trees as far as the eye could see.

His father was an electrician, and his mother was a stay at home mom, who would be waiting for his younger brother and him every day when the school bus dropped them a quarter mile from their home. On five acres, officially, they did not live on a farm, but it seemed like it at times. They had chickens, ducks, rabbits, hamsters, a cockatiel, two dogs, two cats, and even a mischievous ferret.

Michael had always been shy but bright and a bit of an athlete. In middle school, he joined the wrestling and track teams where he quickly became a fierce competitor. He was a late bloomer and was bullied often until his wrestling skills got so good he embarrassed Chad Cooper when he pinned Chad to the ground in various submission holds the day Chad decided he wanted to pick a fight. The bullies left him alone after that.

Michael was never on the chess team, but he liked to play from time to time. He realized he was decent at the game when he beat Zach Nelson, who placed third in the state championship that year. During his junior and senior years, he was a League and Regional wrestling champion and captain of the team. After high school, he went to community college for two years where he met his best friend, Matt Richardson. After that, he went on to the University of Washington to finish his Bachelor's degree, where he continued and also got his medical degree.

As he now walks down the warm orange and white painted halls of the hospital, it is difficult to ignore the colorful flowers and birds painted on the white sections of the walls. He thinks they clutter the walls but tolerates them because the kids seem to like them so much. He walks into Natalie's room to find her sitting up, almost as if she is anticipating his arrival, which she not so secretly is.

The moment she sees him, she can not help but grin. Natalie is an 11-year-old girl with stage two leukemia and on an aggressive treatment plan. She is pale and has already lost her hair from the chemo treatments, but her eyes now sparkle as Dr. Bauer approaches her bed.

"How are you feeling today Natalie?" he asks, with his charming smile while lowering his clipboard to his side.

"Wonderful . . . Michael!" she says with a childish giggle.

It is clear she has a little crush on the doctor.

"Natalie!" he replies with a slight authoritative tone and playful tilt of his head.

"I'm sorry, Dr. Bauer," she corrects herself.

He continues, "Your white blood cell count is looking better. I think the treatment is working." His eyes are caring.

"Does this mean I can go home soon?!" Her grin broadens even more.

"I hope so." His face is warm. "We need a little more time to make sure we have things under better control. You'll be home before you know it!" He pats her on her smooth bald head.

"Do you have a magic trick for me today?" she asks with excitement!

"What makes you think I have a trick ready for you?" he asks playfully.

"You always have a magic trick!" She claps her hands in anticipation.

Gladly he reaches beside her head and pulls a small silk handkerchief from behind her ear, apparently from thin air. She squeals with excitement! He had learned a few tricks in college because he thought it would be an excellent way to impress the ladies. He was a little wilder in his college years but, has given up his reckless ways for more important pursuits. After all, he is a respectable doctor now.

"Nothing on this side!" He shows her both sides of the silk hankie carefully demonstrating that there is nothing on either side. He then carefully places the silk over his empty hand, pauses, then waives his other hand over the handkerchief. Quickly he reaches under the silk and pulls out a small yellow flower, her favorite color which he discovered a month prior!

"Is that for me?!" she squeals again with excitement.

"Yes, it's for you," he says handing her the tiny delicate flower. He is out of time and has to see to his other patients, so he turns headed for the door.

"Thanks, Dr. Bauer," she says, clearly disappointed their visit is ending.

"I'll be back to check on you soon." He looks over his shoulder, winks, and walks out the door.

Chapter 3

Back in Green Lake Park, the police have barrier tape surrounding a third of the park, the taped off area is quite significant. Detective Dexter Burton heads the investigation and is on the scene. He is straightforward and by the book and does not like anyone disturbing his crime scene. He crouches over the body, grimly taking in every detail.

The body lays face up, and a frozen look of horror is on his cold, grey face. The stiff body of the tall man lays on the neatly cut grass beside a large tree like a toppled over statue. Dexter's dark brown eyes scan the area looking for clues that will tell him what happened last night.

Now in his early thirties, Dexter is a bald, black man who stands about five nine and was once a high school track star. Even back then, he had a dedicated, disciplined, and unrelenting personality. He used these traits to achieve his goal of being the fastest person in the state, which for a while he was. Dexter joined the force just after graduating from Western University and quickly excelled at his job.

He made detective in just six years which was unheard of in his department. Now a seasoned detective he rarely missed a clue. As Dexter carefully leans over the body, he also is mindful not to soil his new, dark grey suit. The investigation has just started, but he is not confident he will come up with any witnesses or anyone who might have been in the park at that time of night.

He can see the man's left hand has been crumpled like a tin can. Most of the bones are broken. Other than that, there is no clear sign of other injuries. It is unclear to the detective what the cause of death was at this point. Dexter's partner, Ben Sutton, walks up to Dexter staring into a small electronic pad in his left hand.

"We identified our John Doe as Carl Dunn," Ben begins. "He was a suspect in several crimes including possession of a controlled substance, breaking and entering, kidnapping, and rape."

Ben is a young, plump man recently promoted to detective. He has short, dark hair and is slightly taller than Dexter and outweighs him by more than a hundred pounds, probably because of his steady diet of fast food and doughnuts.

"Looks like he finally got a taste of his own medicine," Dexter says bleakly, not genuinely feeling he received justice.

"What the heck happened here?" Ben finally takes his eyes off the pad and gives his partner his full attention.

Dexter glances at Ben for a moment, and Ben can clearly see the wheels turning in Dexter's head. Dexter looks back at the corpse.

"I'm still working on it," Dexter replies, rubbing his chin.

The corpse still has his pants around his waist, and his male member is exposed.

"Is this a masturbation gone wrong?" Ben asks curiously. One of his many attempts at humor.

"Definitely not." Dexter points to the ripped panties on the ground. "It looks like he had a victim."

"Where is she?"

"I don't know. We will have to do a DNA test on the garment to see if we get a match."

Ben did not seem enthusiastic. "Fat chance of that."

Dexter looked closer at the body. "Something isn't right this time."

"Like what?" Ben inquires, truly interested in Dexter's thoughts.

"How was his hand crushed like this? It would take a vice or some machine to do something like this."

"Maybe someone used a hammer?"

Dexter winces. "I don't think so. Look at his hand." Dexter takes out a pen so as not to touch the body and points to the hand.

"There are no marks and the skin isn't broken. Something squeezed his hand so hard that it broke most of the bones, and yet the force was applied soft enough as not to damage the skin. Dexter points out the spots where there should be damage to the skin but there was none. Whatever did this, wasn't made of metal or anything that has a hard surface. This wasn't done with blunt force, but by brute strength. It is almost like we are looking for a man with incredible grip strength. But I'm pretty sure even bodybuilders would have a hard time doing this." Then Dexter notices, something on the victim.

He leans in closer to get a better look but is careful not to touch the body or disturb anything. Two small puncture wounds are barely noticeable, and make him wonder, he appears to have a sudden bought of acknowledgment and Ben notices.

"What is it?" Ben asks.

"Too early to tell, but I'm curious to see what we get back from the toxicology report."

"Do you think he was high and O.D.ed?"

Dexter stands and gives the body some room; he looks a little nervous. "No."

"Then what is going on here?" Ben is getting a little frustrated.

"That information is given out on a need to know basis."

Ben is confused. "Don't I need to know. I'm part of this case."

Dexter did not say a word and walks away leaving Ben to his frustration.

Chapter 4

A few nights later, close to 1st Avenue in downtown Seattle, a grey BMW pulls up to a corner where several prostitutes are waiting. Probably the busiest and most fought over spot by the ladies of negotiable affections. The tinted passenger window of the Beemer slowly rolls down as the women all huddle around the car, jockeying for position. All of them want this John because driving up in a new BMW typically means a good pay off.

A host of scantily clad women simultaneously call out to the driver of the car when a deep, dominant voice emerges from the vehicle.

"I'm in the mood for a redhead tonight, ladies," the powerful Scandinavian accent dictates.

Instantly, most of the women move away from the car as there is one redhead that stands out from the rest. It is apparent to the entire group who he probably wants. A stunning redhead in a short, black, one-piece low cleavage dress that opens in the back stands with a coy smile as the crowd parts.

The rest of the group walks away in disappointment. The passenger door opens as the striking redhead walks to the car. She bends over in a practiced seductive manner and gazes through the open door.

"What can I do for you, sugar?" she questions flashing her most experienced smirk.

The angle of the light makes it is difficult to see the man's face clearly. He seems to be nothing more than a sizable disembodied shadow. He leans forward just enough for his face to finally catch the edge of the streetlight as it enters his vehicle. He is a very hefty, attractive man. He is very fit and muscular with shoulder-length light, blond hair. Even sitting down, he looks tall.

"Get in," the handsome man says, with the hint of a command that prompts her to move quickly.

She gets into the car, closing the door behind her and she can tell he seems pleased by her presence. His flawless teeth appear white even against his light skin. He revs the engine and speeds off into the night.

"So where are we going honey," she asks sweetly.

"You'll see," he replies.

She is feeling a little uneasy; this is always the most dangerous part of her occupation. She does not know this man or what he will do with her.

A few minutes later, they pull into the Hilton Hotel and drive down into the underground parking garage. The blonde man pulls into one of the stalls and parks the expensive car. Like a true gentleman, he escorts the redhead from the car to the elevator, where he pushes the button. She starts to feel a little more comfortable now that they are at the hotel, this is more like her regular routine.

She pulls out her pocket mirror and lipstick and proceeds to apply more as they anticipate the arrival of the elevator. The elevator chimes, and the doors open and the pair can see themselves in the mirrors in the back of the elevator. She puts her makeup back in her purse. The couple enters, and he pushes the button to one of the top floors. She looks him up and down as he stands boldly waiting to get to their level.

She wonders why he needs a professional like herself. He must have women fighting over him because he is so attractive. She figures he must be married and does not want his wife to know about his little deviance. She does not notice a wedding ring, however.

They arrive at his floor, and the doors open once again. He takes her hand, which is small compared to his, and heads for a door down the hall. She can feel the incredible strength in his hand and arm; it is like nothing she has ever felt before.

She has seen and been with lots of men, but she can already tell there is something different about this one. He is almost too perfect. When they get to his door, he uses his keycard to open it and ushers her in.

The lights are already on and illuminate the stylish room. The suite is composed of several small rooms which give it more of an apartment feel than a hotel room. An oversized business desk with dark wood grain finish sits alone in the corner of the living room area. She catches a glimpse through the open door of the king-sized bed with white satin sheets resting in the middle of the adjacent room.

She is impressed with all the space and accouterments. It has a living room area, kitchenette, large open area in the middle and the large bedroom. The crown molding and decorations of the suite give it an almost royal experience. Most of the rooms appear used except the kitchenette and bedroom. Beautiful paintings decorate the various plush halls and areas in the unit.

"Would you like something to drink?" he asks, motioning to the variety of alcohols on display in the small but elegant full-sized bar against the wall.

It is a lovely suite, much more beautiful than she typically frequents. "Ah . . . yeah, sure," she says, a little taken aback and surprised by the gesture. *I'm a sure thing, no need to woo me*, she thinks.

He has waited long enough, as far as he is concerned, so without waiting any longer, he pours her a glass of red wine and hands it to her. She takes it and sits down on the vast, comfortable couch in the living room. His straight, shoulder-length blonde hair shimmers in the light of the room

She notices when their eyes meet, that his dark, green eyes glisten like a pair of emeralds. *They're beautiful, very captivating,* she thinks. *This guy's wife is not going to be happy if she finds out about this.*

He picks up another bottle that looks like a bottle of dark crimson wine. He pours himself a glass of the deep, red liquid in a crystal glass. She notices it seems a little strange, but then again, she is not too familiar with wine. He takes his drink and holds it up to hers. She gently touches the rim of her glass to his. A beautiful tone rings between the expensive crystal glasses.

"Cheers," they say in unison before they drink.

He never takes his eyes off her while he takes his long, deep drink, she has to shake off a creepy feeling. Most people as she recalls sip wine, he nearly finishes the entire glass in one lengthy, slow gulp. He sets his drink down on the oval glass coffee table in front of the couch, and he reaches for her hand. She does not doubt as to what he wants next. She has been in similar situations many times before. She takes his hand, sets her drink on the table, and he pulls her to her feet. He leads her down the long open area towards the bedroom.

The area between rooms is very sizable and expansive. Once in the bedroom she walks over to the king-sized bed and poses seductively for a moment, trying to excite him. Not that she needs to at this point, but it makes her feel like she is doing her job. She carefully reaches behind her neck and slowly begins to pull on the drawstring of her short dress methodically. He watches her every movement, his green eyes sparkle. She can tell this pleases him and continues her meticulous task, pulling the string with her long, slender fingers.

She flashes a demure grin in his direction as the top of the dress comes undone and falls to her waist revealing her voluptuous breasts. He takes off his expensive black suit jacket and begins to unbutton his shirt.

As he opens the garment she is amazed at how flawless his chest and abdomen appear, he obviously works out often. His muscles are round and bulging. She can see trace amounts of hair scattered on his chiseled chest. He pulls his shirt completely off, and she finds it difficult not to show her apparent attraction to him.

She did not feel attracted to most of the men she was with, but this guy is fantastic! She resists showing her attraction or even admitting it to herself. She has a strict rule which governs her behavior. On the rare occasion that she is attracted to a client, her self-preservation instincts kick in. She believes that it is not in her best interest to fall for the men she encounters. They will leave in less than an hour, and she refuses to allow her heart to go through the torment of continually being broken.

She works her dress off and is completely naked. She positions herself on the center of the cozy bed. Her smooth, fair skin seems to shine. He is unmistakably pleased and continues to watch her as he removes his slacks. It seems to her he is resisting the urge to pounce on her right away.

Now that he is naked, she watches his firm muscles ripple as he begins to crawl towards her on all fours like a lion moving in on its prey. He positions himself over her as she leans back onto the still tightly-made bed. He kisses her soft, full red lips. She knows she is going to enjoy this encounter for once as the anticipation continues to grow.

Moments pass as they wrap their arms around each other and continue to kiss each other passionately. He thrusts himself inside her, and she is ready. She is right; she is enjoying this, more than she thought she would. She can not help but wish all her encounters were like this one.

They continue to move together in a rhythmic manner that makes them moan with pleasure! Moments of complete bliss pass and she tries to hold back, but she can not stop herself, she begins to climax! He immediately moves his mouth to her neck where she feels him kissing her. For a moment, she thinks he might have bitten her, but is not sure. She is helplessly caught in the moment like a fish in a net, and it is so good she can not think about anything else.

He begins to inflict an even deeper pressure on her neck, and now she is sure he is biting her. It does not hurt; however, the sensation is pleasant in a strange way. Her head swims in the ecstasy of the moment, and she can feel her strength to resist in any way leave her body and mind. She finds it more and more difficult to concentrate. It almost feels like she is now entering a dark tunnel, her strength is leaving her body.

What's happening to me? This has never happened before, she ponders.

She can feel the darkness closing in around her, and the light at the end of the tunnel is getting smaller. Finally, the darkness completely engulfs her, and she knows no more. The man lifts his lips from her neck as the last drops of her sweet, dark blood drip from his lips. He gazes down at the beautiful woman who is now pale, her body now void of blood. Her open eyes look hazy and lifeless. He can taste the fresh, pleasant endorphins in her blood that have been generated by their passion. It makes her blood the most tantalizing and delicious of desserts.

This moment is one he loves most, the rush of life and strength filling his veins. He is a cold-blooded monster, who enjoys the moment of the kill. During their passion, his eyes turned to a ruby red and remain so. His eyes now caress her as he looks up and down her lifeless, pale face.

The thrill, excitement, and power are what he lives for. Her life energy is coursing through his ancient body like electricity. Then he notices it, slowly something strange starts to demand his attention. He continues to gaze at his lifeless victim as he contemplates the sensation. He can not place it, but something is happening, something is not right.

The sensation continues to grow as does his concern. He leaves her lifeless body in the middle of the bed and sits on the edge. He attempts to figure out what he is feeling. His body is becoming feebler by the moment. He should be gaining vigor not the opposite.

The experience brings back a distant memory he has nearly forgotten. He has felt a similar sensation over two centuries before. The recollection of an unusual blade piercing his flesh enters his mind. The injury itself was not very painful, but the sword's composition caused an intense burning in the wound. He recalls it was a silver blade, which had produced the burning impression. He looks over her body for any jewelry made of silver; there is none to be found.

How can I feel this way without silver around, he wonders?

He searches his own body to see if there is any silver in contact with it. Once again he finds nothing, he is as naked as the moment he was born. His stomach aches as his muscles continue to weaken. The sickening feeling continues to gain strength, and he makes a move towards the bathroom, but it is too late. He spontaneously vomits blood all over the carpet!

Now he knows something is wrong; this has never happened before. When silver had touched his skin, it burned, but had never made him vomit in the past!

What's wrong with me, he wonders?

The door to his room unexpectedly busts open! Several men in riot gear and automatic weapons spurt through the door screaming, "FBI"! They order him to get down on the floor.

Two agents grab him by the back of his neck, not waiting for him to comply, and violently throw him to the carpet. He lands in the vomited pool of blood and grunts as they hold him to the floor and drive several knees into his back. He tries to resist but is unable to. He can not understand how this is possible.

Why am I so weak, he wonders?

Usually, he would be able to toss them off him like rag dolls. For some unknown reason, he is too weak to get up. He wonders if he could rise even without them on top of him. Two men in black suits enter the room. The younger one in front is missing a tie, unusual because all agents wear ties. The disgruntle, naked man on the floor strains to look up as the agents on his back handcuff him.

"Well, you're not so bad now are you . . . Lucius," the younger man says triumphantly.

The youthful man is about five-ten has short light brown hair and hazel eyes. His most distinguishing feature is the three red scares under his left eye, forming three parallel lines over his high cheekbone as if a tiger had raked his face.

"William!" The naked man on the floor blurts out disgustedly, glaring at the younger man.

"How did you like the silver nitrate?!" William asks with glee. "Didn't see that coming did you?"

"What are you talking about?" Regularly, he would read a person's mind in this situation but for some reason is unable to.

"The hooker you picked up. We injected her and every girl on the corner with silver nitrate." He pauses to let the words sink in. "Look at you now. Weak as a little schoolgirl," William taunts. "We came up with that new trick just for you!"

"You son of a bitch!" the prone man roars with what little strength he has left.

William pulls out his gun and paces over to Lucius. He points the gun directly at the vampire's head. Lucius can not believe this is the end. How could his extraordinarily long life come to an end like this. William wants to pull the trigger.

The middle-aged man in a similar black suit then chimes in, "That's enough, William. Get him out of here!" He orders the other FBI agents.

The middle-aged man has short black hair, dark blue eyes, and is two or three inches taller than William. He is fit for his age and emotes confidence and authority. The agents in the riot gear pick the large, naked man up and carry him out the bedroom door.

William holsters his weapon as his smile fades. He looks at his partner who is now standing next to him with an not so friendly look. "What now, Agent Grey?"

"Now we interrogate him, with extreme prejudice," Grey replies.

He pauses and waits for the remaining agents to leave the room. Once they have, he takes his eyes off the doorway and focuses on William. "What were you thinking?"

A puzzled look comes over the young man's face. "What are you talking about?"

"You injected silver nitrate into the prostitutes?!"

"Well yeah . . . ," William replies, shrugging his shoulders.

"Are you out of your mind? Silver nitrate is toxic to humans in large amounts!"

William turns as if shrugging off the comment. "People use it often, and it has no ill effects. Besides, if we hadn't used silver nitrate, everyone involved in the arrest tonight would be dead now."

"How can you sure of that? Now we'll have several prostitutes suing the government for injecting them with toxic levels of silver nitrate. We've been injecting them for weeks with colloidal silver. How do you know if the two together won't have issues? I trusted you."

William took a few steps towards the exit but stops short of the door and shakes his head as he faces Grey. "I wanted to be sure we would get the results we needed. I wasn't confident in the effects of the colloidal silver alone. I asked our doctor, and he assured me the doses were within survivable limits."

Grey visibly reacts to this comment. "Survivable limits?"

William seems unfazed. "Yes. As in the prostitutes will all survive."

"What kind of side effects are we looking at?"

William seems reluctant, "Well, possibly some burns and maybe their skin will turn blue."

"Turn blue! Great!" Grey's not impressed.

William continues to argue his point, "Oh, and for your information, colloidal silver is toxic in large doses too. Besides, they're just hookers. No one cares about hookers. No one will even listen to them. If they complain, arrest them. Then no one will even hear their complaints."

Grey's look is stern. "Don't ever do anything like this again without clearing it with me first. I must approve any moves you make. You're not an agent. I have given you leniency. Don't make me regret my decision to bring you on board," Agent Grey pushes passed William on his way out.

Chapter 5

At Children's Hospital, Dr. Michael Bauer is finishing his morning rounds when he runs into his good friend and colleague, Dr. Matt Richardson. They had met when they sat next to each other in Biology 101 at Green River Community College, where they studied for two years before moving on to the University of Washington.

They quickly became best friends and studied together and supported each other through many tough exams and fun diversions as well. Most of their distractions involved playing pool, alcohol, and women. Despite the fun activates, they managed not to get into too much trouble.

They developed a mutual motto which saw them through stressful times, "work hard and play harder." It was their young college years and their first time on their own. Having fun was a must. Those fun times were all but nonexistent now that they have everyday life and death situations to deal with at work which require them to stay more focused than ever.

"Hey, Mike!"

Only Dr. Bauer's closest friends and relatives call him "Mike".

"Hey, what's up?" Dr. Bauer replies with a slight nod of his head still looking at his clipboard.

Matt has short, curly, brown hair and sterling grey eyes. Matt is a few inches shorter than Michael but weighs as much as Michael does. He is not obese, but he is a little thicker than he would like. Dr. Richardson stands next to Michael with his stethoscope draped over his shoulders and his white lab coat. His coat is not buttoned revealing his blue button-down shirt and his tan slacks.

"I don't know about you, but I'm getting hungry. Do you want to go to the Lincoln Town Center for lunch?" Matt asks as he scratches his neck.

"Sure. Why not."

"It's been way too long," Matt adds and is pleased.

*   *   *

Down in the Seattle police department building, Ben Sutton navigates the labyrinth of scattered desks on the floor and arrives at Detective Dexter Burton's table. Ben sets a report in front of him.

"You're not going to believe this." Ben's beside himself.

Dexter caught onto the concern in his voice and looks up from the file he is studying. "What's up?"

"This is the medical examiner's toxicology report on Carl Dunn."

Dexter opens the report folder; it is empty. Dexter seems puzzled for a moment. "Is this another one of your jokes?"

"No."

"Why's it empty. I've been waiting for this?" Dexter asks. "This isn't the report."

"No, it's not the report, but it might as well be. They can't do it."

"Ok, I'll bite. Why?"

"His body doesn't have a drop of blood in it."

Dexter does not seem shocked or have any obvious response other than acknowledgment. Ben becomes even more confused by his lack of reaction.

"Don't you find that strange?" Ben lifts his hand in a dramatic gesture.

"Ordinarily I would find that very strange." Dexter turns and starts spinning the dial on a small safe behind him.

Once he has put in the combination, he opens the door and pulls out a set of files. Ben has never seen him open the safe before. He has secretly wondered what was inside ever since he became Dexter's partner. Dexter only keeps the most important and confidential records in this safe. All others go into his personal filing cabinet which sits next to the safe. He sets the records down next to the blank file on his desk.

"What are these?"

Dexter opens the file on the top of the stack. "These are the files of 28 other victims who all have had their blood completely drained from their bodies."

"What?" Just when Ben thought he could not be more puzzled, he is hit with Dexter's announcement. "Why didn't I know about this?"

"To be honest, I'm shocked that we've been able to keep this a secret. Now what I'm about to tell you is to be kept completely confidential." He waited for an acknowledgment. "Ten months ago, we started finding bodies, all completely drained of blood. We were finding two per month until four months ago."

"What happened four months ago?" Ben asks.

"Four months ago, we started finding four per month."

"Why'd they suddenly double?"

"I haven't figured that out yet. Whoever is doing this is very careful not to leave enough evidence to track them down."

"What do we know about this guy so far?" Ben asks.

Dexter tries not to show his frustration. "Not much. The killings are typically prostitutes and career criminals. They usually are the type of person that isn't missed by anyone for days if not weeks after the killing. Associates of these people are not the type to talk to police. The bodies of the prostitutes are typically found in the woods, usually naked and well on their way to decay. The hardened criminals are normally found at the scene of the crime."

Ben thinks about this for a moment. "The m.o.s are completely different. So, we are dealing with two killers?"

"That's my thought. The only connection is the manner in which the victims are killed."

"It almost sounds like a cult," Ben suggests.

"Possibly. We could have a group collecting the blood for rituals. It's hard to say what's going on. There just isn't enough evidence yet to tell. I've yet to come up with a single eyewitness or a security camera that caught the crime on video."

"So they are careful."

"Very," Dexter said.

Chapter 6

Lincoln Town Center is only a short bus ride from Children's Medical facility in Bellevue. They did not need to take the bus if they did not want to, but neither of the doctors are in the mood to walk across the overpass that separates them from Lincoln Square. The Square has condos on the top three quarters of the building and shops and entertainment on the bottom floors. The building also houses a bowling alley, comedy club, restaurants, and shops.

One could almost live his or her entire life in that building, although Michael can not imagine anyone ever doing that. The two friends hop off the bus, and onto the busy sidewalk where they now stand on the corner of NE 8th and Bellevue way. Simultaneously, they glance up at the towering green and blue glass building as they have done what seems like hundreds of times before.

"What do you feel like?" Matt asks.

"I don't know. I think I might be in the mood for a hamburger," Michael replies.

"Red Robin?"

"Red Robin." Michael answers knowing what Matt's going to say before he says it.

They were doctors now, but both had come from families with little money, so they never acquired the taste for expensive restaurants. They make good money now but are still up to their eyeballs in student loan debt and do not have the budget for it yet, even if they wanted it. They typically go to the same place and are content with keeping the status quo.

They walk into the restaurant and pass the rows of classic bright red chairs, and dark wood finished tables, and are seated. The place is filled with a melting pot of various customers. At one table, there are men in three-piece suits, and at the table next to them there is a young mother and her two kids. It is an assortment of people from all walks of life. That is one of the reasons they like coming to this restaurant.

The young, blonde waitress comes to their table, and she starts to hand them menus when Matt stops her in mid-motion. She is new and does not know they are regulars. She winks at Matt, and he tries not to react. He wonders if she is only interested in him because he is a doctor, but how would she even know that. Before he can start his order, she winks again. He pauses and looks at her name tag; it reads, "Winky".

"We already know what we want," Matt insists with a short but polite gesture, she winks again.

Matt begins to realize her winking is nothing more than a tick she can not help. She pulls back the menus and pulls out her order booklet.

"What will you two gentlemen be having today?" she says with a trained smile.

"I'll have the Western Burger," Matt replies with a polite grin.

She turns her attention to Michael. "And for you, sir?" The wink.

"The same."

"I'll get that right out to you!" She jots the order down and heads for the kitchen. By the look on Michael's face, he too can not help but notice the winking. They dismiss it with a mutual grin.

"So, how are your patients?" Matt asks, turning his attention away from the attractive waitress.

"Well, Natalie is making great progress, and Tim is doing better." He pauses and shakes his head. "We lost Samantha."

Matt can see the deep sadness in his eyes.
"Oh no. She looked like she was doing better."

"I know, I don't know what happened. One
day, her cell count was normalizing; the next, it
went down so fast it took us all by surprise. We
didn't have time to adjust her treatment. She was
gone before I could do anything to stop it."

Matt knows what it feels like to lose a
patient. "I'm so sorry man," he says sadly. He
wants to comfort him but is not sure how. He
thought about putting his arm over Michaels'
shoulders but did not feel comfortable doing that.
*Men don't comfort each other with physical forms
of affection*, Matt told himself.

"Sometimes this job seems too hard,"
Michael admits.

Matt takes in a deep breath and
contemplates what Michael's going through. "We
aren't miracle workers Mike. We can only do the
best we can and let the chips fall where they may.
You know what they say, 'God works in mysterious
ways'."

"God . . . Yeah, he sure does."

Michael is not much of a churchgoer,
neither is Matt. They both believe in God but are
not regular church attendees. Michael's younger
brother John, however, is a different story. John

has five children, all of whom live in a small house out in the middle of nowhere in a rural area in northern Washington state. John is a devout Christian and makes sure his whole family attends church every week. His kids are well-behaved and love God.

Although Michael has an underlying love for the Being he calls God, he feels no one really knows just who God is, and religion is nothing more than a form of mass social control. A bit of a sham, for lack of a better phrase. John has called Michael a "pagan" on one occasion for his lack of faith, but Michael just shrugged it off saying, "That's my brother for you."

Michael knows in his heart, he has his own personalized relationship with God, and no one is going to tell him how he should commune with him.

"You know what you need?" Matt says in a cheerful tone.

Michael's eyebrow raises for a moment. "No. What do I need?"

"You need to go out with me and have some drinks tonight. Let off some steam. Remember back in college? We use to go out after every test."

The corner of Michael's mouth perks up.

"Yes, I remember." His eyes seem a little

brighter now, enjoying the flashback to a simpler time.

"Let's do it then!"

"I can't. I have too much work to do. My patients need my full attention right now," Michael says, the corner of his mouth leveling off.

"How good are you to your patients if you're not able to bring your 'A' game? You've been so stressed out that you've lost your edge. You need to get out and let go. Besides, the game's on tonight!" Matt exclaims using his best persuasive tone. He can see he is beginning to convince his friend by the look on his face. "Come on; you know you want to!"

"Has that line ever worked for you before?" Michael asks with a small chuckle.

Matt playfully tilted his head. "That doesn't matter. What matters is, as your doctor, I am giving you a prescription for fun tonight!" Matt speaks in his doctor's voice squaring off his tie.

Matt has a narrow face even though he is slightly heavy set with broad shoulders which served him well when he played football in high school.

Michael chuckles louder. "You're just not going to give up, are you?"

"Nope," Matt says defiantly with a friendly smirk.

"Fine, let's go." He shakes his head in mock distress as he begins to rearrange the condiments on the table in just the right order, tallest to smallest.

"Tonight it is then!" Matt slaps the table playfully, louder than he had intended and draws more attention than he wanted. Matt notices Michaels obsessive behavior and smiles. "You still do that!"

"Do what?"

"You're arranging the condiments again."

"So, there's an order to things. Most places don't seem to understand that." Michael quickly finishes as not to give more credence to Matt's assertion.

Matt just laughs in a playful gesture.

Chapter 7

Deep in the heart of downtown Seattle, the FBI state headquarters stands quietly like a guardian of the city. The building is very dull looking with its countless rows of rectangular windows that scale the twenty stories. The building's exterior is constructed mainly of concrete, down to the thick window frames. The only part of the external structure that isn't concrete is the triple pane tinted glass windows.

The FBI enjoys privacy in their headquarters even though it does not seem to blend in with all the buildings around it. It is the odd duck in the row of buildings. Strange because it is too plain for the rest of the beautifully designed buildings surrounding it. On the top floor of the building, in a dimly lit interrogation room, a single, bright light hangs over a rectangular metallic table with a large man strapped firmly to it.

The restrained person, despite his enormous stature, is much more dangerous than he appears. Agent Grey and William stand on either side of the confined man. The man's arms, wrists, legs, ankles and neck all firmly held to the table with cold, shiny thick steel bands that lock him down. His large frame encompasses almost the entire surface of the table, leaving little visible under his girth.

The prisoner is tired of the little games the Agent and his companion are playing and peers through the bright light above him. The beast of a man can only make out shadows of the two men who now lurk about him. William, he knows well, a hunter from a family of hunters. Agent Grey is a wildcard and is somewhat new to him.

"So, what now dickheads?" Lucius blurts out. He has never been trapped like this and is feeling anxious.

"Now we start our little experiment," Agent Grey replies.

Stacked in one corner of the white, sterile room are several complicated pieces of equipment with blinking lights. A large, metal grey cabinet stands guard nearby. The door to the interrogation room opens, and a man with long, grey hair, wearing thick black glasses and a white lab coat breezes through the door. The newcomer is carrying a small, metallic briefcase.

Agent Grey looks up when the man enters. "It looks like we can start now!"

The man in the lab coat is of average height and build and walks with a slight limp in his right leg from a soccer injury he received a few years before. He sets the briefcase down on the small table next to the equipment in the corner. Then he carefully opens the case and pulls out a syringe-like device. It looks more like something from a sci-fi movie than a syringe.

Lucius can hear the man with the grey hair working, but he is just out of his range of vision.

"What the hell are you doing?" Lucius is becoming impatient.

"Glad you asked," Agent Grey begins, "What we have here is a technological breakthrough. Something the government has been working on for years. Unfortunately, the project was shut down because all the test subjects died. Neither animals nor people have survived the experiments so far. But we believe you can, with your regenerative abilities. Dr. Thompson here was the lead on the project," he explains gesturing to the man in the lab coat. "He managed to acquire for the FBI, the last remaining samples of the amazing product developed for the project. Sad that only twelve doses of this research are all that remains." Agent Grey continues as he holds one of the precious vials up to the light that the doctor has just handed him.

Lucius laughs in a manner that is quite frightening. "I'm only half human. You think that crap is gonna to work on me?" His Scandinavian accent is stronger than usual.

Agent Grey did not even pause. "Guess we will find out." He hands the syringe back to the doctor and motions for the doctor to administer the injection.

Dr. Thompson moves into position standing next to Lucius's arm. Lucius can now see more clearly the Doctor's narrow weasel like nose that protrudes from under his thick, dark glasses. The doctor moves the needle towards its intended vein. Lucius struggles with all his might but is firmly held in place by the thick, steel restraints. The doctor pauses a moment and then continues his task, penetrating the vein and injecting the contents of the syringe into Lucius's arm. The captive bursts into a ferocious rage, controlled only by his restraints as he lurches towards them, his ruby red eyes and his vampire teeth flaring brightly.

"I am 3000 years old. You have no idea what I'm capable of! I sat idly by while you killed my children one by one!" He roars. "My merciful days are over. Now, I will kill all of you, and I will enjoy drinking every drop of your blood!"

William smirks callously. "We'll see how you feel after these nanites take effect." He pats Lucius's head condescendingly.

Lucius relaxes a little as he is bewildered by the comment. "What the hell are nanites?"

William leans in very close. He wants Lucius to see him clearly; he enjoys tormenting the vampire. "They are thousands of microscopic machines that are now in your bloodstream. Once they reach your brain, they will each attach themselves to their own, individual neuron. When this happens, they will lock down on the axon. The axon is where the electrical impulse of the neuron travels in order to send a signal to the adjacent neuron. They will then attach a permanent electronic probe into the axon and will be able to insert an artificial electrical impulse of its own.

"This will give the nanites the ability to control the firing of that neuron in your brain. Thousands of nanites are now entering your brain." He pauses and can tell it does not mean much to Lucius by his expressionless face. In case you haven't figured it out yet, that means they'll control your mind. Since we control the nanites, we'll control you," he says with a sinister grin. "You probably don't have anything to worry about though. No one has ever survived the implantation process."

Lucius's mind fills with terror. "When I get out of here, you're a dead man!" he screams in a deep, inhuman voice.

"Temper temper," William jeers.

Lucius moves his head as if trying to free himself. "I'm going to enjoy killing you the most. I should've killed you years ago, but I became too fond of our little game."

William is unfazed. "Looks like I win!"

"The only reason you're even here is due to my mercy. I could've killed you, your father, or any of your great grandfathers. I watched the Van Helsing family from afar for almost 600 years. It would have been so easy to have ended your family line. Now, this is what I get for my mercy." A blood tear rolls down his face as a feeling of helplessness overtakes him, a sensation he has never experienced before.

William cackles, "Well I appreciate your mercy, as do my future children, . . . but your children killed my brother and my father. That makes you and them responsible."

"Your father and brother killed a dozen of my children between the two of them. Your family has killed nearly 300 of my children over the last

600 years. They were only defending themselves," Lucius continues. "Before you take your last breath, I will end your entire family line. I will make you watch as I bathe in the blood of your children. Then when you see that your line has ended, I will end you."

Even restrained, Lucius is very intimidating. His threat strikes fear into William's heart as if a stake had been driven into it. Lucius can feel William's fear, and for the first time since his arrival, the corner of Lucius's mouth turns up. Terror is something he craves, he loves the smell of trepidation, especially when it comes from a hunter like William Van Helsing.

Suddenly, Lucius starts to feel strange; he notices Grey working on an electronic pad of some kind. He seems like he is trying to figure something out. Lucius turns his head away from William under its metal restraint and faces the light; he is not sure if he has done this on his own or something made him do it. His tense muscles relax. He tries to move them, but with each attempt, he finds some invisible force countering the control over his muscles. He tries to make a fist but notices that his fingers only twitch a little, as if some unseen presence prevents him from doing so.

"What have you done to me," Lucius screams, a little surprised he still has control over his speech.

Agent Grey looks up from his pad noticing the changes. "Looks like the nanites are taking effect," he says, thrilled!

Lucius wants to reply but is still in disbelief over his powerlessness and tries to fight the nanite's effects.

"Now let's start with something simple." Grey pushes a few buttons on the pad. "Who are you?" Agent Grey asks.

"Bite me; you know who I am!" Lucius immediately replies, defiantly staring at Grey.

Agent Grey barely notices! He is too busy trying to figure out just the right settings to get the controlled response he wants. The FBI man frowns. "Now we'll have to see about that." Grey touches the screen of the tablet and makes some adjustments. The display illuminates Grey's face with an unnatural light blue glow. Lights flicker on the equipment in the corner of the room in response to the change in settings. Suddenly, a sharp spasm radiates through Lucius that brings with it a new reality to the definition of real pain. His body tenses and contorts still held down by the restraints.

After a few moments, Agent Grey touches the pad again, and the pain instantly vanishes, leaving only the terrible memory behind.

"That was level one." Grey pauses for effect. "Let's try this again. Who are you?" he repeats.

Lucius catches his breath for a moment.

"Who are you?" he asks again.

Lucius turns his head towards his interrogator once again. "You know who I am, ass hole!"

Grey touches the pad again, and the pain instantly returns, this time it is much worse! Lucius feels his muscles contract in ways he didn't think possible. He fears his muscles might rip themselves loose from his bones. The pain is the worst he has ever felt in his extraordinarily long life. Agent Grey touches the screen again after watching him contort for a minute and the pain leaves as quickly as it had come. Lucius is out of breath. He can feel the tremendous effect this process is having on his body.

"Who are you," he repeated?

Lucius coldly stares at him. He pauses, catching his breath. "Bite me!" he finally shouts rebelliously, panting.

The FBI man sighs deeply, glances at William who shows no sign of knowing what to do at this point. "I see this is getting us nowhere. Let's try something else." He touches the pad again.

Once again, the lights on the machines in the corner flicker in response to the change in settings and starts a new series of neurons in Lucius's mind firing.

"Who are you?"

Lucius tries to refrain from answering, but something seems to compel him to answer. "I am Lucius," the vampire replies, surprised by his own answer.

"Now, that's more like it," William interjects with approval and a sense of accomplishment. "We know only a little about your kind. Thanks to your favorite vampire, Helen, we've known about your weaknesses for generations. However, she didn't tell us much about where you come from or who you really are. The more we know about you and your children, the better we can fight you." William states.

Agent Grey glances at William with agreement and then goes back to his interrogation. "Where do you come from?"

"Scandinavia," Lucius replies.

Tell me something I didn't know, Grey thinks. "What are you?"

"I'm a vampire."

William looks at Grey with a little frustration. Grey caught his glance and agrees internally, that he needs to ask better questions. "Where does your kind come from?"

"I am the beginning," the vampire answers.

Grey considers this for a moment. "You're the first vampire?"

"Yes."

"How did you come to be. I want every detail from the very beginning."

"It all began about 3000 years ago," Lucius starts.

"Go on."

Chapter 8

"My earliest memory is of my mother cooking over the open fire that lay just outside of our small, wood thatched shelter. Her blonde, neatly, braided hair flowed down the center of her slender shoulders and back. She was in her mid-twenties, which was getting close to middle-aged back then. My mother was said by many to have the most beautiful, clear, green eyes in the village.

Our average-sized shelter was about thirty feet long, ten feet across, and nine feet high at the peak of the roof. The base of the structure was made of stone held together by hardened clay and had an oval shape to it. The steep-pitched roof came nearly down to the ground and was supported, in part, by the short rock wall base. The shelter's roof was composed mostly of thick layers of grass, branches, and animal hides. I must have been around four-years-old at the time.

I can remember my mother cooking the fish my father had caught earlier that day in the inlet waters of the Baltic Sea near our small community. The area my village was located is known today as

Stockholm, Sweden. I was big for my age and was nearly as big as my older brother Arne, who was almost two years my senior. The settlement we lived in was nothing more than a few hundred-people scattered over the small peninsula.

I had a normal childhood for the times and thought there was nothing unusual about myself despite the slightly atypical treatment I received from our neighbors and friends. I had these extraordinary, green eyes that sparkled in the sunlight like dark green emeralds. People didn't know what to think about my odd appearance. Some seemed nervous when I looked at them, but others found me intriguing.

Had they known the truth of my origins and the horrors that lay in wait beneath my youthful pale skin and startling green eyes, they would have ended my life for sure. Most of the community was very superstitious and were quick to destroy anything they thought was evil or a threat to the society. Their beliefs dictated that the gods demanded the destruction of all evil. For, as was foretold by their gods, 'if evil is allowed to live among the people it will destroy them.'

Everyone in the community worked together to help one another survive the hard life we all shared. It was through strong social ties and teamwork that we all held hope for the future. As I grew, people took notice of my unusual physical gifts I possessed. I was taller, stronger, and faster than any of the other children my age. My father was always very proud of my accomplishments, particularly with the bow and was quick to show me off to his friends. I was his pride and joy. He favored me even more than he favored Arne, from a very young age.

It was the tradition for the oldest son to be the future leader of the family, who was called the Jarl. When I reached the age of twelve, my father broke with tradition and made me the family Jarl. Putting me in the position of being the future patriarch and owner of most the family assets. When our father made the announcement, Arne stormed out of the family meeting. He did not talk to me for a whole month afterward. He rarely treated me with any form of kindness after the announcement and was quick to point out any of my mistakes no matter how small.

Once I reached adolescence, and my body started to mature, my life changed dramatically. The fish, deer, and various nuts and berries that made up most of our diet began to lose their appeal. I no longer wished to have my meat cooked well, but preferred it rare. It got to the point that I did not want my meat cooked at all. My parents' concern grew as time went on, and the traits they hoped were just a phase, only became more pronounced.

Chapter 9

According to my father, pastimes in the village had stayed very much the same since the time of my grandfather's grandfather. All of that was about to change dramatically. With the new development of forging iron, some of the locals built more massive boats and began exploring the channels and inlets that eventually led out to the open waters of the Baltic Sea. Our world was expanding, and we wanted to explore it.

The men who came back from these relatively short explorative trips returned with treasures we had never seen before! The most lucrative of these treasures appeared when one of the groups of sailors brought an enormous fish larger than the new 20 foot boats they had recently made. Thus, our introduction to whales.

Then began a new type of fisherman, the whaler. The whales these new fishermen brought back made them both local celebrities and wealthy beyond anything they could have imagined. The newly wealthy whalers could afford luxuries that few others in the community could provide, chief among them was their larger huts. One or two were so wealthy that they could even afford a house with solid wood beams held together with iron spikes that today are called nails! Nails were new and very rare and expensive back then.

The whales the fishermen brought back were used for a multitude of purposes including food, butter, candles, and making our fires burn hotter and longer. The discovery of these whales and the great abundance of useful purposes caused an explosion in the population of our little community.

Because of better nutrition and living conditions, most families grew more massive and began to live longer, and the mortality rate dropped dramatically. As the community expanded, so did the need for whales. The size of the ships also grew, and the distance they had to travel to find new whales increased.

These concerns were of little interest to me in my youth. My troubles overshadowed any thought of our community's affairs. My problems had only begun, and they got worse as my cravings for raw meat increased. The whale meat the explores brought back did nothing to satisfy my increasing hunger.

Fortunately, I had many distractions to keep my mind off my troubles. My father continued to teach me how to hunt, and it was clear after only a few lessons that I was a natural. I moved silently and fast. My aim with a bow was getting to be so good it rivaled my father's, who had hunted his whole life. Arne was always invited to go hunting, but our father always focused on making sure I was trained properly and was extra strict with me demonstrating proper form and technique.

The hunters in our community had a tradition of cutting the liver out of a freshly-killed deer and eating it raw; it was my favorite part of the kill. I could not wait to taste the fresh, warm liver in my mouth each time I made a kill. I did not know why at the time, but something about it that made me feel stronger. It was as if I could feel a little of the life force of the deer enter my body when I ate the blood-infused liver. In a short time, I found myself hunting on my own. I relished the kill and the taste of its liver each time.

After one of my kills, I cut the neck as I always did to bleed the deer dry. On this morning, I noticed for the first time the tantalizing aroma of the fresh blood as it drained onto the ground. I had never made the connection between the smell of the blood as the source of the cravings I was having. At some point, an urge overpowered me, and I began to drink the blood as it slowly leaked out of the massive buck. The thick, red blood tasted so good. I could sense the difference it made in my body, and I could not help but think that I was doing something wrong, despite the fact it made me stronger and more alive than ever.

After drinking, I noticed my heightened senses. My hearing was enhanced, and it felt like the entire forest came to life with an orchestra of animal songs. I could see fine detail in everything I observed. Everything seemed more beautiful. All of these wonders distracted me, and I often would come home late at night having lost track of time. As always, my parents were happy to see I was bringing fresh food home but dismayed as they noticed I was eating less and less, with no signs of my body weakening. I only seemed to grow stronger. Often, my father and mother talked about the fears associated with my odd behavior.

As their concerns grew and she could no longer hide it, my mother told my father of a terrible nightmare that occurred just before I was conceived. She did not want to tell my father about it when she was pregnant because like the rest of the community, he was very superstitious and she feared he might decide to kill me as a baby.

On this fateful night, Arne and I overheard my name mentioned by my mother. We crept nearby, secretly listing to the story my mother was about to express.

"I have something I have to tell you, my husband."

My mother's tone caught his attention, and he knew it was something serious.

"What is it?"

"Promise me you will not do anything rash," My mother pleaded.

He became only more concerned. He let out a deep sigh. "I will control myself."

"The nightmare came to me one night about the time Lucious was conceived. As I slept, an enormous, naked brute, with eyes that shined like bright red rubies appeared to me. He was riding a mighty, brown bear as he approached. The large, strong man with pale skin wore an enormous jewel-encrusted crown. Two long, ivory horns protruded from his forehead. He had long blonde hair that flowed from under his royal crown. The powerful man called himself Balam. After dismounting the brown bear, he forced himself upon me.

"Afterwards, he told me I would give birth to his son. He warned her that his son would be a terrible plague upon all of man. He foretold that this child would be the destroyer of lives, immortal and vicious. That he would lay waste to man and death would surround him. Balam and his bear then vanished in a bright flame of searing fire! When I awoke from the nightmare, I discovered blood on my clothes and inner thighs. I cleaned myself up, careful not to wake you."

After hearing the incredible story, my father was dismissive. "That was only a dream. Dreams are not real."

He encouraged my mother never to speak of it again, and not to tell anyone about it. He did not want anyone to get the wrong idea of his future Jarl.

After hearing the story, Arne and I looked at each other in unison. I was horrified by the story and horrified further when I realized Arne looked pleased.

"You're a demon spawn. I knew there was something wrong with you. There's no way we will let a demon be the future of this family," Arne said.

From then on, Arne decided it was time to watch me more carefully. He also mocked me openly in front of his friends every chance he got calling me "demon spawn". I had many friends and admirers in my youth, but most of them abandoned me after hearing the dreadful stories my brother spread about me.

I quickly found myself without a single friend. I tried to make new friends, desperate to undo what my brother had done, but no one would listen to me. No one would give me a chance. My strange appearance and behavior helped give my brother the ammunition he needed to make people fear me. I spent more and more time alone and felt more alienated as each day passed.

Arne secretly followed me on several of my hunting trips. I was now only a year or two from being considered a man myself and was almost as tall as my father. One fateful evening, my brother followed me into the darkening forest as the sun began to set. He wanted to find anything he could on me to spread more stories to the community.

My brother watched as I stalked a large, six-point buck with lethal skill. I took my bow, and aimed for the magnificent animal's heart, and let go of the string. My arrow found its mark and brought down the mighty buck with just one arrow. He watched as I approached the stag with my flint knife drawn. I cut the buck's neck and began to drink the blood as it poured out of the buck's neck.

My brother was horrified and terrified by my behavior. He could barely watch the grotesque

ritual. He burst from his hiding place, and I looked
up from my kill my eyes glistening ruby eyes! The
sight of my red eyes only frightened him further.
He believed the story my mother had told was only
a story and wasn't real. He used the story as an
excuse to discredit me and take his rightful place as
the family Jarl. Now he knew the story was true
for the first time and was disturbed beyond
measure. He startled me, and for a moment I
thought I heard him say something.

"Ki . . ."

"What did you did say, Arne?" I asked.

Completely stunned, he said nothing.

I had no idea that my eyes looked any
different from usual. I was very concerned with
what my brother might be thinking after catching
me with a mouth full of deer blood as he had. I
knew it probably wasn't good. Then I heard it
again, this time a little more clearly.

"Kill."

This time I was sure Arne had said
something, but I was confused because I did not
see his lips move. "What are you going to kill?" I
asked him.

"What makes you think I'm going to kill
something?" he asked as he carefully drew closer.

I was even more bewildered and put on the

defense by his gesturing, which resembled a cat moving in on a mouse. "Nothing. I just thought I heard you say you were going to kill something." I was hoping he would calm down a little.

"I didn't say anything." He looked carefully into my eyes, and I could tell he was thinking something terrible.

I then heard him again.

"Kill the demon spawn."

Again, I heard his voice, but his lips had not moved. The fear was building in my mind, and the pressure became intense. He pulled out his sharp flint knife and came at me with a violent lunge! I could not believe he was attempting to kill me. We had our differences, but this was taking it too far! I grabbed his wrist in a half-hearted attempt to stop his attack, believing his slightly greater size would be difficult for me to stop!

We were both completely surprised when I easily arrested his hand with the knife in mid-motion. No one was more astonished than my brother, who made a second attempt to force the sharp flint into my chest, he was overpowered again. He then put his empty hand on the hilt of his knife and the back of his hand and tried again with his full strength to plunge the knife into my chest, no success. My single arm was stronger than my brother's entire body!

"Why are you doing this?!" I yelled.

"You must die you demon spawn! You are an evil sent here by Satan himself. How could father make you the Jarl? You're evil and must die! When the people hear about your thirst for blood and see your demonic eyes, you'll be stoned," he yelled back, now more fearful of me than ever.

I could tell his apprehension of me would never end, and I would not be able to convince him that I was still his brother. I had grave misgivings about his intentions for my future, even if he had not found out about my secret. He would have found a way to take his rightful place as the family Jarl, no matter what the cost. Now he had what he needed to take back his birthright once and for all, but at the same time he now for the first time believed that I was something that needed to be destroyed and not just an obstacle.

Once he told my family and the village of what he had seen everything would be different. There would be nothing my father could do to stop the community from destroying me. I would not be safe at home. The town, led by my brother, would only be focused after that on ending my life.

My father would likely give his life to defend mine. My mother would be exiled from the city if she tried to help me. My parents and my life was now in jeopardy; I would not be able to live with that. There was only one thing to do. I pushed Arne to the ground and ran into the forest without my prize buck. I left my brother and my life as I knew it, far behind. That was the last time I saw my family.

Chapter 10

Leaving my family behind was the hardest thing I ever had to do. From then on, I lived in the forest and fed on the blood of the animals I found there. Several months passed, and, I had given up all hope of ever going back to my old life.

Convinced they probably were better off without me, I headed south along the coast. When I arrived at the southern tip of what is known today as Sweden, I encountered an elderly fisherman, whose eyesight was beginning to fail him. He was struggling to thread a fishhook when he noticed me.

"Young man, could you help an old man out." He handed me the line and the hook.

I took the items from him and quickly threaded the hook and handed them back.

"Impressive! You have good eyes son." He noticed I was alone. "What's a young man like you doing out here alone?"

I was slow to answer, but he patiently waited for my reply. "I don't know. I have nowhere to go."

He seemed surprisingly pleased by my answer.

"Would you like a job son?"

I had never had a real job before, but I had nothing better to do. "What kind of job?"

"Have you ever fished before?" His cloudy eyes seemed to twinkle.

"Of course."

"Well, then you're perfect! I want you to help me with my fishing business."

I was scared, a little lonely and had nowhere else to go, so I decided to take him up on his offer. I spent months working with him and saving my money. The fisherman tried to pay me in silver, to begin with, but the silver burned my skin and made me feel sick. I was unable to touch it without suffering great pain, so I insisted on gold for payment.

I worked with him for nearly a year, when other people began to take notice of my appearance. My trepidation grew with each passing day. I knew it would not be long before I was forced to leave again. One day a group of fishermen cornered me. The largest of the men pushed me against the wall of a shop in town. His wife had taken a liking to me and she was my only other friend in the community. Over time I could tell she was becoming attached to me. I thought this was not a good thing but I did not want to lose my only companion. I could almost feel his thoughts and they told me he objected to our friendship. He was worried that I would take his wife from him but I had no intention of doing so. I only wanted a friend.

"You're not welcome here," he said coldly.

"I don't want any trouble," I said.

"Then you better leave, before we beat you to death. Something that isn't right about you, and we don't like it." He threw me to the ground. "Next time we see you, we won't be so nice."

As I lay in the cold mud and watched the unruly men leave, all I wanted was to be left alone. I wanted to live in peace and treated like a respectable human being. It was something that was harder for me to find than I ever thought possible. I realized it was time for me to leave again. I convinced the old fisherman to take me across the Baltic Sea, in which we fished daily. He took me to a small town, known today as Copenhagen, Denmark.

I spent several years roaming aimlessly around Denmark. Eventually, I continued my exploration south into what would become Germany. Although I was frugal with my earnings, the gold spent much faster than I expected. Moving from town to town was costly. It was not long before I was penniless and had nowhere to stay. I found people were much less tolerant of you when you have no money.

This did not slow me down much though. I was young and restless, so I continued exploring. I had no idea the world was so vast! I spent almost a decade traveling the coasts of Europe. I avoided the few people that occupied it as much as possible for I feared they would try to hurt me like my brother and the men in town had. I had matured into a full-grown man for some time now. I filled out and was much larger than almost everyone I encountered. I spent most of my waking time at night and slept through most of the daylight hours.

For some reason unknown to me, I felt much stronger at night and much more lethargic during the day. Being active at night did have its advantages. It was easier to avoid people because they were in their huts asleep. From time to time, I would enter small towns and villages after dark, free to roam about unnoticed among the sleeping huts.

One night, I was drawn to one of the larger towns by some strange sounds. I heard loud songs and music that played late into the night. As I

approached the village I could see a massive
bonfire lighting up the night sky. Judging by the
number of huts and people at the celebration, I
guessed there must have been about five thousand
people in the town, which was sizable back then. I
could hear cheering, laughing, music, and dancing
as I drew nearer.

I peered from the dark and watched as the
celebrants, drank and danced around the fire in the
center of the town. Men, women, and children all
took part in the joyous occasion! I could sense
their thoughts, and they all seemed happy and
carefree. A piece of me sincerely wanted to take
part in the celebration. The other part of me
dreaded being attacked, beaten, and treated like an
outcast or perhaps worse, killed.

I was about to turn away and back into the
darkness when I saw her. A beautiful woman,
maybe twenty years old, dancing gracefully around
the warm fire. I could not take my eyes off her; she
captivated me. An unfamiliar feeling overwhelmed
me. All I wanted was to join her and dance around
the fire with her. Her long, beautiful, brown hair
flowed about her as she moved completely
carefree.

She was tall for a woman in that period, and
her blue eyes twinkled in the firelight. I could feel

a profound desire to touch her smooth, olive skin as I continued to watch from afar. Gathered on a big, flat log were several old men, harmoniously played strange-looking instruments, creating a unique form of music I had never heard before. I found the melody and festivities quite enjoyable and entertaining.

Finally, I could take it no longer. I left my hiding place in the dark shadows and entered the circle created by the firelight. Illuminated by the fire, my massive silhouette caught the attention of the entire gathering. The music abruptly stopped, and everyone looked at me with fear. Several of the men stood to their feet. Some of them grabbed their sword which lay nearby. Back then a smart man never was far from his sword. Now that I stood amongst them, it was clear to me I must have been the tallest and largest man there.

I wore a rough-cut bearskin over my shoulders. I made wolf skin into a pair of trousers. The large wolf attached me a few months before and I was force to kill it. I was not sure why but the animal almost seemed to have a grudge against me. My feet were wrapped in dark, brown, hardened leather, and my large bow hung over my shoulder. By comparison to the dark-haired girl's neatly made black and tan cloth dress, I looked like a barbarian. I could hear the peoples' frightened thoughts sting me like a thousand bees. I did not want them to be frightened of me so I spoke.

"May I join you."

This did not seem to help as much as I would have liked. The young woman I had watched moved away from me frightened. She went back to a man who I assumed was probably her father. I stood alone by the warmth of the large bonfire, my immense, terrifying shadow flickering in a rhythmic dance. I had no desire to alarm the group any more than I already had. Slowly, I turned and disappeared back into the shadows from which I had emerged.

A deep curiosity and fascination remained in my mind for the young dark, haired beauty. I was unable to explain even to myself the feelings that were developing because I had never had them before and had nothing to compare them.

Days passed, and I continued to watch the young woman from afar, hidden in the forest nearby. During the day, she would work her daily chores, which consisted of taking care of a young girl. Her thoughts eventually told me she was her little sister.

Most of her time was spent cooking and preparing meals. Judging by her size, her sister must have been about 12, plus or minus. The younger girl looked like a miniature version of the older girl. One day, the young dark-haired girls were on their way to the lazy creek at the edge of town to fetch some water in a wooden bucket, one of their daily tasks. When they reached the stream, I watched as the older sister filled her bucket with fresh water. Her stunning hair caught in the gentle breeze. The feelings I felt as I watched her that night at the bonfire were stronger than ever.

"Cressia!" a middle-aged man's voice called out.

It seemed he must be calling to the dark hair girl, but it was hard to tell. I was not sure because she showed little interest and she barely acknowledged him with a slight turn of her beautiful head. The man was short, filthy, and fat with matted brown hair and a scraggly beard. He wore a tattered, grey tunic over his grey, shirt, and the neck was open. His light brown, knee-high boots were covered in dry and caked on mud. He had been following them for some reason. Once her bucket was full, she stood and turned to head back home, still showing no interest in the fat man who stood directly in their path.

"What do you want, Firmin?" she asked, clearly annoyed at the man's intervention with her chores.

"I just wanted to talk to you." He stumbled for a moment but managed to hold his balance.

"About what?" she asked, maintaining her annoyance.

She could smell the pungent odor of lousy wine on his breath.

"You know, young girls like yourselves shouldn't be out alone like this." he slurred.

She looked at him with a little suspicion, "Oh?"

He grinned, revealing several gaps from missing teeth. "A girl could get hurt out here."

She shifted her weight, suggesting she was starting to feel a little uneasy with the whole conversation. "Thanks, I'll be more careful in the future," she said, making a second attempt to walk past him, but her path was blocked again by the slovenly man.

"What if there is no next time," he said with a creepy smirk.

She could tell, at this point, that Firmin clearly had less than honorable intentions, so she grabbed the bottom of her bucket with her free hand and dumped the water all over the bedraggled man. She dropped the bucket, grabbed her little sister's palm and raced back towards the safety of their home! The water blinded Firmin momentarily, but he shook it off and quickly caught up with the duo and grabbed Cressia. He forced her to the ground, she lost her grip on her sister's hand as she fell.

"Run, Appoline!" Cressia yelled looking up from under the weight of the unruly man.

Appoline ran as fast as her little feet would carry her, screaming at the top of her lungs.

"Keep quiet!" Firmin said forcefully.

He began to pull up the folds of Cressia's dress and was about to unbuckle his pants when he felt a massive force lift him off the girl and roughly toss him to the side.

Firmin was stunned when he hit the ground hard, knocking the wind out of him. Rattled and angry, he promptly got to his feet with the intent to fight back when he saw the intimidating stature of a massive man standing head and shoulders above him. Fear quickly squelched any desire to fight. Outmatched, Firmin did not hesitate to run in the direction of the town.

After rescuing her, I turned and offered my hand to Cressia; she was still lying on the ground in shock. She did not know what to think or do since nothing like this had ever happened to her before. Strangers were always met with apprehension, but this stranger had just saved her from the ravagings of an intoxicated, begrimed man.

She did not want to insult her rescuer, so she gingerly took my large hand. I stood above her blocking the morning sun. I carefully pulled her to her feet, and she finally saw my face clearly as she brushed off her dress. She recognized me as the man who attempted to join the festival bonfire a few nights earlier. Hard to forget someone like that in my distinctive bearskin and wolf outfit.

"Who are you?" Cressia asked softly.

"I am Lucius." I felt awkward and unsure of the proper thing to do in this situation.

"Thank you," she replied, filled with mixed emotions.

I gladly picked up her bucket and, without another word, filled the bucket back up with fresh water.

"Thank you again," she said with a little more confidence. *At least he is a gentleman, despite his outward appearance. Not bad on the eyes either,* she thought.

"May I carry this for you?

The situation made her nervous again because she knew nothing about me, but she still did not wish to offend. She did feel a little safer with me by her side, despite her apprehension.

"Sure," she answered, with a graceful tilt of her head.

I escorted her back to her home where her father was already running in their direction with a sword in his hand. As he approached us, her father aggressively pointed his sword at my chest, his sword arm tense and fully extended as he held the blade ready to gravely wound or kill.

"Back off! He demanded.

I sized up the man now threatening me. Her father had long black hair and was about five inches shorter than me. He was middle-aged and seemed fit and robust despite his slightly bulging belly. He had a finely-made, clean, light tan tunic with a dark brown belt and metal buckle around his waist. His dark brown pants were equally splendid and met his black knee-high shiny leather boots. My first impression was that he must be wealthy, for he resembled the whalers back home.

"Father no!" Cressia cried.

Her father hesitated, confused that she would defend a man who had just attacked her.

"He saved me!" Cressia continued.

Her father relaxed his sword arm a little, still trying to figure out what was going on.

"He stopped Firmin from violating me!' Cressida explained.

Her father lowered his sword. "Firmin? Firmin did this?" he hissed, raising his voice.

He looked into my eyes as if seeking confirmation; I could only look away.

Cressia nodded her head, which only intensified his outrage. It was clear by his tone he was not going to let this go without a fight when he came across Firmin again.

Her father embraced her. "So, you are well? Did he hurt you?" he asked.

"No, he didn't." Cressia answered.

"Thank the gods!" he cried. After a long embrace, he released her and looked up at me. Her father's demeanor changed, his rage was gone. "I have you to thank for my daughter's safe return?"

I nodded.

"Then I am indebted to you. You must dine with us this afternoon! Come . . . come!" he insisted as he put his hand on my back and urged me to follow them back to their home.

Chapter 11

Their dwelling was unusually large,
Cressia's father led me to the door and then inside,
where her little sister was quietly sitting at a table.
I was impressed further, an actual house and not
just a hut. It had solid wood beams, and cedar
shakes on the roof. Her father closed the wooden
door held by iron hinges, which was remarkable for
that time! Most homes back then used twine to
serve as hinges, and the doors closed clumsily, this
door was smooth. This family must have been
moderately wealthy to be able to afford such
luxury. Their father toured me around the fantastic
home.

"My wife died in childbirth with my second
daughter, so it's just my daughters and me."
Appoline sheepishly turned her head down as I
looked in her direction. "Cressia is a wonderful
cook and will make a great feast for us," her father
stated.

I set the bucket of water down beside the
stone fireplace held together with mortar, another

sign the family was well-to-do. Cressia and her sister began preparation of the meal as her father and I sat down at an oak dining table in the center of the house. The table had a smooth, hard finish with several fancy designs carved into the sides and legs. I had never seen such a beautiful piece of furniture! Surrounded the table were several individual chairs and not the typical benches you would find in most homes. I sat in a chair of my own. I could not help but be slightly distracted by the luxury.

Her father suddenly realized he was impolite. "Forgive me; I have not introduced myself. My name is Gerbaut," he said, holding out his hand.

I took his hand and shook it. "I am Lucius."

Her father asked me where I was from and what I was doing here. Gerbaut was very curious about his daughter's rescuer. I told him I was from up north and was exploring. He was intrigued for he had not seen much of the world and began to ask me all sorts of questions about my explorations so far. I could not tell him much, because I had kept to myself for the most part. I told Gerbaut a few short stories about my experiences, careful to leave out the drama of my past. He seemed more and more interested as he got to know me better.

We had an amiable conversation for over an hour when Cressia and her sister began to set out bowls made of baked porcelain. The dishes had a glossy, smooth finish and were pleasant to hold. I had never seen such riches as fired porcelain bowls, hinges, and stone fireplaces except in the homes of the wealthy whalers back home. Nearly everything in my childhood home made entirely of wood. The only family possessions I could remember not made of wood was my father's hunting knife and our arrowheads, which were a rare expense.

Cressia then set something on the table I had never seen before, a metal spoon! When I saw it, I immediately picked it up. I studied the dense, smooth material in my fingers and could not believe my eyes.

How is it possible to build such a thing, I wondered?

Cressia's father could see I was very impressed and captivated by the spoon and could not help but show his approval.

"You like it?" Gerbaut asked.

"I do!" I replied with astonishment.

"I made it myself," he boasted.

The statement shocked me more than the spoon did. Cressia then filled the bowls with a hot stew that steamed with a wonderful scent.

Cressia's dad leaned in close and deeply breathed in the aroma, the fragrance pleased him immensely. "Doesn't it smell amazing?" he asked.

I leaned in close and inhaled deeply as well. Although the aroma seemed pungent, it did not appeal to me much. I lied and told him it smelled wonderful. Cressia and her sister joined the pair of men, and they all began to eat. I did my best to fake enjoyment of the food that must have been a rare treat in those days.

After dinner, Cressia and Appoline began to clean up, and their father invited me to sit with him by the fire. Near the fireplace were two solid oak chairs that were also beautifully decorated with intricate carvings. By my standards, they were worth a small fortune. He directed me to one of the handsome seats as he took the other, which I got the impression was his favorite.

It would have been my favorite too with the soft plush skins that cushioned the seat, I thought.

Gerbaut pulled out a metal smoker's pipe and began to fill it with some sort of small black crushed plant! The treasures in this house never seemed to end. He began to puff on his pipe, and then he spoke, puffs of smoke emanated from his mouth as he did.

"What are your plans?" Gerbaut asked.

"Plans?" I asked.

"Yes, what do you plan to do with your future?"

I paused for a moment. I had never been asked this question before. I never put much thought into the future. "I don't have any plans."

"Do you think you will stay here in the village?"

I paused again. "I don't really have anything keeping me here."

Gerbaut exhaled a long slow puff of smoke that billowed from his mouth. "I must say that I'm very impressed with you."

I was surprised he felt this way about a man dressed in crude animal skins. He must have been judging me by my actions more than my appearance.

"We need more people like yourself in this village."

I was further shocked by this comment; I had not felt needed in a long time now.

"Would you be interested in working for me at my shop?" He held his pipe in a dignified manner.

I was utterly taken back by his offer. Not only had he not rejected me, but Gerbaut was treating me like someone of value. I had forgotten what it felt like to feel accepted and granted respect. Gerbaut could tell I was pondering his request.

"You'll be paid, of course. And if you do well, you may earn enough to afford to have your own hut soon." He carefully studied my face for a reaction.

The idea of having a home to call my own appealed to me greatly. I was tired of being constantly on the move, with the uncertainty of not knowing where I would be tomorrow.

Staying close to Cressia would be wonderful too, I thought.

I only hoped she felt the same way, or at least that she might someday. One thing I did know was I was willing to find out. If I were capable of living in a village in peace and accepted by others, I would be able to stop running. I could live my dream of having a family and living a normal life.

My chance to start all over, to be an honorable and respectable man had finally arrived. I couldn't believe my change of fortune. I gratefully accepted Gerbaut's offer. He notified me I would be starting in the morning. I was excited for the first time in as long as I could remember.

Gerbaut allowed me to stay in the hut that stood behind his house. It had been his mother's before she died two years earlier. He told me I could stay there as long as I needed to and be ready to work in the morning.

Chapter 12

The next morning, Cressia's dad started by showing me around his shop. I saw the new forge he built himself. It gave him the ability to superheat iron ore more efficiently to a temperature high enough to melt it so he could work with it. I now understood why he had so many items made of metal in his home.

Forging was the new discovery of the age, and he was at the forefront of the men who were developing the skills and knowledge for this innovation. His forge, made of a particularly fired brick allowed him to superheat metal. He used newly discovered black rock-like objects he called coal to fuel the fire of his forge. He had a device made of animal hides that pumped tremendous amounts of air into his forge and made the fire extremely hot.

Gerbaut's shop was large and made with similar construction techniques as his house was. He had several men working for him, and they all seemed very busy at work like harmonious bees in a hive. Gerbaut wasted no time and put me to work right away.

One of the first things he showed me how to make was a nail. Nails were the easiest thing to create in his shop, and he wanted to start me with something simple. After several attempts and hours, I made my first spike! It was not pretty, but it would do the job if needed.

I felt a tremendous sense of accomplishment with this achievement. I could see why Cressia's dad was so sturdy and fit, especially in the arms and shoulders. The heavy hammer used to pound the metal into shape took great effort to wield especially after working with it all day.

Days passed into weeks, and eventually, after making several progressively more challenging items, Gerbaut finally showed me how to make a sword. My first sword was short, and it was a bit crooked. But I worked on it for days until it was straight, smooth, and sharp.

As time went on my feelings for Cressia grew. I visited her nearly every day and had dinner with her family often. She also developed strong feelings for me, and it was clear to me we had something wonderful and a possible future! We went on countless long walks beside the creek and through the meadow at the edge of town. We created numerous precious memories that I often recounted when I was away from her. One, in particular, was nothing more than a look she gave me right before she kissed me one night. The look in her flush cheeks was that of complete surrender, trust, and love. I had never felt anything like it before. It was something I would do anything to keep.

After a year of working for Cressia's father I had finally established myself, I even saved enough to buy Gerbaut's hut. I worked long hours and nearly every day to improve any flaw in my technique and work. Word spread about my new skills at the shop, and people came to the shop often to purchase my works. People began to ask me if I was going to open a shop of my own, my skills become so well-known. I told them I would never do that to Gerbaut and they understood, loyalty was something everyone in the village respected.

Eventually, I built up the courage and confidence enough to ask for Cressia's hand in marriage. Her father was expecting it when I made the request and gladly gave his permission. I was so excited I could not wait to tell her. One late evening, I had dinner with her family as I had done many times before.

After supper, I took Cressia outside and, under the light of the full moon, I asked her to marry me. She said yes without hesitation. In our excitement, we took a walk together in the warm, summer air. The stars shone brightly, and it seemed the whole world was ours. We stopped for a moment to kiss; I could feel her soft lips pressed firmly against mine. I had always liked the scent of people for some reason that eluded me, but her smell was unusually intense and enjoyable on this day. Perhaps it was because of the intensity of the emotions at that moment. We were caught up in each other. I could smell something about her that drove an urge that I had been subconsciously repressing for decades now.

It was a craving that terrified me so much I kept it deep inside. But while she was in my arms, I had a tough time keeping the compulsion buried and repressed. The urge began to overwhelm me as I began to kiss her neck. I wanted her in so many ways I could not begin to think where to start. Finally, I felt the strong desire to bite her take over, and I pulled away from her. I was horrified by what I almost did. I had no idea why I wanted to taste her so badly, it almost felt like hunger or thirst.

Was it my desire to be with Cressia physically bizarrely manifesting itself? What kind of monster must I be even to have such an urge? I wondered.

I told myself I was not a monster and would never harm Cressia. I swore never to allow myself to even think about hurting her again after that night. It was an atrocity I was not willing to commit or even contemplate. For the first time since I had arrived, I felt the shadow of my past creeping in on me.

*   *   *

Several days later the entire family was sitting down to eat a late dinner in Cressia's father's home when we heard a commotion coming from outside. I could see the sun was setting on top the far hills through the window. It would be dark soon.

Men were screaming, "To arms! To arms!"

I saw a look of great concern come over both Cressia and her father. They seemed to have an idea of what it meant. Cressia's father opened an old wood box, that was reinforced with metal straps and lay near the entrance to the house. He reached in and pulled out two well-crafted swords.

"I hope you know how to use this!" He nervously tossed the gleaming, new sword in my direction.

I caught the sword by the handle and looked down at it, confused. The shimmering metal mesmerized me; it was a beautiful sword. Never had I seen such an amazing weapon. It was the end of the bronze age, and every sword I had ever seen before had been from that era. This was the first iron sword I had ever seen or held. A sinking feeling quickly gave me the notion we were about to enter a life or death fight!

Gerbaut opened the door and motioned for me to follow him. I hesitated for a moment then followed him out and encountered a large group of men clad in leather armor, bronze swords were drawn, attacking the town. Cressia's father charged into the fight, raising his sword as he did. I followed him holding my sword similarly. I did not have much experience fighting with a sword, so I mimicked him as best as I could. Gerbaut struck down a man right away, and I watched as the enemy lay on the ground, and his blood colored the ground red.

I could smell the pleasant aroma of fresh, warm human blood fill the air. It was like a banquet, nearly impossible to resist, but I found the strength not to succumb. I swung my new sword at the first assailant I encountered with a powerful downward swing with all my might. My weapon struck him through the shoulder and nearly cleaved him in two.

My strength shocked me and all who witnessed my blow. I was much larger than most of the men in the fight. Several of the intruders who saw my death blow stopped fighting for a moment to assess the new threat. They were clearly intimidated by both my size and apparent strength. Transfixed by my shiny unfamiliar weapon, they wondered about its composition.

The enemy held their bronze weapons at the ready when the largest of them swung his sword at me with all his strength, with a backhanded death swing. I slashed at his sword with mine and when they struck his bronze snapped in two. The man back away in disbelief, just staring at his broken blade.

Another man swung his weapon at me. I spun out of the way and quickly swung my blade in return, severing his free arm at the elbow. The man could only stand in complete shock as Gerbaut then thrust his iron into the large man's belly. After observing this, the three remaining men in our vicinity fled to fight elsewhere; they wanted no part of me. Gerbaut seemed in awe with my fierce fighting but did not have time to express it in more than a quick look of admiration.

We continued to fight, cutting men down like wheat in a field. The smell of blood got stronger, making it harder for me to resist the urge to indulge in my hunger. Something deep inside me began to take over. After nearly an hour of fighting, we heard the voice of a neighbor which sent a shudder through my heart, "They are raping the women!"

My heart sank! "Cressia!" I yelled. I immediately turned and headed back to the house, fighting my way as I went.

The sun set some time ago, and darkness surrounded us as I approached Cressia's dwelling. In the light of the nearby torches, I saw a man attempting to break into Gerbaut's home. He was a large, black-haired man, with dark, leather armor.

"Stop!" I yelled as I drew near.

He immediately turned and swung his sword, catching me off guard. His weapon sliced through my left arm, leaving a deep, gushing wound. I let out a terrifying yell as I swung my steel, ignoring to the pain in my arm. My blade sliced through his neck, and his blood sprayed all over my face and body. I could taste the sweet flavor as a steady stream of blood dripped into my mouth and filled me with sensations I had never felt before! Human blood was amazing! All I could think of was I wanted more.

Ultimately, I lost control, I bit the dying man over the hemorrhaging gash on his neck and began to drink. His life force filled my mouth and then my body, making me stronger than ever. Animal blood empowered me, but I had no idea that human blood could be like this! The blood brought my strength and senses to new heights. At that moment, a part of me wished those drops of blood had never touched my lips, for the temptation had completely taken over my mind, and I knew there was no going back now. Before I could stop, I had consumed all his blood. The first thing that came to my mind was I wanted more.

His body became limp and lifeless in my arms as Cressia opened the door. I pulled my mouth from his neck and observed the horror in Cressia's eyes. The shock of the sight of her blood-soaked fiancé, drinking the blood of the enemy was more than she could bear. The damage had been done and nothing could change that now. My sparkling ruby eyes forced fear into her heart. I was a monster in her mind, a bloodthirsty demon. I knew right away her feelings for me had changed forever. I could sense her thoughts clearly now, the human blood coursing through my veins, made my abilities stronger. Where love once resided in her heart, disgust and terror took its place. She looked into my red eyes with complete dread.

What have I done, I thought. *I've ruined my perfect life. How could I have given into my dark urges?*

Blood tears streamed down the sides of my face. I was completely devastated, my face begged for forgiveness!

Why did I do this? Why didn't I stop myself?

My brother's words reverberated in my mind like a hundred thunderous drums, "Spawn of Satan!"

My brother was right; I am evil. I am a monster. They should have destroyed me!

Suddenly, I heard footsteps approaching me; it was Cressia's father. I could now hear the thoughts of everyone around me more clearly than ever before. He was coming to help us when he saw for himself what kind of monster I was. When I turned in his direction, he saw my ruby eyes and my elongated incisors with human blood still dripping from them, his jaw dropped. I released the body of the dead man in my arms, and it fell to the ground limp and lifeless.

Gerbaut did not know what to think; he was in complete disbelief. "What are you?" Gerbaut screamed, as he carefully walked past me on his way to his daughter's side.

The superstitions of the day ran through his mind. I could only look back at him with nothing to say in explanation.

"What are you?" he screamed even more loudly. His look of dread was like a hundred expletives describing what I was.

His words blasted in my head and in my heart like a deafening explosion.

I now knew what I was, a heinous monster.

Just as I had feared and just as my brother had said. A plague, a disease on man just as my mother's dream had predicted, something to be eradicated. I could sense their fear, and rejection sting my whole body like countless needles. I did not blame them. I hated myself for what I had done and for what I was.

"Leave!" he screamed.

Unexpectedly, a sharp pain radiated in my back and continued through to my abdomen. I saw in horror as the tip of a sword burst from my stomach. Despite the extreme pain, I turned with the sword still lodged inside of me to find the attacking enemy who'd driven his weapon through my back.

My anger drove me to slash his neck deeply with my sharp claw-like hands, leaving several deep gashes behind. The man fell to the ground writhing in pain as he bled out. I was shocked by the unexpected damage I had caused and looked at my hands for an explanation. I almost could not believe my eyes for my hands had somehow changed. Although they still looked somewhat human, they had sharp, claw-like nails that protruded from each of my fingers like sharp, curved daggers. I reached behind me and pulled the sword out by the hilt. I felt a sharp pain radiate through my body. I internalized the pain, for I deserved it, and I wanted to die. The emotional pain was so severe I became numb to the physical pain.

I turned back to Cressia as blood oozed from my wounds. Her aversion and distress radiated from her like the intense heat from Gerbaut's forge. I knew she no longer wanted or loved me. She only wanted me to go, so I turned and headed into the dark woods with the full moon overhead. After several hundred feet, I fell to the ground. I knew my wounds were deep and life-threatening, so I decided to allow death to come for me.

Chapter 13

Hours passed, I was surprised death had not come. As time went on, I began to feel my strength return. When it was clear I was recovering, I sat up and examined my wounds. They were well on their way to healing! I could not believe my eyes!

What am I? I wondered.

I stood to get a better look at my injuries to find they had stopped bleeding and were beginning to pull themselves closed. Rage and self-hatred began to overcome me. I could not even die to escape the pain. I was an indestructible, unlovable demon! I no longer cared about anything. I fled further into the forest, looking for an escape from my pain but found nothing that could comfort me.

*   *   *

As days and nights went by, the emotional pain did not subside but began to consume me. I started to feel less and less human.

One night while walking through the forest, I could hear the voices of men in the distance. I crept towards them as if unconsciously compelled to do so. I cautiously approached the camp, my heart emotionless and empty. It was dark, and their campfire lit the night sky. It was easy to find them, too easy. I sat there watching them for several minutes as I felt the anger and rage build inside of me. It was men like them who had torment me my whole life. I hated them, and all I could feel now was hate. I burst into their camp and quickly killed all three and drank their blood.

My mind filled with unusual sensations generated by the effects of their blood. I found solace in the drug-like effects of the blood; it was my opiate. The blood was the only thing that distracted me from my pain. It was the only drug that dulled the devastation of my heart.

I started feeding on the solitary men I randomly encountered and in time my empty heart entirely callused over. It was not long until I began feasting on a few women as well. Eventually, I started using sex to lure women into my trap. I did not know it for some time, but women found me very attractive. I used this to my advantage. Sex also made the feminine blood taste even better.

Women quickly became my victim of choice. I had became the creature of folklore, all men and women feared at night. I became the monster of their nightmares. As time went on, I became comfortable with killing, and the pain inside was replaced with the pleasure of the kill.

Eventually, it became a game for me. I would often toy with my potential victims and see if they could find a clever way to get away from me before I delivered them to death. As I grew older, wiser, and stronger, I noticed that time seemed to pass more quickly. The months, years, and decades began to blend. Before I knew it, centuries had passed, and as always, I was alone. A chance encounter with a skilled swordsman changed everything. I was feeding on a beautiful, young woman of Troy. I found out later her name was Helen. I wanted to know if royal blood tasted better than the peasant blood that made up the bulk of my diet. The swordsman spilled my blood for the first time in centuries, and Pandora's box was open.

My blood covered my beautiful royal victim. In doing so, my blood infected her with my curse. At first, I had no idea what was happening to her. Curiosity overpowered me once again, and I watched her from a distance, studying her. I observed as she changed, careful to ensure she did not notice my presence. It took some time before I realized what was happening to her. She was transforming into a monster like me, a creature of the night.

Before this event, I had no idea how to make one like myself. I thought for the longest time that I would be the only one of my kind ever to walk the earth. Having discovered my blood was the key to make children of my own gave me hope. I studied my prodigy from afar, fascinated by her behavior. Years later, she also learned about this secret and produced a child of her own.

Before long her mate, who was her only creation, made numerous immortal children of his own. They roamed the earth spreading my disease across the whole world. They grew like wildfire. Starting with Dracula, my children were hunted down and killed, mostly by the Van Helsing family. One by one, my children were slain until only one now remains. Desperate to stay alive and to avoid the Van Helsing family, Helen changed her name to Roslyn.

Agent Grey and William glance at each other. They have no idea how many vampires still exist. "So, how many vampires did you say there are there now?" William asks, narrowing his eyes?

"Other than myself there is only one remaining."

Agent Grey and William both look at each other again with astonishment. They had no idea how successful at irradiating the vampire infestation they had been.

William stares at Lucious intently. "So, Roslyn is the last vampire?" William's excited by the thought and wanted to make absolutely sure he heard him right.

"She is the last."

The two men are curious.

"How can you be sure?" William asks.

"I can sense all my children."

"If you can sense them, do you know where they are?" William asks.

"Yes, I know where they are."

"Where is she, where is Roslyn?" William questions.

"She's here, in Seattle." Another blood tear trails down Lucius cheek. He resists with all his might but can not keep from betraying his oldest and only remaining progeny.

Chapter 14

A few days later at the Seattle Coroner's office, Jack Turner is finishing the autopsy of Carl Dunn's body. Suddenly, two men in black suits burst into Turner's workroom.

Jack's startled by the intrusion. "What are you two doing in here?" Jack demands.

"FBI. Special Agent Grey!" The tall man in front says quickly flashing a badge and then tucking it away in his breast jacket pocket.

William stands next to Grey with a cold demeanor. Jack can not help being distracted by the three thin parallel scars that run from the just below William's left eye and down the side of his face to his jawbone.

"This is most unusual. I haven't finished my report yet." Jack protests.

"Don't worry. We aren't interested in your report. We'll conduct our own investigation," William replies.

Jack tries his best not to stare at the scars and has to force his eyes away. "What are you talking about?" Jack protests.

"We only need a couple of minutes with the body, please."

The pair motion for him to move away from the table. Jack reluctantly moves aside as the two men quickly go to work. William turns the head of the corpse to the side and carefully examines the neck, while Agent Grey keeps his eyes on Jack, the two men stare each other down. After a moment of careful examination, William notices two small punctures in the skin of the neck.

He looks up. "It's her!" he says.

Grey brakes eye contact with Jack and looks at the corpse for a moment. Without another word, the two men turn around and head for the door.

"Thank you for your time," Agent Grey says over his shoulder.

"Right, no problem," Jack responds, clearly unhappy.

*   *   *

Grey and William walk into the FBI building in downtown Seattle. They push the button, and the pair enters the waiting elevator. Agent Grey puts his encrypted key card into the slot, which gives him access to the top floor of the building. This floor is the maximum-security floor, which only a handful of Agents with the appropriate clearance can access. The elevator opens to a small room, where a robust armed Agent greets them. The security Agent knows the pair well and allows them to pass through the door behind him, which leads to the rest of the floor.

Agent Hwan Cheong is briskly walking towards them in the corridor. He reaches the pair just on the other side of the bulletproof glass security door they just walked through. Cheong's apparently in a bad mood. Agent Cheong is an unusually large Korean with striking eyes. He is very fit and muscular and is an inch or two taller than agent Grey. He fills his navy-blue suit well and is wearing his trademark red tie.

Cheong has always stood out, even as a young man, because of his considerable stature. He is also the youngest Agent ever to be put in charge of a state branch headquarters for the FBI. One of the reasons Agent Grey has a hard time respecting Cheong, as he is much younger than Grey. Grey feels Cheong is too green to be in charge. William and Agent Grey glance at each other and try not to look concerned.

"What the hell is going on here?" Cheong demands.

Cheong has a hint of a foreign accent, he has been working hard to rid himself of it.

"To what are you referring, sir," Agent Grey asks.

"Why have you been torturing a prisoner in my facility, and why has he been strapped to a metal table for nearly twenty-four hours straight?" he roars, his face turning red.

"Sir, he's not a prisoner, he's a terrorist. I'm interrogating him, and he is under my supervision."

"This isn't Guantanamo, this is my facility, and I say who supervises what!" Agent Cheong barks.

"Sir, with all due respect, I have the President's authority in this case because of the prisoner's status as a terrorist. As you already know, I'm an agent of the President's special terrorist task force, and that puts me in charge of this individual."

Agent Cheong's eyes narrow. "Cut the crap! You can't just label anyone you want as a terrorist, just to circumvent the constitution, and more importantly . . ME!"

Grey strains to remain calm. "Sir, all of the paperwork you need on this case is on your desk."

Cheong does not want to back down, but his curiosity about those documents is growing.

"We'll see about this."

"I'm sure we will, sir. But in the meantime, I need every agent's cooperation. I'm the only one who's to have any contact with this detainee. I need you and your agents to provide security and make sure he is under lock and key at all times."

Agent Cheong coldly stares at him, analyzing his options. He realizes he has hit a brick wall. "This isn't over." Cheong marches off in the direction of his office, on a mission.

He is not going to let this one go easily. He is not the type of person to allow a violation of the constitution of any kind in his facility or let anyone challenge his authority.

"We're running out of time," Grey says to William without looking at him. His resentful eyes follow Cheong down the hall.

The pair let out a deep sigh and head for the interrogation room.

Chapter 15

They enter the room where Lucius still lays confined on his cold, metal table.

Lucius looks over barely able to move his head because of the restraints. "Well if it isn't Tweedle-dee and Tweedledum."

William glares at him. "Very funny, Lucius. We'll see how funny you are in a moment."

Grey moves over to the locked cabinet. He pulls out his keys, opens it, and pulls out the electronic pad. Lucius tenses almost unconsciously at the very sight of the menacing pad now in Grey's hand. He closes the cabinet and walks over to the table where Lucius lays.

"I'm going to kill you very slowly," Lucius growls.

"Good luck with that," Grey replies with a cocky smile. He touches the tablet and sets the device to the settings that'd given him the results he wanted in their last session. Lucius's body suddenly goes limp.

"Now we need to see about your abilities. If this works the government will have a powerful weapon," Grey pauses. "Now what number am I thinking of?" he asks looking curiously into Lucius's eyes.

Lucius looks back and reaches into Grey's mind. "2,947," he states confidently.

Agent Grey smiles. "That's correct."

William is standing at the door, his arms folded. A half-hearted smirk perks the corners of William's mouth. He has never said so out loud, but he just wants Lucius dead. *It is a bad idea, turning him into a weapon. There are too many things that could go wrong and if they do it will mean disaster. As far as I am concerned, the only good vampire is a dead vampire*, Willian thinks.

Grey continues his experiment. "Now, what's the name of the person I'm thinking of?"

Lucius reaches into his mind again. "Sonja Mallard," he states.

"And who is she?"

"She's the first girl you ever kissed, on your sixteenth birthday," Lucius replies.

"Very good!" Grey replies, pleased with his progress. With his curiosity satisfied he decides to change the subject. "By the time we got to the location you gave us, Roslyn was gone. We need to know where she goes, so we can be there waiting. Where can we find Roslyn? Where does she go?"

Lucius fights to restrain himself. "S . . . S . . She frequents several bars. Her favorites are the Dub Pub, Bill's and St . . ."

A knock at the door interrupts Lucius. Grey looks toward the door and then at William who stands next to it with his arms still locked.

"See who it is, will you?" Grey motions with his head.

William reluctantly uncrosses his arms and opens the door. It was Agent Farmer, a young blonde who received her badge only last year.

She pokes her head into the room. "Agent Cheong wants to see you both in his office right away!" she says in a practiced, professional tone.

"We're in the middle of something!" Grey protests.

"He said it's urgent and to have you report immediately. Both of you!" she insists, casting her eyes in both of their directions.

The two men look at each other; they are confident this means trouble.

What does Doogie want now, Agent Grey thought.

He has always thought of Cheong as a Doogie Howser type because he had achieved so much at such a young age. Grey reluctantly sets the electronic pad down, and the two men exit the room, close the door behind them and ensure Agent Farmer has left.

Farmer starts down the hall in the opposite direction of Grey and his minion. She glances over her shoulder as they turn down the hall, heading directly for Cheong's office. As soon as they are out of sight, Farmer stops in her tracks and heads back for the interrogation room. She waves her badge in front of the electronic sensor at the door, the light turns green, and the door opens much to her relief.

She had only been granted clearance for that room minutes before. Cheong changed the clearance setting on her badge to allow her access. Without pause, she flies through the door and to the metal table. She releases the metal clamp that restrains Lucius's right hand and then the one on his bicep. No sooner has she done so, Lucius grabs her by the throat with lightning speed!

"Got you!" he roars.

She grabs his hand with hers and struggles for a moment, but quickly realizes it is futile. His hand feels like a metal vice because it is so solid.

"Stop! I'm here to help you. I'm getting you out of here. I'm moving you to a secure facility. Agent Cheong is taking custody of you," she explains.

Lucius thinks about this for a moment and confirms her intentions with his dark gift, then releases her. She lets out a deep sigh of relief and wonders if she is doing the right thing now that she knows he is capable of such violence. She hopes Cheong knows what he is doing. Despite her reservations, she continues to free him. As soon as he is unfettered, the pair head for the door.

"I have a car down in the garage. I'll take you to our Tacoma office where you'll be safe." she continues as she begins to put her cuffs on him, he pulls back.

"I need to put these on you to get you out of the building without drawing suspicion from other agents."

Lucius hesitates but realizes she is probably right. He allows her to put the cuffs on, figuring his vampire strength is more than enough to break out of the cuffs if he wants to. The cuffs are nowhere near as strong as the restraints on the table. It would not be the first time he has broken out of shackles. He has not had blood in several days and wonders if in his weakened state if he is strong enough to bust out. She locks his hands in front of him and leads him out of the room.

Lucius fights the urge to flee without her; he is not convinced he needs her help any longer now that he is out of the room. One thing he is sure of is he is not going to let them put him in another cage. Any thought of bolting changes once he is out of the dark, interrogation room. He feels his great strength leave him as soon as he steps into the corridor. It takes him by surprise when he notices the sun shining through the far window. He strains against the cuffs to free himself. He now does not have the strength to break himself out without his abilities. With his plans dashed, he has no other choice than to take advantage of Farmer's help.

"We have to move quickly!" she stresses as she leads him to the stairwell.

She opens the door and leads him into the entrance of the stairwell just as Grey and William come around the corner. The meeting with Cheong has been short, too short. The Agents' eyes meet at the same time. Farmer looks like a deer caught in headlights, her eyes widen.

Grey can not believe what he is seeing. "What are you doing!" he screams.

Farmer turns and darts through the door and down the stairs with her prisoner, like a bandit with her loot.

Chapter 16

Farmer and Lucius have raced down half a dozen flights when Grey and William finally enter the top of the stairwell! Her heart is pounding; her anxiety is peeking! She runs as fast as her slender legs can carry her. Seconds seem like hours, it feels like forever has passed by the time Agent Farmer and Lucius finally reach the underground parking garage. She opens the door and rushes the prisoner to her black SUV.

She puts him in the backseat and darts for the driver's side! She starts the car and slams it into gear. Tires squeal and smoke as the car lurches into motion, just as Grey and his partner burst through the stairwell door!

"STOP!" Grey yells. "You don't know what you're doing!"

Farmer's vehicle is almost to the exit. Grey and William pursue her on foot for a few seconds but quickly realize they will never catch her. The two men change directions and speed to Grey's SUV and screech into action as her vehicle leaves the garage. Grey's car bursts out of the garage. In seconds, they are in sight of her as she speeds down the crowded downtown streets.

Farmer plans to get to the freeway, the on-ramp is only a few blocks away. She is desperate to get there! She blows through red lights narrowly missing other cars as she drives like a woman possessed! Within a few minutes, Grey is right on her tail, swerving in and out of traffic, causing a bicyclist to tumble to the ground to avoid a near collision.

She reaches the I-90 ramp and flies around the loop, tires squealing. She pushes the pedal to the floor as she approaches the straightaway, cars honk their horns as she flashes by! Agent Grey isn't going to let them get away that easily. He too pushes his gas pedal to the floor.

Within minutes, Farmer can see the floating bridge ahead of her. Two of the longest floating bridges in the world lay right ahead of them as she races down the freeway. She can see the traffic is somewhat clear ahead; only a few scattered cars are on the bridge. Her heart fills with hope.

I'm going to make it, she thinks!

Her SUV's engine roars as she races onto the bridge. Her vehicle reaches ninety miles an hour and beyond as she contemplates her escape route. She quickly gains on two large trucks and a car positioned right next to each other in adjacent lanes, blocking all three lanes of traffic ahead. She decides to go around the large tow truck that occupies the outside right lane by driving on the shoulder.

As she enters the shoulder, her speed is so high it causes the SUV to swerve on the loose gravel and debris, and she struggles to regain control of the vehicle. The back of the car fishtails as she battles the wheel. The left rear of her SUV slams into the back of the large tow truck as she completely loses control of the car. The impact sends her vehicle careening into the side barrier of the floating bridge, loosening one of the concrete walls.

For a moment, she can see nothing but ocean water in front of her when another violent impact with the side barrier causes her vehicle to spin violently in a complete circle. Several of her side windows shatter spraying them with small pieces of glass. Grey's right behind her and slams on his brakes, but it is too late. His automobile crashes into her spinning vehicle and sends it into the barrier again. This time Agent Farmer's crumpled car knocks a section of barrier over the side of the bridge and into the ice-cold water of the

Puget Sound, it sinks like a rock. The back window smashed on impact.

Farmer's automobile comes to a sudden stop, teetering on the edge of the bridge, right where the missing barrier was moments ago. The back end of the automobile is facing the water and Farmer now faces Grey's vehicle. She is dazed and confused, as she looks around the crumpled cab and then to the backseat. Lucius is still sitting in the back seat and isn't happy. He does not appear to be injured but is a little stunned himself.

"Get me out of these cuffs!" he is nearly yelling at her.

Farmer seems too disoriented to comply or even to be able to rationalize his request. Grey's automobile's momentum had completely stopped in the impact. He hops out as all the remaining traffic on the bridge comes to a screeching halt behind him. Farmer strains to regain her senses and looks out of her cracked windshield and notices Grey standing beside his vehicle. Their eyes meet for a moment as her thoughts suddenly start to clear, the tense moment shocking her to her senses. There's nowhere for her to go now.

"It's over. Get out of the vehicle and surrender the prisoner!" Grey demands.

The teetering vehicle shifts and tilts over the side of the bridge. Grey lifts his hand as if it would somehow steady the vehicle.

"Don't move!" Grey yells.

Farmer has no intention of moving. She can feel the weight of the vehicle shifting below her. She knows it will not take much to send the vehicle into the water taking her and her prisoner to their deaths. The odds of survival will be very low if she is in the automobile when it hits the water. The waters of the Puget Sound never get much above fifty degrees even in the middle of summer.

"Get me out of here!" Lucius yells trying his best to break through his restraints, unable to do so.

Farmer carefully reaches for the keys in the ignition. The car shifts again, she freezes, hoping the automobile will stop. She turns the ignition and frees the keys. The car stabilizes again, as the keys drop and can feel the cold metal in her small hands. She tosses them back to Lucius. The keys to freedom bounce off his knee and fall to the floorboards. The car shifts again and slips off the edge of the bridge and begins to fall towards the cold, dark water.

Both agent's eyes widen as the peril of the moment strikes them at the same time. The car falls, and the two opposing agents can only watch each other, in their helpless visual embrace. Then, the SUV plunges into the Puget Sound, and begins to sink!

"No!" Grey screams, knowing there's nothing he can do.

The broken windows allow the car to fill with water quickly. Within a few seconds, the car sinks beneath the surface of the dark, green water and is gone, taking its occupants with it. Grey races to the edge of the bridge, knocking a couple of loose chunks of concrete into the murky water.

"NO!" Grey screams again, as he reaches for the bubbles that now percolate to the surface.

William casually walks up behind him, and they peer down into the gloomy depths with no signs of survival. William looks up at the sun as it dips below the Olympic mountains in the west, then back into the dark waters below with a smirk. The water becomes much darker with the setting of the sun.

"Well, I guess that's that," William says coldly. He is not sad to see the end of another vampire.

Grey continues to stare into the water and is clearly beyond upset and William's comment does not sit well with him. His new powerful weapon is gone.

Chapter 17

A few hours later, Matt and Michael sit in their favorite spot at the Dub Pub, one of their college hangouts. The Dub Pub was just remodeled a couple of years ago and looks very modern now. Rows of black and grey matching tables and chairs are neatly lined up in rows. The bar has a variety of alcohols carefully stacked on shelves, brilliantly backlit by the new lighted panels behind the bottles.

The bar has all the usually amenities, new dart boards, pool tables, and a small hardwood dance floor. Back in their UW days, the pair of friends fancied themselves as pool sharks. The University of Washington frowned on such behavior because gambling was not permitted on campus. So, they had to take their skills here to avoid getting in trouble. They weren't the best but good enough to make a few extra bucks for college tuition.

Now, years later, their connection with the purple and gold Huskies has never been stronger. They love all the U.W. sports teams. Football is still their favorite sport to watch. Since it is baseball season now, they loudly cheer the squad on! Any Husky squad is worth cheering for as far as they are concerned. The game is now in the sixth inning, and the Huskies are at bat. The purple and gold are down by three when the Husky batter hits a home run with one on base.

The bar erupts in a loud simultaneous cheer! Matt and Michael hit their feet, raising their arms and screaming at the top of their lungs! They turn towards each other and high five like they had countless times before. Much to Matt's relief, he can tell Michael's feeling much better.

"See. I told you this's what you needed!" he says giving Michael a firm pat on the back.

Michael's unable to argue with the fact he is feeling more relaxed than he has in ages, he too thinks that Matt's right. The seventh inning stretch arrives, and Matt gestures towards the pool tables.

"Think you still got it?" he asks with a challenging tone.

"Let's see!" Michael replies.

The friends leave their chairs and head for the tables. "I have one thing to say. You're going down my friend, down!" Matt reaches for a pool stick, clearly excited to have a cue in his hand once again.

After racking and breaking the balls, Matt sinks several before finally missing his fourth shot.

Satisfied with his performance he glances at Michael. "Bet you can't sink more."

"We'll see," Michael replies with a steely determination.

Michael quickly sinks three balls and then also misses his fourth shot. He remains in his shooting stance and shakes his head, closing his eyes in disgust. Still, he can not remember the last time he has had so much fun!

"Dude! That chick's totally checking you out!" Matt says in a hushed tone.

Michael looks up at Matt who is gesturing his head towards the bar. Michael stands and turns; he notices a young woman with long, light brown hair sitting at the bar. Her back is to them, and she is not looking in their direction. She is wearing a long, slender, black dress that makes her look like she might be slightly overdressed for the bar.

"Whatever." Michael shakes his head again and returns his attention to their game.

"Seriously. I saw her!"

"She's not even looking at me."

"Not now, but she was."

"Yeah right. You're just trying to get me to talk to

her." Michael knows Matt well, and his tactics won't work on him.

"No! I'm dead serious this time! She's into you man!"

"Let's just play pool," Michael replies, he isn't in a mood for Matt to mess with him. He is finally in a great mood and wants to stay that way for at least the rest of the night.

"Chicken!" Matt says putting his hands in his armpits and moving his elbows up and down, making a small spectacle of himself as he chuckles.

"Really. What are you, six?"

"Come on. When was the last time you were on a date?" Matt inquires.

"For your information, I was on a date last week. "Michael states, knowing he could not count lunch in the break room with a female doctor a "date". He just wanted to save face.

"What! Are you serious? With whom?" Matt asks surprised and very curious.

"With Beth."

"Dr. Stevens?" Matt asks disappointed.

"Yes."

"Lunch on break doesn't count," Matt retorts.

"We had a deep, meaningful conversation about her dog."

"What? Her dog?" Matt shakes his head; he is further disappointed. He hoped Mike had actually been on a real date.

"Her dog is very important to her."

"Doesn't count." Matt is firm.

"Yes, it does," Michael insists, still trying to save face.

"Does not."

Michael tilts his head. "Now you're trying to make both of us six."

"Just do it! Go talk to her." He gestures at the woman at the bar.

"Oh wait, now I'm truly persuaded." Michael rolls his eyes. "Your argument was too compelling," he adds sarcastically.

"I'll pay you a hundred dollars if you go up and talk to her."

"You don't have a hundred dollars," Michael replies.

Matt pulls a one-hundred-dollar bill out of his wallet and places it on the table. Michael eyes the bill half surprised.

"It's yours if you talk to her," Matt says, playfully taunting him.

Michael considers the prospects. *What's the worst that could happen*, he thought. *I end up with some of Matt's money. I guess I win either way.*

"You're a jerk," Michael chuckles, picking up the bill.

"Happy hunting!" Matt says slyly.

With a sigh, Michael walks to the bar and sits down next to the woman. His first thought is she must be younger than him. Only by a couple of years though.

"Can I get you something to drink?" he asks bravely.

The woman turns her head slightly in his direction, gazing at the full glass in front of her, playing with the small umbrella inside.

"You can't afford my drink," she said softly still not looking at him. "Besides, I haven't finished the one I have."

"I'm a doctor, and I'm sure I can afford whatever drink you'd like." Michael feels a little insulted; she seems to pick up on this.

"I meant no insult. A doctor you say." She turns further and looks directly at him but does not look him in the eyes. She wants to mend the feelings she hurt. "So, you save lives, do you?" she says playfully.

"I do. Or at least, I do my best to," Michael answers confidently.

"Who would save your life if your life hung in the balance?"

"Well, I guess another doctor. Perhaps, my friend over there. He is a doctor, too." He motions to Matt who is moved back to their seats.

"You might want to call him," she affirms with a lighthearted air. Their eyes meet for the first time, and they both feel a connection.

"Why's that?" Michael says curiously a bit distracted from their instant connection.

"Because you're in trouble," she says with a teasing wink.

Michael chuckles, her unusual humor seems to encourage him. "My name's Michael," he says holding out his hand.

She turns and gracefully takes his hand. "I'm Roslyn."

Their connection only gets stronger when their hands touch, it radiates through them like an electric wave.

"So, where you from?" Michael asks.

"Back East."

"Ok, so, what you do for a living?" He is undaunted by her short response. "I work in pest control."

He is puzzled by her comment, it did not make sense. When he pictured someone in pest control, he thinks of a man in a jumpsuit with a dog catcher's stick or maybe a canister of bug spray in hand. She does not seem to fit the picture at all.

"You live here now?"

"You ask a lot of questions." She flashes her gorgeous, pearly whites again.

"How else can you get to know someone?"

"You want to get to know me?"

"Sure."

After a moment of thought, her smile fades and she turns back toward her drink. "You don't want to know me."

"Why do you say that?"

"Trust me, I'm trouble." She sounds a little sad.

"Oh, so you're married?"

"No. I'm not married. Or at least not anymore."

"You're engaged or have a boyfriend?"

"No and no." She looks back at him.

Her eyes are a clear blue with a gemlike quality that makes his heart melt. He had not felt initial chemistry like this in a long time. He does not ever remember feeling a connection this strong with anyone. He feels she has a compelling charisma and charm that is very rare. She looks like she is hesitant, but turns towards him again.

"You're single?" Michael asks.

"You could say that." She reaches up and runs her fingers through his dark hair; the touch is exciting. "You remind me of someone I once knew."

"Really!" He is surprised.

"Yes."

"What was his name?" Michael asks, thinking it was probably stupid to have asked.

She pauses and her forehead wrinkles. "Are you sure you really want to know?"

At this point, he realizes it is probably a mistake to seek more information but urges her anyway.

"Vlad," she replies quietly.

"Did you love him?" *Now, I've really gone too far, just keep digging your hole*, he thinks.

"Yes, very much. Too much, as it turned out." She is saddened by the memory and turns back to the bar.

"What happened. If you don't mind my asking?"

"No harm in asking," she answers, her grace shakes him to his very core.

"Well?"

"He turned into a monster?" her reply is cold.

"He abused you?"

"Not really."

"What made him a monster?" Michael's intrigued.

"I did."

"I'm afraid I don't understand," Michael says with an uneasy chuckle.

"There's no way you could understand."

"You're an unusual woman!"

"You have no idea," She says with a mischievous grin.

He could not help but realize the conversation is bizarre, but, for some reason unknown to him, he is compelled to know her more.

"So what brings you to the Emerald City?" he questions with his best charm.

She tosses her hair to the side with a slight flick of her head and turns back to him. "I like it here. It's almost like the city was calling to me."

"Calling to you?"

"Yeah, it was like I was compelled to come to this city."

"And you have no idea why?"

She pauses in thought. "It feels like I should, but for the life of me I can't quite figure it out. I do love the weather here."

Michael thought she must be kidding. Who in their right mind would like the constant cloudy weather? "You're joking?"

"No, actually I find the weather rather pleasant."

"OK." Michael's trying hard to figure her out. "You're a little mysterious, aren't you?"

"Why do you say that?"

"You don't like to give out many specific details about yourself."

"You already know everything you need to know about me. Whether someone is from Japan, America, or from Australia, people are just people."

"But everyone has his or her own unique little quirks," he continues.

"Sweetie, when you get as old as I am, you don't have quirks, you're eccentric."

"Old as you are?" He laughs. "You can't be more than 25?"

"That's very kind of you. But you're way off."

He looks more firmly into her eyes as she looks back at him, they twinkle like sapphires, and are deep with an old soul look to them. Older than any soul he has ever seen before. She has a wisdom and grace about her that does not come from someone who looks 25. She has an unrelenting stone cold confidence about her that causes him to question his own. Despite her self-assurance, she does not come across as arrogant. She has an overpowering poise that is completely solid.

"So, can I have your number?" he asks politely, as he starts to rearrange the condiments scattered in front of him.

"I'm afraid I don't have a number." She shakes her head slightly, casually noticing his awkward behavior.

"You don't have a phone?" his voice resonates with disbelief. He finishes his organizing and refocuses his attention on her.

"No, never have."

"How do people stay in touch with you?" he asks perplexed.

"They don't."

"Don't you have friends and family you want to talk to?"

"No. No one."

"That's sad." He moves a little closer to her, for some reason he feels the need to comfort her.

"In my line of work, people who get close to me end up getting hurt."

"I didn't know pest control was so dangerous."

"It has its moments."

"If I wanted to see you again, how do I go about doing that?" Michael tries to lay on the charm.

"I don't think that's a good idea," she says, clearly conflicted.

"Why not?"

"Because I like you," she says slowly, looking into his eyes.

"That's kinda the point."　His brows furrow.

"I would like nothing more than that, but I think I'll have to pass.　For your sake," she affirms with a refinement that only makes him want her more.

Michael is confused.　"I'm a big boy.　I can take care of myself."　He pushes his chest out slightly.

She pauses, scanning his face.　His attention pleases her in a way that's both exhilarating and troubling.　"I'll think about it."

"OK.　Here's my card."

"It was a pleasure meeting you," she says reaching for the card.

An overwhelming urge overtakes him.　He takes her hand as she reaches for the card and gallantly kisses the back of her hand. Sparks fly, he can feel every nerve in his body tingle. He thinks she can feel it too. He lowers her hand. Her eyes twinkle as if she can not fight her feelings any longer. She moves in close to him and kisses him on the lips. The kiss is breathtaking, like a bolt of electricity running through their bodies! She finally regains control and pulls away from him, and leans back in her stool. They pause, not sure what to say as they look into each other's eyes intently. There is something here between them, but neither is ready to admit it.

He finds himself uncharacteristically silent for a moment. "The pleasure is all mine," he says finally.

The thought of seeing her and having her touch him again is all that is on his mind. She places the card in her jacket pocket. Every fiber in his body beckons for him to stay. His intellect kicks in, and he remembers he has ignored his best friend for far too long. Michael reluctantly says a short goodbye and walks over to Matt, looking over his shoulder at him as he approaches their seats.

Chapter 18

"Dude, you missed the top of the seventh! I assume it all went well?" Matt is trying to be patient with Michael. He had no idea the talk would go this long. He is glad Michael has finally talked to a woman but is a little disappointed he missed half of the 7th inning. Matt's happy, however, that he appeared to have a good time.

"Yeah, I guess," Michael responds nonchalantly.

"Did you get her number?" Matt Asks.

"No."

"What? Why not?" *After all of that time the least he could have done was gotten her phone number. Then it would have at least been worth missing part of the game,* Matt thinks.

"She doesn't have a number."

"What? What kind of person doesn't have a number?"

"Apparently, her." Michael glances back at bar for a moment.

She has her back to them and looks amazing sitting there, he longs to be with her. Another man moves in on the young beauty, who is left unattended.

She must get lots of attention, he thinks. He returns his gaze to the game in which he now has little interest.

"She's probably just not interested," Matt says roughly.

"Oh, I wouldn't say that." Michael can not help but feel a little jealous over the attention she is getting. He is confused by these feelings. He has just met her, no reason to feel this way.

"Why? Did she give you some reason to think she was interested?"

"You could say that," Michael answers.

Now his interest is peaking. "What happened?" Matt grins like the Cheshire cat.

"Well, we kissed."

"You dog! I guess you still got it." Matt was impressed.

Michael turns back to look in her direction, but she is already gone. He scans the bar, frantically looking for her, but she is nowhere in sight.

Had she left with that other guy, he wonders?

Outside the bar, Roslyn stands peering through the bar's window. She can see Michael's eyes searching for her. Her heart sinks, and although she knows little about the game he is watching, she wishes she could be inside cheering with him. She imagines his strong arm draped over her shoulders, his amazing laugh dancing in her ears. She has refused to allow herself the luxury of a companion in many years. The last time she found love it ended so terribly it took decades for her to recover. In fact, the world itself had just recovered from the aftermath of her last love affair.

With that thought, she pulls out an old gold locket that hangs around her neck. She gazes at it with longing and sadness. A bittersweet memory is hidden deep inside the heavy gold locket. It has intricate designs and is very valuable both monetarily and sentimentally to her. She opens the locket and gazes at the two-small hand-painted faces on opposite sides of the locket. The paintings are of Vlad and herself.

She can not help but notice how much Michael resembles the man she once loved, part of her still does. Perhaps that is why Michael caught her attention. She looks back up to the two men watching the game. That could be a good thing; it also could be a terrible thing. She knows it would be a monumental mistake to bring Michael into her world, but that does not stop her from wanting him just the same.

"Roslyn!" a man's shrill voice pierces the darkness, breaking her concentration.

She does not have to look to know who it is. It is a voice she knows well.

"How can I help you, Mr. Van Helsing," she says callously, still looking at Michael through the window.

"You can help by ending your life. That's if you can even say you're alive," William replies.

"I'm afraid I can't help you with that." She kisses the locket and allows it to hang from her neck as she turns to face him.

He stands about 40 feet away from her on the other side of the narrow street. She can clearly see the signature scars under his left eye. He is wearing his usual black suit, and his colleague stands beside him.

"I see you're still working with Agent Grey." She notices William Van Helsing is holding a long Bowie knife; he just pulled from its sheath.

He seems to have competently ignored her comment.

"It's silver plated, just for you!" William grins, gesturing to the knife.

"Good to know." She does not show an ounce of fear.

The pair of men walk across the street towards Roslyn.

"And I thought this was going to be a friendly visit," she says sarcastically, standing her ground with a sigh.

The two men continue relentlessly towards their prey.

"How long are we going to do this dance?" she asks politely.

"Until you're in a cage or dead. You've killed far too many people to walk away scot-free." William has a hint of anger in his voice.

"I've only killed people who truly deserved it. Never have I harmed an innocent person." She shows little emotion to his comment. "Why now a cage? Why the sudden change? You've always wanted only to kill me before."

William increases his pace and again seems to have ignored her comment. "Everyone's guilty of something. Who decides who's guilty enough for death? You, I think not! What were my father and brother guilty of?" he screams, the anger in his voice increasing.

"I had nothing to do with either of their deaths."

"It doesn't matter if you did it or not. You are a monster just like the one who killed my family. You have killed, and will kill again. As for the cage, I still want you dead, but Grey here has plans for you."

Roslyn senses Grey's thoughts which dwell on his recent loss. His feelings are of near desperation; he must have her for some nefarious reason. She shutters when his thoughts reveal that Lucius is dead. The man who was always her safety net is no more. He seemed to always show up and save her when she needed him most. Now he is gone, but he was much more than a source of safety to her. He was her maker a fact she had only discovered a few short years ago. She can see the vision in Grey's mind as Lucius sank beneath the cold depths of the Puget Sound.

"So, you finally killed Lucius," she states remorsefully, a blood tear drips down her cheek.

She begins to feel uneasy for the first time since the Van Helsing family has started their pursuit of her. She has never been aware of Lucius following her, so she did not know how he always found a way to be in the right place at the right time. Whenever her foes were on the verge of delivering her onto death's door, he had managed to find a way to stop them. But he was gone now, and there is no one to save her this time. She is on her own. Another blood tear slides down the side of her face full of the remorse for her fallen creator.

"Ironically, we didn't want to kill him. He wouldn't play along, so we had to extinguish him just like all the others," William replies. "And the same will happen to you if you don't behave."

They fearlessly approach her, and yet she does not move.

"Don't do this. I don't want to hurt you," she warns.

"I'm going to enjoy carving you up, bitch!" William slashes violently at her with his silver knife.

Roslyn effortlessly moves out of the weapon's path with time to spare. He slashes at her over and over but only catches air, she is much too quick. He might as well be standing still, but he is earning an "A" for effort. Undaunted, he desperately attempts to inflict serious bodily harm on the girl.

Grey becomes more concerned with each moment that passes, for William's attack appears more and more futile.

"Careful!" Grey pulls a gun out of a shoulder holster which catches Roslyn's attention.

William's next slash almost connects, she is distracted by the gun. The knife catches her jacket ripping it open.

Grey aims the gun at Roslyn's head. "Don't make me kill you!"

With lightning reflexes, she pushes the gun away from her head, when it goes off. The bullet passes through her hand, barely missing her head by an inch or two. Roslyn lets out a blood-curdling scream, blood splatters across her face. She darts away from the two men through the alley behind the bar with unbelievable speed. She is gone in a flash, like a shadow disappearing into the night.

William helplessly watches as she quickly vanishes into the darkness. He is used to vampires staying in the fight and giving him a chance to kill them, not fleeing. Grey points his weapon and resists the urge to fire, he does not want any civilian casualties on his hands.

"You want . . . me . . . to be careful?" William states, obviously annoyed, breathing heavy from the exertion. He could not believe Grey was being so careless and yet asking him to do the opposite. After a few deep breaths, William looks down and notices a piece of paper on the ground that had not been there a moment ago. It is a business card, it must have fallen from her torn jacket. He picks it up and reads it. "Dr. Michael Bauer. Children's Hospital," William reads aloud.

　　The gunfire attracted the attention of the bar patrons, including Michael and Matt. They are peering out the windows, wondering what has just transpired. The two men put away their weapons and walk away, hoping not to draw any more attention.

Chapter 19

The next day at Children's Hospital, Michael is making his rounds when he hears a voice over the intercom, "Dr. Bauer, you're needed at the front desk. Dr. Bauer, you're needed at the front desk."

That's odd, Michael thinks. Seldom has he been called to the front desk. *What's this about?*

When he arrives at the reception desk, two men in black suits wait for him. A tall, dark-haired man and the other has three parallel scars on his face.

"Dr. Bauer?" The tall man asks.

"Yes? How can I help you?"

"FBI, Special Agent Grey." The tall one flashed his badge and then puts it away. "We need to ask you a few questions."

"Ok. Let's go to my office," Michael suggests, wondering what they could want.

"Great," Grey replies.

The three walk down the hall and to Bauer's office where the physician opens the door and allows them in. They follow him, and Michael sits down in the black leather chair behind his comfortable desk. He motions for them to take the two seats in front of his workstation. These chairs are much smaller and swivel.

"How can I help you?" Michael begins, leaning forward and folds his hands on the desktop.

"We understand you've been in contact with a woman named Roslyn?"

Michael unfolds his hands and sits back in his chair. The uneasy movement triggers a response in Grey.

"Yes. I just met her last night."

"What's the nature of your relationship?" Grey asks sternly.

"Relationship? I don't have a relationship with her. As I said, I just met her." Michael's defensive.

Grey's years of training tells him he is telling the truth. "If you're smart, you'll forget you ever met her and stay as far away from her as possible." Grey's adamantly forthright.

"Why?"

"She's a murderer."

Michael's brow furrows. "She's no murderer."

"I thought you said you didn't know her?" Agent Grey leans forward in his seat.

"I don't. But I can tell she's not a

murderer," he replies confidently.

The man with three parallel scares chimes in, "Things aren't always as they seem, I assure you. She is directly responsible for hundreds, if not thousands, of deaths."

Michael shifts in his seat again. "Hundreds? Really? That's impossible."

"It's true," William answers coldly.

"Hundreds? What is she? A mass serial killer of some kind?" Michael asks. His concern is growing.

"Worse."

"Worse than a serial killer?" Michael wonders where the conversation is leading.

"I can see that you don't believe us. If you go near her, we will be forced to intervene." Grey's very serious.

"Intervene?" Michael shifts again uneasily.

"She's been classified as a terrorist. If you have any contact with her or assist her in any way, you will be deemed a terrorist as well," Grey explains.

"Are you out of your mind? This must be some kind of joke, right? Did Matt put you up to this?" Michael barks.

Grey is unmoved. "As a terrorist, we'll ship you out of the country where you'll no longer have your constitutional right for a trial or an attorney."

"That's ridiculous! You can't just label someone a terrorist and ship them off just to take away their rights. As an American citizen, you can't take those rights from me!"

"Yes, we can, and we will if you force our hand," Grey replies grimly.

Michael sizes the men up carefully. "Who's this with you? He points to William. "I never saw his badge."

"This is William, and he's none of your concern," Agent Grey is stern.

Michael picks up on the situation. "Isn't it unusual for a civilian to accompany an FBI agent on a case?" Michael's grasping at straws, but his statement is on the mark.

"The FBI doesn't answer to you." Grey pauses. "But for your information, he's a special consultant."

"Consulting for what?"

"That's none of your concern.

"If you see her again, you'll let us know, immediately. Won't you?" William asks.

"Of course," Michael says disingenuously.

Grey hands Michael his card. "Call me the moment you see or hear from her."

"A . . . Alright."

The two men stand up, starring Michael down, and attempt to intimidate him. Without another word, they turn and walk out of the office, leaving Michael to his thoughts.

*   *   *

As a vampire, Roslyn needs to feed a couple of times a month. She chooses her prey carefully. She only preys on people she refers to as "monsters". Rapists and murderers are her favorite victims. She feels they are the worst of the worst. Her dark gifts make it easy to find evildoers. Able to read their minds, she can know their true intents and what they are going to do before they do it.

Tonight she has found two men who fit her criteria for food. Both who have killed before, according to her special abilities. She can tell they have committed worse acts, but can not be sure on the details because those thoughts are presently too deep in their minds for her to reach clearly.

It does not take much to get them to follow her. She leads them down the street, late at night, much later than she prefers. She normally aims for midnight meal. The early morning is quickly approaching. She has called off hunts at this late hour in the past, but she has not fed in over two weeks. These two are particularly bad men, so she continues the chase. Hunger is starting to become overwhelming. She is beginning to feel the effects of not enough nourishment. Her strength is waning. She is still several times stronger than a powerful man.

The two men she coaxed into following her are gaining fast. She looks for the perfect place to spring her trap and ensure no one sees what is about to happen. She never likes taking on two people at the same time, as it leaves far too many variables. She makes an exception in this case because she feels slightly drained from hunger, and these two deserve what they are about to get.

Two birds with one stone this time, she thinks.

She walks ahead of the men as they attempt to corner her in a parking lot. She does not like the visibility of the open lot and avoids being trapped. Despite the hour, there are still people out and about. It is a weekend, she hoped people would have gone home by now and is irritated by the night owls.

She scans the area for the perfect place while they continue to trail her. She is in a part of town where she has not hunted before. Good spots for a clean kill seem to be few and far between here. She darts through the lot, down a back street, and through an isolated neighborhood with the two men hot on her tail. Each time she thinks she has found an excellent place to do the deadly deed, people seem to pop out from nowhere, or there is too high of a chance a video surveillance system might catch the killer. That is all she needed, to have her kill caught on video and put on YouTube.

Finally, after she has nearly given up, she finds an appropriate spot. It is an empty parking lot with high retaining walls on two sides, no cameras either. She allows the men to move in on her. She enters the semi-enclosed lot, and the area feels isolated. There is no one to be seen. She now feels relaxed. As quickly as she calms down, they corner her, leaving no escape.

"You gave us quite the chase." The ugly, short man is out of breath.

"Leave now, and I'll let you live," she warns.

The men glance at each other, chuckling in unison, and move closer.

"This is your final warning."

"What're you gonna do, little girl?" the short, ugly one says sarcastically.

He is heavyset and bald and smells like stale beer. He is wearing old, dusty jeans and a grey Grateful Dead t-shirt. She finds this very ironic, given the situation.

"I'm going to kill you," she states matter-of-factly.

"Oh really." They continue to laugh. "Now, be a good, little girl, and this will be over before you know it," demands the ugly one who produces a pair of handcuffs while the older man holds up a black bag he intends to use as a hood for her head.

The older fellow is also wearing jeans and has long, grey hair that creeps out from under his black, knit hat. He has on a red and black flannel long-sleeved shirt and has deep wrinkles that crease his face. It seems like he has had a hard life, as he looks much older than he probably is.

"And if I don't?" she asks.

"You don't have a choice." The old one is missing a tooth on the upper right side of his mouth which makes him look even creepier.

She responds without emotion. "You're welcome to try."

The men move in for the capture. The ugly man grabs her wrist and tries to twist her arm behind her back; her limb does not budge in the slightest. He is confused, how can a little woman possibly be strong enough to resist him. He puts all his strength into twisting her arm; still, it does not budge.

The older man notices his partner struggling and moves in to assist. He grabs her other arm and puts all his force into the struggle. Both men strain, but it is a futile effort to subdue her in any way. Perplexed, they look at her with disbelief when she shoots an eerie gaze back at them. They notice her eyes are ruby red. She pushes them back, knocking both off their feet.

"What the hell are you?" the ugly one yells from the ground a little dazed from the fall.

She walks up to the ugly one, grabs him by the throat, and squeezes. He can feel the blood rush to his head and knows he is undoubtedly going to die. She moves in for the kill. Suddenly, the clouds part over the Cascades in the east revealing the early morning sunrise. Morning sunbeams illuminate the man's face and strike Roslyn. Her grip rapidly weakens. Her eyes fade quickly from red back to her original blue. A wave of dread sweeps over her.

The older man gets back on his feet. He rushes towards Roslyn and tackles her, breaking her grip around the ugly man's neck. She falls to the ground, striking her head on the hard asphalt, and the world goes dark.

Chapter 20

Michael's mind is going wild as he contemplates the recent strange events. The only one he can think of with the answers to his questions is Roslyn. He can not explain even to himself why he has this sudden obsession with her and the truth. *Why do I even care who she is or why she's in trouble. Why do I feel the need to help her? he* wonders.

Agent Grey's threats ring in his mind, giving him caution. It has been almost a week since he has seen her, now he finds himself determined to find her. That night he is back at the Dub Pub and waits for Roslyn to show up. Hours pass and, there is no sign of her. He continues patiently waiting and it is getting late and still no Roslyn. The bar closes, yet no sign of her. He returns the next day, and again, waits for hours. The time seems to crawl as his anxiety grows, but still Roslyn is nowhere to be found. The bar closes again, and he leaves, disappointedly pondering what to do next.

Roslyn awoke a few hours after the two men captured her. The sun shines in her eyes through the bars of the single window in the small, confined room. She checks the solid, metal door; it is locked from the outside with no way for her to escape. The door has a closed slat right at head level. The firmly mounted bars of the window prevent any attempt to leave. The walls are made of cinder blocks and are a cold, grey, and unpainted. The room is lit only by the sun through the window and a small light in the center of the room. There are two tiny foam pads for sleeping and several dusty blankets scattered about the floor.

A dark-haired girl huddles in the fetal position in the corner. She is wearing a light pink t-shirt, grey jeans, and white sneakers. She has several fresh bruises and scrapes, and her clothes have several small tears, telltale signs of a brutal struggle. She must have fought her assailants, but failed. She appears to be in shock, shaking like a leaf. Hard to tell at first if it is from the cold or the trauma of the abduction, or both. Roslyn moves over to the girl, who does not even seem to notice her.

Roslyn suddenly realizes she is feeling something she has not felt in a long time. There is a pain, coming from her forehead. She rubs her head for a moment, and when she pulls her hand down, she is surprised to see it is covered in dark, red blood; her blood. She has not seen her own blood in over two hundred years, and it is a queer sight. She must have split her head open when she was thrown to the ground. She vaguely remembers being tackled by the smelly, older man. She looks up at the sun through the barred window, the light blazes in her eyes. The sun's still up.

That's why I haven't healed yet, she realizes.

Trapped in this room with someone who probably can not help her, she contemplates her options. The girl in the corner looks like she needs some serious help herself. Roslyn's great strength along with her dark gifts are gone. From the sun's position in the sky, it is not going to set anytime soon. She sits down beside the young girl and looks her over for injuries. The traumatized teen cowers, quietly moaning.

"Where are we?" Roslyn asks the young woman.

The girl does not stop her rocking motion or answer. She still does not seem even to realize Roslyn is there. The girl's in worse shape than she thought.

"Are you ok?" Roslyn continues.

The girl makes no sign she hears her. Roslyn puts her arm around her.

"It's going to be ok." Roslyn attempts to comfort her.

The adolescent still makes no response. A few minutes later, a man with a round, bald head opens the sliding slot on the door at face level. She assumes he is one of the guards and is probably from down south judging from his dark complexion and accent.

"You're gonna fetch a nice price, despite that ugly cut on your head!" The man cackles in a thick, Mexican accent.

Roslyn glares back at him with a defiant look.

"Attitude! We'll see what kind of attitude you have after you've been sold, chica. In a couple of years, you'll be all used up and no one will want you." He closes the small opening coving his smirk.

*   *   *

The next night Michael's back at the Dub Pub. When he walks in a woman with light golden brown hair sits with her back to him at the bar. Roslyn! He walks over to the woman.

"I was beginning to think I'd never see you again," he says.

The woman turns around, and her green eyes jump out at him.

"Excuse me," she says.

It wasn't Roslyn.

"I'm sorry. I thought you were someone else," he replies.

He walks away from the bar, a little embarrassed over the whole thing. He orders a soda and sits in the corner waiting for Roslyn to show up. He wonders if he will ever see her again. He remains until the bar closes and ends up leaving disappointed yet again. As he goes, he realizes he can't do this forever.

Chapter 21

Several days pass and Roslyn awakes again, startled when the metal door suddenly opens with a loud squeak. A large fat, bald man walks in with handcuffs. Roslyn recognizes his eyes and mouth as the same man who had spoken through the door slot on several occasions before. He has slid two meals that went untouched through a slot at the bottom of the door a couple of days ago.

The first night Roslyn tried to break down the door when her vampire strength had returned, but the reinforced door was too strong. She might have been able to do it if she had just eaten, but she was not strong enough now. The metal bars were also too much for her, so she is trapped. The only light in the room comes from the single light bulb in the center of the ceiling.

Roslyn glances out of the barred window to see only darkness and the dim glow of the city lights far away. She guessed the city must be at least twenty or thirty miles away.

"Time to go, little one," he says coldly in his thick, Mexican accent.

"I'm not going anywhere with you." Roslyn rises to her feet.

"I'm not talking to you, bitch," he says roughly. "This one has been sold for a hefty price! I wanted to have some fun with her myself, but we can get more if she is not violated."

Roslyn looks down at the girl with the dark hair, who is sitting. The young girl had started talking on the second day. Roslyn discovers that she is a runaway who found herself seeking help from the wrong people.

"Don't let them take me," the girl cries.

"I won't, Roslyn replies and then looks back at the fat man. "She's not going anywhere with you."

The fat man looks at Roslyn with a malicious grimace. "You want to play, little girl. I guess I have time to break you in. I'm sure our clients won't know the difference if I loosen you up a little." He starts to reach for Roslyn but stops suddenly. His smirk quickly dissipates when he notices the cut on her head is completely gone, no scar of any kind.

Roslyn pulls out her gold locket. The guard's fascination with the disappearance of her injury is interrupted when he notices the necklace.

"How did we miss that! Give that to me," he demands.

She kisses the locket and lets it hang. "Come and get it."

"Chingada!" He reaches for the pendant.

She grabs him by the throat, squeezes, and he can feel the blood pooling in his skull. He can not breathe, and his head feels like it is going to explode. He struggles to pull her off him, but she is like a stone statue, unmovable. He feels the darkness creeping in and panic sets in as he fights frantically to get free but is helpless. The darkness consumes him, and he falls to the floor with a loud thud. She immediately feeds upon him. She can feel his fading heart pumping his lifeblood into her.

The girl in the corner screams, and races out of the room more scared of Roslyn than of the guard. Roslyn senses life filling her body as her full-strength returns. Another guard shows up at the door when he notices the other young girl fleeing. He had heard the scream and came to investigate. He wants to chase after the young girl running down the adjacent corridor but stops when he sees Roslyn hanging over the body of the dead man.

"What the hell's going on here," his accent was Russian. He was a higher up on the food chain, a lower level boss.

Roslyn stops feeding and peers up, flashing her red eyes. "I'm putting an end to your little operation here," she states.

He does not notice her red eyes at first; he is too distracted at the sight of the lifeless guard on the floor. "You're not doing anything but what we tell you," he replies. He does not know how she managed to kill him but he is going to stop her.

She displays her dagger-like whites.

He stops in his tracks. "What the hell?" He feels fear for the first time in years. He is used to instilling fear, not receiving it. She bolts in his direction ready to inflict pain.

*   *   *

Michael spends all his spare time at the Dub Pub for a full month and still no Roslyn. He becomes mentally and physically fatigued from his late nights out, and his work at the hospital begins to slip. He decides he needs to take a couple of his sick days to continue his search.

Where did she go? Is the FBI's story true?

He has to find her at any cost. He has always been level-headed, but now he is starting to feel like he is more obsessed and does not know why.

I've only met this woman once, so why's she so important to me? Why do I feel such a strong connection with her? Why do I need to do this?

He must find the truth. After closing the bar yet again, Michael walks to his car. He is fishing for his keys when he notices a hooded, shadowy figure standing in the dimly lit alley next to the Dub Pub. He almost does not see the person at first because it is so dark.

"Who's there?" he yells into the darkness.

There was no answer.

"Who's there?" he repeats.

Then the shadow moves towards him. He is startled, and he stumbles, trying to keep his composure. The eerie person comes closer and closer. Panic fills his veins, and he prepares to defend himself when the shadow removes its hood and speaks, "How are you, Michael?"

The street lights illuminate the figure's face. It is Roslyn!

He tries to talk but finds himself speechless. He clears his throat and tries again. "R . . Roslyn."

She smiles, and he can see her beauty now illuminated by a nearby streetlight. It seems to lighten his mood, after long last he has found her, or she has found him. That does not matter to him now, only that they are together now.

"You seem well," she continues.

"I'm ok. Where have you been?" He tries to hold back his frustration and anxiety.

"Oh, I've been around."

"I've been trying to find you."

"I know."

"How do you know?"

"A woman has a way of knowing things like that," she replies playfully. "I also know that you've been coming here for some time now. I need you to stop," her demeanor and voice became serious.

"Why?" he asks, a terrible foreboding fills his heart.

"We can't be together. It's too dangerous for you."

"If it's so dangerous, why are you here?" Michael asks.

"Because I care about you," she insists. "I don't want you to waste your life looking for me."

Michael pauses and then says, "I've heard some terrible things about you?"

"I know." She can see his thoughts clearly, her dark gift probes his mind.

"So, they're true!" he replies in disbelief.

"No, I wouldn't say you've heard the truth about me."

"What's the truth?"

"I really can't tell you," she responds.

"Why not?"

"If I told you, your life would be in more danger than it already is."

"So, you're a terrorist?"

"No, I'm not a terrorist." She chuckles lightheartedly. "The FBI rarely tells the whole truth."

"This isn't funny. The FBI's after you."

"I know."

"They're asking me to turn you in."

"I know." Her face does not change expression. "But I also know you have no intention of turning me in."

"How do you know that?"

"I can tell. It's written all over your face." Although truthfully, she read his mind.

"So, if you're not a terrorist what are you?"

"I'm a woman."

"Well, I can see that you're a woman." That brought some romantic thoughts to his mind.

He is trying not to allow those ideas to creep in, but they are very persistent. He moves closer to her, and she does not resist. He raises his hand to her waist, and she does the same. Their free hands meet, and their nerves tingle. An overwhelming urge to kiss her begins to take over. He pulls her closer. He feels her hand move to his shoulder, and his entire body aches with anticipation. For some reason beyond his understanding, he wants her more than anything.

Why do I feel this way, I hardly know her? he wonders.

She appears to feel the same way. He touches her face with a gentle caress. His finger moves to her chin, he tilts her head toward him, so that he can kiss her. Their lips are nearly touching when a thunderous explosion erupts, knocking Michael off his feet.

It was a concussion grenade, often used by police to stun suspects! Michael lays on the ground dazed and looks up and sees Roslyn still standing. Somehow, she was unfazed despite the blast. Two men in riot gear with assault rifles rush from the darkness, screaming for Roslyn to get down on her knees. The blast only slightly dazes Roslyn.

Noticing the weapons, she realizes she is no match for a pair of semiautomatic assault rifles, she bolts for the alleyway beside the bar. With speed faster than any human possesses she disappears into the shadows. The two men fire as she vanishes into the darkness. Michael can only watch from the ground still stunned.

The men stop shooting and walk over to Michael, more men in black riot gear rush from a nearby van with dark-tinted windows. Roslyn is gone before they can engage her. The two shooters pull off their dark hoods and reveal it is Grey and William. They stand triumphantly over Michael almost gloating. The men from the van pick Michael up off the ground and hold him firmly as Agent Grey and William supervise.

"You should have left good enough alone," William says putting handcuffs on Michael as he pulls the doctor's arms behind his back.

Simultaneously, Grey puts a black hood over his head. Still stunted, Michael's still having trouble putting together coherent thoughts and lays silent as the men carry him to the back of a black SUV.

Chapter 22

Several hours later, Michael has regained his bearings. He still has the black hood over his head and senses he is in a small, enclosed room. He is handcuffed with his hands behind his back and sitting in a hard, steel chair that is bolted to the floor. His cuffs are secured to a chain bolted to the floor. He can make out a low bright light pointing directly at him that faintly brakes through the fabric of the hood. Other than the illuminated bulb in front of him, he can not see much. He struggles to free himself, but it is no use. The cuffs are secured and do not budge.

A short time later, he hears a metal door open and close to his right. Someone pulls the hood off, and the light suddenly seems bright. The sound of two people's footsteps breaks the uneasy silence. One stands to his right, hood in hand. The other walks over to the table in front of him, and he hears the person pull a chair out as he takes a seat behind the table in the shadow of the interrogation light. Michael's eyes begin to adjust.

"Michael Bauer," Grey's deep voice rings out.

"That's Dr. Michael Bauer to you."

"Still a little defiance in you. That won't do you any good in here."

"You can't do this. I'm an American citizen," Michael pleads.

"Yes, we can. You're aiding a terrorist and thus have been labeled a terrorist yourself. You'll be shipped out of the country where you'll have no rights."

"I'm in the country now; you can't just ship me out to remove my rights," Michael protests.

"It's a technicality, but rest assured, once you're out of the country, you'll have no ability to complain about your rights."

Michael thinks about this. He can feel rage building. "Who are you? You're not FBI!" Michael doubts a federal agency can get away with such treatment.

"Oh, I'm FBI alright," Grey sits confidently in his chair.

Michael looks to the man on his right. It was the man with the three scars. "I know he's not FBI."

"Oh, my friend here? William's a Hunter," Grey begins.

"A Hunter of what?"

"Vampires," William answers.

"What're you talking about?" Michael does not believe a word he is hearing.

"Yes. The woman you know as Roslyn is a vampire," Grey continues.

"You guys have just gone from crazy to cuckoo?" Michael replies, attempting to jump up from his chair but instantly failing. The cuffs firmly restrain him.

"We don't have a lot of time here. Please just listen," Grey explains.

"Ok . . ." Michael realizes he has no choice in the matter.

"According to our records," William begins, "Roslyn changed her name from Helen about 600 years ago. We believe she was born in Persia nearly two and a half centuries ago. We believe she was also married into a royal family in the ancient city of Troy."

Michael thinks this through for a moment. "Wait a minute, are you trying to tell me she's the Helen of Troy?"

"Yes. Don't interrupt me again." Grey's getting hostile. "We'd like to capture Roslyn, preferably alive. We need your help to do that."

"How'd the FBI get involved in killing . . ah . . vampires?" Michael asks, still having a hard time even being a part of this unusual conversation.

His mind is still trying to wrap itself around the idea that Roslyn could be the Helen of Troy.

"The FBI is not involved in an official capacity. I was investigating a suspected terrorist and was hot on his trail when the killer ambushed me. William here happened to be hunting my suspect too. He showed up just in time to terminate the suspect before he killed me." He points to the man with the scars. "William's been a Hunter his whole life."

"My family's been hunters for hundreds of years," William interjects.

"As I was saying," Grey continues with a glance at William. "The suspect I was after turned out to be a vampire. When William saved my life, I felt I owed him. Plus I felt compelled to learn more about these creatures. I started helping him track down and kill vampires, which I now have a personal interest in."

Michael's thoughts race as he notices the scars on William's face. "You were attacked by a vampire?

"Clearly," William was a little uncomfortable with Michael staring at his scares.

"Why aren't you a vampire then?" Michael asked. He had watched several vampire movies in the past and thought he knew a little about the lore.

"The vampire slashed me with his claws," William responds. "We've learned from years of experience and confirmed our information through the original vampire himself, that the Nosferatu infection is a blood borne pathogen. We believe it's transmitted by direct blood to blood contact. One must either ingest the blood, or it can enter the body through an open wound. The vampire's blood never came into contact with me, so I was spared the infliction."

Grey continues his explanation, "After the vampire's failed attempt on my life, I started using my FBI authority and resources to help hunt down and eradicate vampires ever since. We've found every last one of them, only Roslyn remains. She's the last vampire. She must be caged or killed, ideally caged. This infestation must not be allowed to spread. Our original mandate was to simply eradicate vampires, but because of recent developments, our mandate has changed. We've come across a technological advancement that's made Roslyn of particular interest to the government. We want to study her once we have captured her."

"This is very interesting. I didn't know the FBI employed lunatics. Oh, wait, yes I did. Sorry, my mistake." Michael's condescension is not taken well.

"This's no joking matter. It's very serious," William replies.

"Oh, I'm sure you believe that. Now, let me out of here," Michael demands.

"I don't think so," William states.

Grey opens a metal briefcase. Michael's eyes can vaguely see as they adjust to the light. He puts on some latex gloves and pulls out a vial with dark red fluid in it and holds it up for Michael to see.

"This is a vial of blood we acquired from the original vampire," Grey explains. "We believe it can be used to create new vampires. If we don't have your help and get what we want from Roslyn, we'll start experimenting with this and create a vampire of our own. If it works out, we will make an army of invincible soldiers."

Michael is getting a bad feeling by the look on Grey's face that he might be part of their experiments. Michael thinks that he might be their first vampire.

"Why would you create the one thing you've been trying to destroy?" Michael notices William seems to agree with him.

"We'll be in control of these new vampires," Grey explains.

"It's in your best interest to help us," William states, clearly in conflict. "Either way you'll aid us. You see, the best way to catch a predator is to use bait and you're the bait." He seems pleased with himself.

"She's not going to come for me. She doesn't even know me," Michael insists.

"You better hope she does. You'll find your life will be very difficult if she doesn't," Grey replies.

"What're you going to do . . kill me?!"

"Make no mistake; if we wanted you dead, you would be," William says.

"You can't kill me," Michael's voice begins to shake.

"The FBI has been killing people for a very long time," William states. "Who do you think killed JFK? If they can kill a President, they can kill anyone."

The gravity of the situation finally sets in as Michael quietly contemplates his odds for survival, they are not good.

"Anyway," Agent Grey interrupts with a displeased look. "As you know technology gets more advanced every day." Grey sets the red vial back in the metal briefcase. He then reaches for something else that's inside. "We've made new advances that have unlimited potential." The agent pulls out a very high tech looking syringe. It's mostly glass but has electronic components embedded in the clear material. "Do you know what this is?" He motions to the syringe.

"No, should I?" Michael asks.

"These are nanites; it's the latest advancement in nanotechnology. The creators of these machines designed them to enter a living cell and repair it. It accomplishes this by attaching to a cell and rebuilding it from the inside restoring it a state where it functions properly. Unfortunately in humans, the machines destroy the cells they attach to. The creators designed them to work on any cell in the body, even brain cells. Imagine a little machine attaching itself to a single neuron in the brain," Agent Grey states.

Michael relies on his vast medical knowledge. "If you were able to attach to the axon of the neuron you could control the firing of that neuron. You could prevent seizures. You could cure Parkinson's!" Michael thinks of all the diseases that it could cure.

"That true, but unfortunately, there are several bugs to work out and the solutions may not be achievable for humans."

"That's too bad," Michael turns his head? "I hope you don't think I can solve your problem for you?"

Grey ignores his comment. "As you've pointed out, these nanites can be programmed to control the brain cells in which they attach. Once attached to the neuron, it can control the electrical firing of that cell. Controlling when a brain cells fires effectively give us control over someone's mind."

Michael glares at the agent. "I'm pretty sure that's not what they were made for."

"You're right, but that isn't going to stop us," Grey replies. "Regrettably, no human has survived the procedure thus far. A vampire, however, has. We need to study the effects this technology has on vampires. We have two reasons for this; one is to control vampires. A vampire could become a very potent weapon. The second reason is to find a way to make the process work on humans. Once fully developed, we'll be able to make people feel and think whatever we want.

Imagine a world with no war, with no crime. Everyone happy and living in harmony."

"A world of mindless automatons," Michael says with disgust. "You'd take away peoples' humanity, their freedom."

"Peace has its price," Grey replies.

"You're insane!"

"Sadly, we've put ourselves in a bit of a pickle. This infliction is so dangerous that we don't want to risk making a new vampire. We have one last chance to develop this process without endangering the public more. We need Roslyn. She's the only one left we can experiment on."

"You're even crazier than I thought!" Michael's shock is apparent.

"With her regenerative abilities, she should be able to survive the process. If it wasn't for the fact that she's the last of her kind and the promise of this new technology, she'd already be dead. But as you can see, we need her alive for our research. That's where you come in."

Michael pulls at his cuffs again. "I'll never help you!"

"Oh, but you will," Grey seems more confident than ever. "You already are. She's going to try and save you. When she does, we'll be ready and capture her. Once we have her, we'll inject her with these nanites. They'll take control of her mind and her abilities. We'll be able to use her to read the minds of our enemies. We'll discover terrorist's plots and can intervene before they happen. She'll be one of the governments most powerful weapons! We will even have her create new vampires for our arsenal. With any luck, the nanites in her blood will transfer in the process and her children will already be under our control as well."

"You really have lost your mind." Michael hopelessly drops his eyes. "She won't come after me."

"For your sake, you better hope she does.

Chapter 23

A week later in the early evening, a pizza currier stands in the reception area of the FBI's building in downtown Seattle. He has the typical red, flashy jacket and white hat on, worn by the small army of pizza deliverymen scattered around town. He is quite impatient and a little belligerent. The young woman in the form-fitting grey suit at the reception desk sits in her comfortable chair with her arms crossed.

"We didn't order a pizza," she insists. Her light brown hair is neatly rolled in a tight bun.

"That's not what my order says!" the man says raising his voice.

"I don't care what your order says. Get out of here, and take your stupid pizza with you!" Her irritation increases.

She usually keeps her cool in situations like this, but her short fuse may be a result, in part, by the fact that she is fresh out of the academy and feels she should be dealing with more important matters. She has a four-year degree and is a well-trained agent. It is a waste of her talent to be sitting at the front desk. The man's frustration escalates to anger, and he pounds on the grey, marble countertop that separates him from the young woman.

At this point, she has had enough and pushes the button on the intercom. "I need security down here right away," she squawks impatiently.

"You called security over a pizza. What's wrong with you?" the man yells.

"Sir, leave now," she demands, pointing her slender finger at the entrance.

"You're a real piece of work," the man screams at the top of his lungs, veins bulging from his neck.

She gets to her feet and stands her ground. She glares at him as he glares back. Suddenly, the expression on his face changes to one of great concern. He reaches for his chest and clutches it. He lets out a strangled cough and falls to the ground; the woman watches in horror. Her training kicks in and she calls for medical assistance, and is around the marble countertop in a flash!

"Sir, are you ok?" Her demeanor has completely changed to considerable concern.

His eyes roll back, and he continues to grasp his chest and grown, he does not look up at her.

"Sir, can you tell me what's wrong," she pleads.

A small amount of foam starts to leak from the corner of his mouth and run down his cheek and onto the floor! The woman's eyes nearly pop out of her head! She can not believe what is happening! A group of armed men in riot gear burst into the room, weapons ready to fire!

"Stand down! We have a medical emergency," the woman explains.

The men ignore her and continue to secure the room. A few moments later, medical staff arrives on the scene. The moment they arrive, the delivery man begins convulsing like a flopping fresh fish out of water. Chaos fills the room, putting everyone on edge!

"What happened?" the medics ask the woman.

"I don't know. One moment, he was yelling at me, and the next, he was on the floor, foaming at the mouth."

Just then the lights in the facility go out.

"What the . . .!" The young woman holds back what she wants to say!

The emergency lights come on, but the room is still dim.

"What the hell's going on down there?" a voice screams from the radios the security guards have strapped to their waists.

The guard who seems to be in charge replies, "We have a medical alert in the lobby, and we've lost power!"

Back on the 20th floor in a dark questioning room, Michael sits alone and can tell something isn't right. The emergency lights are on around him, and he can hear feet running in the nearby hallway. The faint sound of frantic voices in the hall also clue him in. On the other side of the two-way mirror of the interrogation room, Grey and William are also made aware there is a crisis when the lights went out.

They had been standing there staring through the mirror waiting for Michael to crack when the commotion started. Time sitting alone stewing in one's thoughts is a common tactic used by the government to break down suspects, but now they have more significant concerns than Michael.

"What's going on?" William asks.

"I don't know, but we need to find out for sure." Grey heads out the door and closes it behind him.

William continues to stare through the mirror at Michael. A few moments later, a knock comes on the door. William goes to the door, he guesses Grey has forgotten something and pulls it open, but no one is there. He looks down the hall in one direction and then the other, but finds no one. He dismisses it, and when William nearly has the door closed, it is flung open with great force hitting him in the chest sending him back sliding across the floor. He strikes a set of chairs that are neatly arranged and scatters them across the room like a bowling ball.

William is out cold.

Chapter 24

Michael looks up when he hears the noise through the mirror. He can not see anything but his reflection. Suddenly the door to his room starts to make a groaning sound and is ripped open. A shadowy figure moves into the room and to Michael's side. He can feel the person firmly pull on his shackles. He can hear the metal groan, and the chains on his cuffs snap, freeing him. He stands up and turns to face the shadow; it is Roslyn!

"How'd you find me?"

"No time to talk now. They'll be here any second. We have to get out of here!" she replies with urgency.

The two leave the room and hurry down the dark hall. They turn down an adjacent corridor and see an exit sign glowing brightly at the far end of the dimly lit hallway. Freedom is only a few seconds away! They are halfway to the door when Grey suddenly appears ahead of them; he is as surprised as they are.

"Roslyn!" Grey yells.

The couple stops in their tracks and immediately start back the way they came.

Grey lifts his radio mic to his mouth as he bolts after them. "The prisoners are trying to escape! They're now headed down the north corridor! Close every exit in the facility; no one gets out of here!"

Most of the security in the building is occupied in the lobby, so it will be several minutes before Grey gets help. Michael and Roslyn turn down one corridor after another but are not able to lose Grey. With her superhuman strength, Roslyn can get away easily, but with her companion in tow, it is no easy task. Grey relays their position at every turn. Within minutes, the duo hears footsteps in nearby stairways and in passage. The sound of feet is getting closer with every passing moment.

It will not be long before the feds are upon them! They have no way of escape in sight, and the shadow of the FBI lurks all around them. They make one last turn into the only corridor that footsteps are not coming from; dead end! The hallway ends with a window and one door. They check the door, but it is locked. They are trapped like rats in a maze.

Grey slides around the corner and stops in the middle of the corridor. Several armed agents emerge from the nearby elevator and form an intimidating, impenetrable line behind him. A cruel grimace spreads across Agent Grey's face.

"There's no way out," Grey says triumphantly. "Don't make us destroy you. We'd prefer to keep you alive."

"I'm still having a hard time believing that," Roslyn barks. "Your only goal has been to kill my kind." She reads his mind and discovers his treacherous plans for her. Her heart trembles with his terrible intentions.

"Well, it's your lucky day. Things have changed. If you surrender, we promise to let your boyfriend go."

She does not have to read his mind to know he is lying. Roslyn tilts her head slightly and sarcastically replies, "You know I can tell you're lying."

Grey lowers his head for a moment then looks back into Roslyn's eyes, "Ah, yes . . . I guess you can read my thoughts. Then you know by now that's why we want you alive."

"I'll never help you. I can see what you want with me. Do you really think your technology can control me?"

"If it can't, you won't live to tell about it." Grey is cold and serious. "This is your only chance for survival. If my men open fire, even you with your regenerative abilities, may not survive."

Roslyn is defiant. "I've survived worse than you Grey."

Grey leads his host of armed men as they slowly march down the hall towards the helpless couple. Roslyn can feel desperation dripping like sweat down the side of her face. She glances around the room looking for anything that can help her, but there is nothing. She spots the fire alarm and looks below the alarm taking notice of an extinguisher encased in the wall. It is not much, but it is better than nothing. She snatches the extinguisher from its case and points it at the approaching agents.

The men momentarily pause their advance to analyze the new weapon she defiantly points in their direction. After a short pause, they continue their march realizing it is no threat. Roslyn pulls the pin and presses down on the fire extinguisher handle, and a large cloud of retardant chemicals sprays out and completely engulfs the agents.

For several moments, the entire corridor is completely obscured. Roslyn tosses the extinguisher through the window. She brakes the remaining glass with her fist and motions for Michael to climb out on the ledge.

Michael hopes she is kidding. "Are you crazy?"

"We don't have time to argue. Go!"

Michael's reluctant to comply.

"Just get out and hold on tight." Roslyn insists.

Michael gingerly climbs out on the ledge and holds on tightly to the edge of the building, there is not much to hold on to, but he has a death grip on the little that is there. She too climbs out onto the small ledge with Michael clinging to the side of the building like a large monkey. The night sky is clear, and the moon shines brightly. With her vampire claws, she has no problem holding fast to the side of the building. She looks down the 20-story drop and knows they can not go down. She might be able to survive a fall of that height, but Michael definitely can not.

She looks up to the roof of the building; it is only a few feet above. She scales the short distance like a spider. Once on top of the roof, she reaches as far as her body can go down for Michael. He reaches up for her hand, but she can not reach down far enough, she is about a foot and a half short.

"You're going to have to jump," Roslyn insists.

Michael looks down for a moment and then up at her hand that is not so close. "You're crazy!"

"I'll catch you."

"You're not strong enough to hold me."

"Yes, I am." She did her best to encourage him.

"That's impossible. I weight twice as much as you."

"Please trust me."

Michael looks down again; the height gives him the willies.

"They're coming, Michael. Jump! Now," she urges.

Michael looks carefully at her hand. "This is nuts!"

"Just do it!"

Michael gives in and jumps, reaching and grasps her wrist, simultaneously she grips his. To his astonishment, she holds his weight. She surprises him more when she lifts him up and onto the roof. He can not believe his eyes. He is grateful to be safe on the roof but confused by what he has just witnessed.

"What are you?"

"I'm getting that question a lot lately," she replies.

"You didn't answer the question."

"You know what I am. We don't have time for this. We have to get out of here."

In the corridor below, the air begins to clear, and Grey finally finds the window. He leans out and points his gun looking for his targets. He looks down, to the sides and finally up. He manages to see Michael just as he disappears on to the roof.

Unable to follow, he yells to the other agents, "They're on the roof!"

Without any hesitation, the group sprints for the stairway.

Roslyn's mind races as she struggles to come up with a plan. She leads Michael to a deployed parachute. It is now flapping in the wind and is tangling on the roof air-conditioning units.

"Thank God it's still here. This is how I got in. It wasn't my plan on how to get out though!" Roslyn used the parachute to land on the roof, gliding from the much taller nearby building, earlier that evening. "Put this on," she says as she takes the straps from the harness and places them over his shoulders.

"But what about you?"

"Don't worry about me, just put this on. They'll be here any second."

She loosens the straps and adjusts them for his height and girth. Her hands move faster than anything Michael has ever seen. Once she has him secured, she moves him to the edge of the rooftop when the chute snags on the sides of the air-conditioner, she fears it will tear. She goes back to the chute and pulls it off the air-conditioner and does her best not to tangle the cords any more than they already are.

The door to the roof burst opens, and a flood of agents pour out. Roslyn drops the chute, and with all her speed, bolts for Michael. She grabs hold of Michael's arm and heads for the edge of the building. Once at the edge, she stops and throughs Michael into the air as far as she can throw him, which is much further than Michael could have thought possible.

"Shit!!" Michael screams. He sails into the air with the tangled mess following him like a streamer.

Roslyn's heart sinks as she watches him fall towards the street with no sign of the chute opening. He helplessly falls with only seconds to go before he hits the ground. The chute violently whips around in the air. Michael's life flashes before his eyes. He can only watch as the earth gets closer. With a vicious jerk, the chute finally balloons open only a couple of seconds before he hits the pavement. Seconds later, Michael lands on the roof of a parked vehicle, crumpling it like a tin can. Roslyn looks for signs of life. Michael moans and struggles to get off the car. Roslyn lets out a sigh of relief. He might be banged up, but she can see he is still moving, he is alive!

"It's all over Roslyn," Grey's voice sounds shrill behind her.

Roslyn slowly turned, not wanting to take her eyes off Michael. "I don't want to hurt you, Grey. Just let me go."

"That's not going to happen. Now be a good girl, and get in your cage."

"I'm not going anywhere with you."

"You don't have a choice." Grey feels more confident having a dozen agents by his side.

Roslyn scans the area for any means of escape but finds none. Once again, desperation fills her body. She has no other choice; she turns towards the ledge to jump.

"What are you doing?" Grey yells.

"If I must die to keep from being your guinea pig, then so be it."

Roslyn lifts her foot off the edge and begins to step off when she suddenly stops herself. She notices a large tree close to the corner of the building. It is tall, but still, the building towers over it. The tree is about 80 or 90 feet tall and stands almost half the height of the building, about eleven or twelve stories down. She turns and races down the edge of the roof!

"You're going to die!" Grey screams! He does not want to lose his last chance for his weapon.

Roslyn ignores him and races to the corner of the building at full speed and jumps off aiming for the top of the tree far below.

"No!!" Grey yells reaching for her over the ledge, watching his prize fall to oblivion.

The wind whips through her hair and whistles in her ears as she plunges towards the tree beneath her. Michael looks up in time to see her sailing through the air, his heart sinks.

What is she thinking? She's a goner, he believes.

She strikes the top of the tree with incredible force! Much harder than she thought. Michael can hear the loud cracks and snaps of the limbs of the tree as she tumbles down in a frightening, awkward tumble! Roslyn lets out a cry when one of the branched tears a large gash in her arm.

She continues to fall through the branches until she hits the ground with a loud thud that Michael can hear from where he is standing. He can not believe how hard she hit. He speeds to her side. She is bleeding badly from her arm and lays awkwardly. He leg is bent in a way that looks very bad. He examines her leg and feels bones and muscles in places they should not be. As a doctor, he has never seen anything like it in a person he loved. She appears to be dead, lifeless and not moving.

Suddenly, a grey four-door Audi squeals its tires in the parking lot and stops right next to the couple. The rear passenger door springs open.

"Get in!" a voice yells!

Seeing he doesn't have any choice, Michael picks Roslyn's mangled body up.

He puts her in the backseat and jumps into the vehicle beside her, not knowing who is in the driver seat. The car speeds off into the night! Michael soon realizes who's driving the car.

"Matt!?" Michael says, surprised.

Matt's wearing a red pizza delivery jacket and a white hat.

"How're you doing buddy?" Matt replies hastily, as he focuses on the road.

"What're you doing here, and what's with the outfit?"

"You're welcome!" Matt says, still focusing on the street. He aggressively turns the wheel as the street whips by, trying to maintain control.

"But how? Michael asks in complete disbelief.

"How do you think? Roslyn told me that you needed my help. She said someone was gonna kill you if I didn't help. I'm not about to let my best friend die." He violently turns the wheel again.

"Wow! I wouldn't think you'd dare stand up to the FBI!"

"What!? That was the FBI?! Roslyn never told me that!"

Chapter 25

Matt pulls the Audi into a cobblestone driveway and to the attached garage of an aged, blue weathered house. The house is an old rambler, has a rusting metal roof and cedar shakes for siding. Many of the shakes are missing, and most of the paint on the home has long since faded away. He pushes a button on the visor, and the garage door opens.

He pulls the car into the dilapidated looking building and turns off the engine; then he assists Michael with Roslyn's body. They move her into the house and lay her gently on the living room couch. The residence on the inside is well-kept, quite modern, too. From the outside, no one would ever know how beautiful it is on the inside. After laying her down, the two men stand over her, pondering their situation and next move.

"Is she dead?" Matt asks.

"I think so," Michael's voice quivers. "I didn't feel a pulse the entire drive here."

"What're we gonna do?"

Michael slowly shakes his head. "I don't

know." Michael notices a gold locket dangling from her neck.

He reaches down and unlatches the small chain holding it. He pulls on the locket, and it comes free. He looks at it closely opening it, revealing the two pictures inside. He can tell one of them is of her, the other he deduces must be Vlad. He realizes now just how much he resembles Vlad. He can not ignore how eerie it feels to resemble the man in the picture. An even more eerie feeling overtakes him as Roslyn's head moves slightly.

"Did you see that!" Matt shouts.

Michael's eyes widen. "I'm not sure?" Michael had been preoccupied with the locket and only saw the moment out of the corner of his eye.

"Her head moved!"

"Are you sure?" Michael's somewhat sure he saw it, but now is looking for confirmation.

"Pretty sure."

Michael watches her intently; she looks as lifeless as before. Her head seems to move a little again and stops.

"Did she move her head, or was it just her body settling?" Matt asks, pointing.

"I don't know!" Michael says.

Matt kneels beside her and checks her pulse, his eyes lower. "She's gone."

They sit in silence for a moment, not knowing what to do, when she groans.

"What the hell!" Michael yells.

Matt jumps to his feet in fright. "What's going on here?" Matt's voice trembles slightly.

Roslyn's head turns again, this time it is more pronounced and noticeable.

"What the hell!" Michael says again even louder.

Matt's hand is shaking. "I just checked her pulse; she doesn't have one. How's this possible?! This is creeping me out, man!" Matt's frightened, the dead coming back to life was one of his worst nightmares as a kid.

Roslyn's eyes open a little and her muscles tense up. Once her head clears, she looks around the room and realizes she is home and relaxes a little. She looks up at Matt and Michael; she is pleased to see them. Michael, of course, has never been to Roslyn's home before, but Matt has. Matt was here only a few hours before getting the details of her rescue plan.

"I'm glad to see we made it!" she says in a soft, weak voice.

"Holy shit!" the two men yell in unison.

Roslyn's eyes open wider, she looks around the room, attempting to find whatever it is that has startled them. "What's wrong?"

The men are hesitant to speak caught in a petrified stare.

When their fear, subsides a little Michael says, "Besides the fact that you're dead . . . nothing!!"

"Oh, yeah. Well, I'm not dead."

"I don't know how this is possible. Matt just checked. You don't have a pulse!" Michael's voice is panicked.

"Of course I do," she says softly. "My heart doesn't beat as often as yours, and the beat is much softer."

Roslyn tries to move when a sharp pain in her left arm stops her; the large cut has almost stopped bleeding. She tries to move her legs but her right leg is not working right, and a sharp pain causes her to pause. She examines her leg, it does not take long for her to discover her femur is at an odd angle.

"Can you help me remove my pants please?" Roslyn looks up at Michael who seems a little embarrassed by the request and still rattled by the fact she is even alive.

"Ummm."

"It will be fine. Please just help me. I need to see how bad it is," she insists.

"Yeah, ok." He awkwardly moves into position to help her.

She unbuttons her pants, and he lowers her pants down to her knees revealing her red lace panties, she lets out a cry of pain. Matt turns his head away and shifts his weight uncomfortably.

Michael suddenly remembers his manners. "I'm sorry. Are you ok."

"Yes. I'm fine. That just hurt."

Michael examines her leg and can see the bone protruding under the skin, it is broken. She lays back down realizing her injuries are worse than she realized.

"Would you mind helping me?" she asks softly.

"Not here. You need to go to a hospital. There's nothing we can do right now!" Matt says over his shoulder; he can see himself losing his license over this.

"Sure there is. You're doctors, aren't you?"

"You don't need a doctor. You need an exorcist! Or at very least, an orthopedic surgeon," Matt replies.

Roslyn lets out a painful chuckle. "Just set my leg, will you please, and I'll answer all your questions."

"Roslyn, this injury could kill you if we don't treat it correctly," Michael explains.

Roslyn was getting a little frustrated. "You know I can't go to a hospital. My vital signs alone are enough to draw unwanted attention. The government will be looking for us there. I need your help, please."

Matt's very uncomfortable with the situation. "Roslyn, if your bone severs an artery when we set it, you could bleed out, and we don't have the meds or equipment here to treat you. If you get an infection, you'll be in a serious world of hurt."

"Don't worry about either of those. My body is not like yours. I can't get infections, and it would be very difficult for me to bleed out."

Matt does not seem to believe her. "How can you not be prone to infection?"

"I don't have time to explain. Trust me; I'll be fine. Please set my leg."

Michael hesitates for a moment but wants to do anything he can to help. Despite everything he still has underlining feelings for her. He hates to see her in any pain. He moves to her feet where he grabs her ankle firmly.

"I have to say for the record, this is a really bad idea. Now I'm guessing this will hurt a lot," Michael warns.

"Go ahead." She braces herself.

Michael pulls down on her ankle, and an audible popping sound emanates from deep inside her thigh. Roslyn lets out another cry! After the pain subsides, she thanks him. Michael sits down beside her and motions to her arm.

"That's going to need stitches."

"No. It won't," she replies. "But I will need some blood," she says reluctantly.

"What kind of blood? A+? B-?" Matt asks, voice shaky again.

She looks up at him. "Human blood, or animal blood, if we can't get any human blood."

"Animal blood?" Matt was still mentally spiraling downward.

"Yes. Any blood would be good right now."

The two men look at each other in confusion. They have no idea what use animal blood could be to her right now.

Matt thinks about it for a moment. "I guess I can get some from the hospital."

"That would be great!"

"What's your blood type?" he asks.

"Doesn't matter. Any blood will do."

Matt's even more puzzled. "What are you talking about, everyone has a blood type."

"I don't."

Matt does not know what to think, but at this point is in no mood to argue. "OK, I'll be right back." Matt nervously picks up his keys to the Audi and heads for the garage.

After Matt leaves, Michael's mind begins to race, but he can not make any sense of the unfolding events.

"What's going on here? Who are you? What are you? Why is the FBI after you?"

"Hold on. Slow down. I know you have questions about me."

"Ah, yeah. To start off with, the FBI says you're a terrorist. Are you?"

Roslyn gazes at him as she rests on the couch. "I already told you I'm not a terrorist."

"Then, what are you?" he demands.

Roslyn pauses and sighs. She can see he'll continue to ask her this question until he gets a satisfactory answer.

"You already know what I am."

"I need to hear it from you," he is persistent.

"I'm a vampire."

Michael's eyes widen again, he was convinced there was another explanation, and the confirmation of the FBI's story shocks him more than he was prepared. "What?!"

"I'm a vampire," she repeats.

He stands and moves a few paces away uneasily. "You're serious?"

"Of course I am. I wouldn't joke about something like that."

"So, the FBI is telling the truth! I thought they were messing with me, trying to get in my head." He contemplates what she has told him when a terrible thought crosses his mind. "You're not going to kill me, are you?"

She lets out a quiet laugh. "Of course not."

"What do you want with me?"

"The better question is what do you want with me?"

"Umm . . . Nothing."

"That's not what you were thinking the other night," she teases.

Michael turns his head slightly. "How can you possibly know that?"

"I read your mind. It's one of the gifts all vampires have."

"Ah, you read my mind?"

"Yes, but a woman doesn't have to read a man's mind to know what he wants with her," she continues.

"So, who are you? Is your name really Roslyn?"

"That's a long story. My name is Roslyn now, but it wasn't always."

"So, who were you?"

"It's a long story. Do you really want to know all of this?" She can tell he does, but she is not sure if she is ready to tell him yet.

"Yes, I do. We have nothing but time right now!" Michael insists.

"Very well." She begins with a deep sigh. "It began about 2500 years ago."

Chapter 26

"2500 years ago!?" Michael cries in disbelief!

"Yes. This is difficult for me to say." She tilts her head slightly.

She has not told this story to anyone before. It has been a closely guarded secret. She is a little surprised that she is now telling him.

"I'm sorry. Continue,"

"I was born about 2500 years ago, as far as I can remember. When so many years go by it's difficult to remember the exact number. My parents named me Helen. My parents were the King and Queen of Persia. My mother's name was Leda, and my father's name was Tyndareus. I grew up in the palace and had a good life. When I was getting close to the age of 20, my parents wished to have me married to King Menelaus of Sparta.

"The King of Sparta was a new ally and my father wanted to solidify this new political alliance with our wedding. He was twice my age, and I had no feelings for him. I think the only feelings he had for me were lustful. I was to be sent to Sparta in four weeks when I met one of the princes of

Troy. He was visiting to build a new trade agreement with my father; his name was Paris. We spent a lot of time together despite my father's objections.

"I had only met the Spartan King, two months before and he'd returned home to make preparations for our wedding. Now my heart longed for someone else."

"Helen!" Paris called out.

He was at the end of his three-week visit and wished to see me one last time before he left.

"Helen!" He called out again! He wore his grey-blue tunic with a purple sash.

Paris stood about six feet two inches and had a muscular build. His dark, brown hair curled tightly just above his shoulders. He searched the courtyard, the dining hall, and then the palace balcony. He had found me in each of these locations on many occasions. The terrace was my favorite. I loved to look from the terrace over the menagerie and take in the sweet smells of the gardens and watch my father's animals play.

Paris was disappointed because I was in none of my usual places. He thought about checking my sleeping chamber, but a young man found in a young woman's room was forbidden, even for a prince. The fact I was betrothed to another only made it worse. If my future husband found out, he would not be happy. He decided he would not enter but would just walk by my chamber door to see if he could hear me inside.

At least, he would know if I was there. He crept up to my chamber and placed his ear to the door. His dark curly hair dangled in his face as he did. He could not hear anything. He did not think I was there. He was about to pull his head from the door when he heard a crash from inside my room as if a metal platter crashed against the floor. Then he heard me scream!

"Helen!" he yelled. No reply.

A scream followed!

"Helen!"

Paris tried to open the large, heavy, wood doors but found they did not budge. They were locked from the inside. He slammed his shoulder into the massive towering ten-foot doors. They moved a little, but it was clear they were not going to open. He looked around for something to assist him and saw a immense, marble statue of Zeus standing opposite my doors in the corridor.

He got an idea, and he raced to the figure. It was two or three times his height. The pose of the figure was a common one used for Zeus. His left forearm rested horizontally and rested against his side. His palm was attached to the statue's belly near the navel. The right arm was raised and held a lightning bolt. He jumped up and grabbed the arm of the half-naked god. He pulled himself up using the left forearm and stood up to where he could now reach the shoulders. He put his arms around Zeus's massive neck and pulled himself up onto the figure's shoulders. Then he wedged himself between the tall wall and the enormous statue's back.

With Paris's back to the wall and his feet on the statue's back, he pushed with all his might. The statue didn't want to budge. He drove again with all his strength, and the statue began to move slightly. He continued to push until the statue started to rock. Finally, it began to fall toward the massive wooden doors slowly. As the statue started to fall, he jumped down to the side and out of harm's way. He watched as Zeus crashed through the doors turning them to splinters.

Paris busted through the rubble, drawing his sword as he did so. What he saw next horrified him. I lay in my beautifully-decorated bed motionless. I wore only my once gorgeous nightgown. It had been torn into pieces and blood was everywhere. Paris raced to my side, only to find the gruesome sight of my half-naked body with several, deep wounds.

He grimly looked down at my once alluring body, a would-be queen. The wounds covering my body were raw and looked as if a wild animal had savagely attacked me. He moved in closer to see if I was alive. My eyes were open, but they were fixed on the ceiling and showing no response or recognition.

Paris feared I was dead. He was afraid to touch me but still moved in closer to see if I was breathing. After a few moments, he could feel the faint heat and moisture of my breath. Soon, he thought he could hear me trying to speak. It was very weak and difficult for him to make out.

"Aaaaaaa...bbbboov . . . yyyyyyy...oo...," my voice was weak.

Paris tried desperately to make out what I was saying when it came to him.

"Above you!"

Suddenly, he felt we weren't alone. Terror crept into his soul like a silent darkness! He could feel his heart beating like a loud drum. He was too frightened to look up but reluctantly forced himself to do so. He turned his head slightly and looked out of the corner of his eye. A monstrous, shadowy figure was directly above them, clinging to the ceiling like a giant spider. He did not know what to do when he realized his sword was still in his hand.

He swung the weapon with all his might directly above his head, striking the creature in the chest! Blood sprayed over me like a warm, creepy shower. Paris quickly moved away following his swing, avoiding most of the spray. He repositioned himself for a better space to fight off the creature, who was still clinging to the ceiling. The brute let out a terrible roar as its blood covered me in a film of red.

The being sprang from the ceiling and landed on the floor with great agility. It now stood before Paris in all its ferocious might! It looked like a formidable man with shoulder-length blonde hair and ruby red eyes! He wore only a pair of ragged pants. The creature stood nearly six foot four with broad shoulders, and his bare chest showed his intimidating musculature.

He was a couple of inches taller than Paris, who still had the slender build of a youth. Paris stood defiantly, his sword still in hand and ready to fight, despite the daunting man who stood before him. Several armed guards burst through the door, yelling as they did.

The bleeding beast saw he was outnumbered. He seemed weakened from his wound and had lost all desire to fight. The monster raced for the window and leaped into the dark and fled into the night with a speed and agility that would have rivaled the fastest of men. The royal doctor was called and rushed to my aid.

The commotion had drawn a crowd, so everyone who did not need to be in my room was ushered out. The doctor carefully removed what little was left of my nightgown and began wiping away the dark, red blood that covered most of my body. There was more blood than he had ever seen, and it was impossible to tell how much of it was mine and how much of it belonged to the creature.

Once the wounds were cleaned up, he could see more clearly the magnitude of my extensive injuries. Several deep gashes could be seen across my weak, naked body. I had so little blood left the wounds were not bleeding much. The physician cleaned the wounds, stitched them, and dressed them. After doing everything he could, he announced to my family that I had lost too much blood and would probably die.

My family continued to care for me, despite the hopeless prognosis. I was unconscious and barely breathing for the whole next day when just after nightfall, my eyes opened. My mother was there sitting on my bed when it happened. Once my eyes cleared, I could see my mother's smile.

"Welcome back Helen!" my mother said softly.

I tried to speak but found I was too weak to do so. My mother gave me a goblet of water. I needed help to take the chalice to my lips, so my mother assisted me. The fresh, cold water dribbled into my mouth. The clear water tasted very strange. Typically, water would have made me feel better and perhaps stronger, but today it did not affect on me one way or the other.

Suddenly, I could smell a tantalizing, fantastic aroma coming from somewhere nearby, but I could not tell what it was, or where it was coming from. I still felt very weak and made an extra effort to sit up. When I did it surprised my mother.

"Feeling a little better, are we?" my mother asked with an encouraging smile.

"Yeees," I said in a shaky soft tone.

I took a few deep breaths, trying to regain some much needed strength. I could feel a deep hunger, but it was unlike any desire I had ever felt before. Whatever it was that I craved, I could smell it. I sniffed the air as to determine where the scent was coming. After a few moments, I discovered it must be coming from my mother's direction. I thought there must be a table full of food sitting behind her, where I could not see it. I leaned forward, trying to catch a glimpse of the tasty cuisine that lingered nearby. But, I could not see a table behind my mother.

"What are you looking for, dear?" my mother noticed my search.

"Food," I replied.

"Are you hungry?"

"Yes."

"Don't worry; I'll have some food brought up right away." She gestured to a servant at the door.

I noticed the door to my chambers had been completely repaired and my bed was freshly made as well. The servant girl at the door wore the typical plain white tunic of a domestic. She had dark hair tightly tied up the back, which was the only style acceptable for a servant to wear. She also had a distinctive silver earring in her right ear that distinguished her as someone's property.

She knew exactly what to do when she noticed the queen's gesture and quickly left the room. A few minutes later the girl returned with a plate full of fruit which was a royal delicacy. She set it down on a small table next to the side of my bed. The food looked so good! I began to eat the fresh fruit because I had quite the appetite. As I ate the fruit, I notice all the fruit tasted very bland.

In fact, it seemed to have no appeal to me at all. I felt that the food just like the water did not seem to give me any additional strength or satisfy me in any way. I could not understand why nothing seemed to make me feel better. I put the cluster of grapes back on the plate.

"Is something the matter." The queen was concerned.

"No. Maybe. I'm not sure. I just don't know what I'm hungry for," I replied.

There was that wonderful smell again. Now it seemed to be coming from the servant girl's direction, who was now standing beside my bed.

She must have walked past something delicious in the kitchen, I thought.

I felt tired again, and the food and drink did nothing to help me. I lay back against my pillows in frustration. "I'm exhausted."

My mother gently caressed my head. "Get some sleep," she said softly.

Her touch rubbed against one of my numerous bandages, and I could feel the soreness of the wound hidden beneath. The pain was sharp and caused me to twitch.

"I'm sorry my love," the queen said politely.

"It's ok," I replied with a short smile.

The beautiful queen then stood and left the room.

Chapter 27

A couple of hours after the queen left, I lay in my bed and looked out the chamber window. I could sleep no longer. Night had fallen, and the light of the moon shone through my window. From out of the dark, I felt something jump up on the bed and walk across my chest. It was Tam, my beloved black cat, who purred as he rubbed his head against my face.

"Tam!" I said with glee but still in a weak voice.

I sat up and embraced him. I had raised the cat since he was a kitten. He purred even louder as I stroked his soft fur. Unexpectedly, I noticed that wonderful smell once again!

Where was it coming from, I wondered?

The scent drove me wild with intense hunger pains. I sniffed the air again, and the aroma seemed to be coming from Tam. I picked Tam up and sniffed him. Something about Tam appeared to smell amazing! I inhaled again, and I felt an uncontrollable urge to bite him. I pulled the cat away from my face applauded by the thought. The cat looked at me and hissed. The animal fought to get away and finally broke free and dashed away in a flash. I had no idea why Tam had acted so strangely, and why he was incredibly frightened by me.

Something was different about me, but I did not know what. Inexplicably, I felt stronger in the dark of night. The night made me feel alive, and it gave me enough strength to get to my feet. I walked over to the mirror in my chambers that stood tall against the far wall and gazed at my reflection. I was right; something was different!

The person in the mirror seemed foreign; it was as if I was looking at a stranger. The person was pale and frail looking. Her hair was dry and brittle. I moved closer to the glass and noticed something different about my eyes. I looked closer and observed they were no longer a brilliant blue but a bright red! I analyzed my eyes and discerned they looked like a pair of rubies staring back at me.

What happened to me, I wondered touching my face!

As I did, I perceived something poked my lip from the inside of my mouth. I gently pulled my lip back and realized my canine teeth were longer than I remembered, they were much longer than normal. I released my lip and peered into the large, round mirror. My face looked cold and lifeless. Something seemed very wrong with me.

A gentle breeze through the window brought with it a multitude of delightful smells. I took in a deep breath and basked in the aromas! Then, something occurred to me; I did not remember ever having such an acute sense of smell. My senses were definitely heightened.

I followed the aroma to the window and stood at the sill. The moon shone, a bright orb in the sky. I could see everything clearly, despite the fact the moon was the only source of light. The soft, faint glow of the stars twinkled in a way I had never seen before. It was like the whole world had changed around me. Everything seemed brighter and more detailed than I remembered. My sight was also more keen than ever.

I could hear the animals moving around the menagerie. Despite their location on the west side of the palace, I could hear them clearly despite my window facing east. This shocked me because the animals were nowhere near me. I marveled at how sensitive my hearing was. The thought of seeing the animals right now seemed to appeal to me more than usual.

It was as if the menagerie was calling to me in some unconscious summoning. I left my room and navigated down the corridors and halls and finally to the stables. I opened the gate, and the animals that were still awake seemed instantly disturbed by my presence. I walked the narrow paths and between the stalls and pens of animals.

My father had spent years collecting these creatures from kingdoms far and away. Animals you would see nowhere else in our land were here for the king's pleasure. That tantalizing smell that fueled my hunger filled the air once more and was stronger than ever! I walked up to a pen; three small goats slept inside.

An overpowering desire beckoned me to enter. I quietly opened the door to the pen and silently walked up to the sleeping goats. They were a gift for my father from the sultan at our western border. I knelt beside one; it still had not stirred. I started stroking the animal, who seemed content to remain asleep. Something about the goat seemed wonderful. I tried to fight it, but the aroma and sensations of the moment began to overwhelm me. I leaned in close and buried my nose in the fur of the goat. It was a sweeter fragrance than anything I'd ever experienced. I began to rub my face across the animal's skin. Up against its back and towards its neck.

Something deep inside seemed to be taking over as if some unknown instinct was directing my actions. My lips slowly opened as I leaned in close. With a compulsive gesture, I allowed my teeth to sink into the flesh of the goat. I noticed my sharp incisors puncture the skin like a pair of hot knives through butter. A moment later a warm liquid entered my mouth. It tasted so good; I could feel life fill my body along with new strength and vigor. I continued to suck the vital fluid, and shortly, it was all gone.

I came out of my trance and pulled my lips away from the beast in horror! I looked down to see the lifeless body of the goat. Its last drops of blood dripped from my lips. In terror, I jumped to my feet with a strength I had never felt before! I ran back towards my chambers. The air whipped through my hair. I found myself running lighter and faster than I ever had before! I was back in my room in a fraction of the time it took me to get to the menagerie.

I expected my heart to be beating hard with all the excitement and exertion, but I could hardly feel it at all. If not for my heightened senses I might not notice my hearts beat at all it was beating so softly. My chamber seemed alive with energy.

I felt free, and yet for a reason unknown to me I also felt trapped, like a caged animal. The nourishing taste of the blood still lingered in my mouth. I felt terror and exhilaration simultaneously. Once again, I walked passed the mirror. The girl in the mirror caught my attention, so I stopped to look. Her appearance had changed in the time I was gone. Her hair was brilliant and shiny, her skin soft and vibrant. She looked more beautiful than anyone I had ever seen. She radiated life and vitality. Her eyes were like luminous rubies in the night. Part of me was terrified by what I saw; part of me wanted more.

*   *   *

The next day, my mother woke me again. I felt drained and sluggish now. I felt like I had slept, but I still felt very lethargic. I could see the rays of the morning sun shining through my window. I thought about it for a moment, but I could not remember when I fell asleep.

After the happenings of the previous night, I was petrified of looking my mother in the eyes. I did not want my mother to see what I saw last night in the mirror. My concerns were vanquished when she had no noticeable reaction to my changes in appearance. I was curious, so I got out of bed and went back to my mirror. There I stood, beautiful and radiant looking quite human, almost more that human.

The queen was amazed when I got to my feet. "I'm glad to see you doing so well, my daughter!" She exclaimed with delight!

I was shocked when I noticed my eyes were a brilliant blue color. The only apparent difference was that they had a gem-like quality now. They looked a bit like the dazzling, blue sapphires I had seen in my father's treasure room. I examined my teeth, and they too looked normal.

Had I only been dreaming, I wondered?

I felt extremely good, despite my lethargic demeanor. The doctor entered the room for his morning visit. He sat me down and asked me how I was doing. I told him I felt fine. He removed to bandage on my upper bicep and froze. He could not believe his eyes.

The queen noticed his expression and became concerned, "What's wrong?"

The doctor suddenly snapped out of his stupor, "Umm . . . Ahh . . . nothing. I'm just surprised. Her wounds have completely closed. I will need to take out the stitches right away. She has had over two weeks of healing in one day."

"How's the possible," the queen asked.

"It's a miracle. Zeus himself must have healed her," he proclaimed.

The doctor carefully removed the stitches from all of my injuries and covered them with new bandages. After he finished, he promptly left.

"It's time to eat," the queen announced her mind still spinning on the miraculous recovery.

My mother led me to the royal dining hall where food was already prepared for us. I did not feel hungry for food at all. The delicious dishes that had been meticulously prepared for me seemed unappealing. I sat down at the great table set in the middle of the hall, and my mother sat beside me.

"You must eat, dear," my mother insisted.

I hesitantly tasted the food to please my mother, but none of it seemed palatable to me. I was confused because my mother's servants had prepared my favorite dishes. I used to love them, but now they seemed abhorrent. I might as well have been eating paper. I choked down most of my food to please my mother who was watching me diligently. Abruptly, a servant came rushing through the door!

"My queen, someone has killed one of the king's prized goats!" the elderly, male servant announced.

He wore a plain white tunic with no decorations. He had short, grey hair and the distinctive, silver earring.

"What?" the queen roared rising to her feet.

The servant led the queen to the grizzly scene, with me close behind. I had to see if it was real. I wanted to be sure I had not just imagined it.

It was just a dream, wasn't it? Was I responsible? I wondered.

Once in the menagerie, the servant revealed the carcass of the dead goat. It lay on the ground just the way I remembered leaving it last night. It was real, it really happened!

The queen was angry. "Who did this?" she screamed with outrage.

"I don't know my queen! It was like this when we found it this morning." The old servant quivered with fear.

"When I find the person who did this, he'll suffer for it dearly!" she roared.

I did not want to be caught in my mother's wrath, so I left the menagerie and went back to my chambers. I figured my mother had more important things to worry about now than to force feed her daughter. I felt tired and just wanted to sleep so I laid my head down and closed my eyes.

Chapter 28

That evening, I awoke as the sun was setting. I felt the hunger once again. I eventually realized the hunger felt more like a deep, thirst. I trembled with trepidation at the thought of killing something or even worse, someone, to satisfy this thirst. In some unforeseen way, I had become a monster who craved blood. As I walked down the corridors of the royal sleeping chambers, I could hear the hearts of my family beating softly and slowly as they peacefully slept. I could smell the sweetness of their blood coursing through their veins.

I had to leave before I did something very wrong, something I would never be able to forgive myself. I raced down the corridor with a stealthy speed that amazed me! It seemed to me that I was faster than any person in the kingdom, possibly faster than any animal in the land! In a flash, I was out of the palace and into the nearby city streets. I silently crept through the dark alleys. I could smell the fragrant aroma of the blood of people I encountered.

Most people I encountered were homeless drifters no one would miss. I fought the temptation to drink their blood too. The temptation to take one of them was getting stronger by the minute. I told myself, I was not a killer! I had to get out of the city before I lost control. I raced for the gates, and through the large columns that supported them, the forest was near.

If I was going to act like an animal, I might as well join them, I thought as I bolted into the forest.

My fear and frustration continued to build as I ran faster and faster whipping through the underbrush and trees, zipping past the unsuspecting animals of the forest. I was right; I was faster than even the animals! I finally came to a precipice, where I stopped at the edge and looked into the night with my new eyes.

In the dim light of the moon, I could see the tops of the trees as they stretched for countless miles. I could smell the variety of plants in the forest and its creatures. Everything seemed so brilliant and beautiful now! I basked in the magnificence of the wild nature surrounding me. I wished I could stay in that moment forever when I heard something moving toward me. I turned my back to the precipice to try to determine where the noise had originated and what it might be. I soon realized it was not one thing coming in my direction but several. In moments, the footsteps were nearly upon me when I could suddenly see several sets of eyes peering from the dark, watching me.

I sniffed the air, but the wind was to my back, so that I could not smell the creatures. I could hear the shadowy animal closest to me begin to growl. The rest of the beasts did not hesitate and quickly joined in on the verbal attack. The eyes approached, and I could now make out the faint figures of the massive creatures as they emerged from the darkness. It was a pack of hungry wolves! Wolves were known to attack humans, but they seemed more determined than normal. Years later I would discover that this attack was no accident, wolves have a primitive hatred for my kind and attack us any chance they get. The pack moved around me blocking any path of escape. I could feel a deep-seated fear build inside of me as if it were instinctual.

There were five of the beasts and only one of me. The largest wolf in the center seemed to be the leader of the pack as he was the most aggressive. He snapped his enormous white fangs at me! I could feel my body intuitively assume a defensive stance to prepare to defend myself. The leader snapped at me again. I surprised myself as I roared back at him with a deep and terrible voice I hardly recognized. The rest of the pack held back in fear, but the leader kept moving forward, undaunted. I could see in his demeanor he was without a doubt, completely committed to the prospect of taking me down.

The wolf lunged at me with great speed. I sprang over his body like a deer over a fence and gracefully landed on the other side of the beast. He squared up as I swung my hand at the fiend as if my hand was a mighty claw. I struck the animal in his massive chest, sending him hurtling head over heels, yelping as he tumbled headlong. The rest of the pack hesitated as their leader got back to his feet. I felt like a crazed, wild animal as I waited for the beast to resume his attack.

The alpha wolf moved forward more determined than ever. He lunged at me again, this time his huge teeth sank deep into my left wrist, causing tremendous pain to radiate up my arm. I tried to ignore the pain as I locked my hands together, pinching the wolves's head in my arms like a vise, my wrist still firmly secured in his teeth. I squeezed my arms together and twisted with all my might. The neck of the mighty wolf snapped, and he fell to the ground, dead. The sight of their powerful leader falling in battle caused the other wolves to bolt back to the safety of the shadows of the forest.

The tantalizing smell of the dead wolf's blood beckoned to me. I finally could not resist the temptation. I rationalized the wolf was already dead, so I did not have to feel guilty. I propped the hind end of the animal upon a boulder so the blood would drain down into his head. I kneeled over the massive beast. I leaned over him and sank my teeth deep through his thick fur and into his huge neck. His warm blood filled my body, and I could feel the life force of the wolf flowing through my veins. Within moments, the wolf was completely drained of blood.

I sat for a few moments with my eyes closed. I concentrated on what I was feeling. I was stronger and more alive than ever! I was in tune with the forest and the world around me. I had a strong urge to run, so I opened my eyes. I glanced at my gaping wound and could see it had already stopped bleeding. I could feel to injury slowly pulling itself shut. I got to my feet, and disappeared into the dark forest, racing like the wind through the trees. I easily leaped over the fallen trees that lay in my path. I whipped through the underbrush with blazing speed! I felt so amazing! I felt blessed and cursed, but, most of all, I felt free!

Chapter 29

The next morning, my mother woke me, again I felt tired and lethargic. I did not want to get up, but my mother insisted.

"The whole kingdom is talking about you, my daughter."

I was surprised. "What are they saying?"

"They are in disbelief at how quickly you've recovered from your injuries. Most people don't survive from such things."

"I guess I was lucky." I shrugged.

"People are saying you're more than lucky. They think you must be the daughter of Zeus himself."

"I'm flattered." Although I was a little embarrassed by the thought.

My mother laughed. "Well, I know exactly where you come from. You're my daughter, and, if Zeus was involved, I think I would know," the queen said with an elegant grace.

As we walked down the great hall, Paris approached us.

"I'm glad you're doing better. I was worried about you," he said.

"Thank you for saving my life." I felt a closer bond to him now that he had rescued me.

The queen seemed a bit disturbed by our emotional interaction.

"Is there something we can do to help you, my Prince," the queen asked.

The question appeared to pull Paris out of a trance. Somehow I was even more beautiful than he remembered. "No my queen. I just wanted to check on Helen."

"Well, my daughter must get prepared for her wedding," the queen insisted.

I did not need to get ready right now, but I think she was trying to tell Paris I was off limits and to get him to go away.

"I will let you prepare," he replied.

My mother's comment also reminded me that I was to be wed, to that old man who I had no interest. I thought about what it would be like to live with him. I felt that in time I would grow tired of his advances and drain him of his blood to rid myself of him. I knew this would be a terrible idea. If I followed this course of action, our countries would go to war. That would mean the end of my family and country. I could not allow this to happen.

How could I prevent this wedding from happening, I thought.

I looked into Paris' eager eyes. I could tell he wanted me more than just as a friend.

Maybe I could leave with him and hide from this man who I didn't love. A man I might end up killing in order to be free. I would have to stow away on his ship when he leaves. No one would have to know. I could just disappear, I contemplated.

*   *   *

When Paris' ship was about to disembark, I made sure I was abroad. He had no idea that I was there until long after they had set sail. Once we were out at sea, I decided to emerge from my hiding place. I had a large hood that I used to cover my face and head. I did not want anyone to recognize me. When I saw him, I took him to the side. He was pleased to see me but concerned too.

"What are you doing here?" he asked.

"I'm not going to marry that wretched man," I replied.

"You can't be here. If the Spartans find out there will be hell to pay."

"I know. We have to make sure they don't find out."

"What did you tell your parents?"

"I didn't tell them anything," I said.

"So you're just going to vanish?"

"Yes."

"Your parents are royalty; they aren't going to stand for their daughter just disappearing and not knowing why. They'll do whatever it takes to find out what happened to you."

"I know, but what was I to do. I'm not going to spend my life with that awful man. Please don't bring me back."

Paris let out a sigh. "You're going to be the death of me." He thought about how to keep this a secret. "You will have to stay in my cabin. We can't let people see you."

Paris tucked me away until we reached shore. He then took me to his palace after everyone else had disembarked and tried to keep my presence a secret. Eventually, my parents discovered what had happened to me despite our careful efforts. It was not long until the King of

Sparta learned my little secret too. During the time I was with Paris, we fell in love. I did not know it at the time, but vampires have a very captivating charisma that is difficult to resist. Paris decided he would not let me go despite the Spartan King's threats. It led to a massive war with the Spartans.

Paris and I eventually fled when the city was burned to the ground. During our escape, Paris was wounded in a fight with a Spartan warrior, who had slain his brother. Paris later died from his injuries, so I escaped. I was presumed dead by most. I discovered later that the Spartan King had taken a woman of Troy who resembled me as his wife saying she was me. This was done to prevent my parents from going to war with Sparta. They would have been very unhappy to find out that I was killed in a Spartan attack.

Chapter 30

"So, you don't burst into flames if you go out in the sun?" Michael asks.

Roslyn chuckles. "That only happens in the movies. The sun robs us of our dark gifts, rendering us as weak as a normal human. We're almost human in direct sunlight. We typically avoid the sun, because it makes us vulnerable. It also makes us tired and lethargic. The only disguising difference between humans and us when we're exposed to sunlight is our gem like eye."

"Your gem like eyes?"

"I'm sure you've noticed them by now. Our eyes don't look quite human."

He gazed into her eyes and observed just how different they were. He knew something was unusual about them before, but must have been too distracted to focus on it. Perhaps he was not using his head, or maybe the wrong one.

"You say that vampires are very charismatic?"

"Yes"

"How do I know that you're not using that charisma on my now?"

"Do you feel like I am?"

He thought about it, "No."

"There you go."

"So, tell me something . . . why did you rescue me. You've put yourself at great risk." He's dying to hear her answer.

"I had to." She looks away from him for a moment. "You're only in danger because of me. I'm responsible for all of this." She pauses.

"That can't be the entire reason?"

"You're right. It's also because you've made me feel something I haven't felt in nearly six hundred years." She sighs.

"And what's that?"

"You know exactly what I'm talking about. You've felt it every time we've been together."

Michael looks down; he can not deny what he has felt. It is exciting and intoxicating and everything he has ever wanted from a partner. *Why did she have to turn out to be a blood-sucking vampire?* He thinks.

She does her best to ignore his internal comment. "I have to leave. I want you to come with me." She takes his hand.

"Come with you? Are you serious? I can't leave! I have patients who depend on me. I can't leave them," he replies sadly.

She softly squeezes his hand, her immortal touch is exhilarating, like fireworks on New Year's Eve! She wants to protect him from her perilous life, but she is paralyzed. As if frozen in her indecision. Only once before in her very long life has she felt something as powerful as her attraction to him. Her relationship with Paris was a childish puppy love. Her relationship with Vlad was a deep and meaningful love. Her attraction for Michael was something different, something better! She will never be free of her desire for him. If she leaves, he will haunt her dreams for as long as she lives, and with her, that could be a very long time.

"Michael," she begins, "the FBI won't rest until they have me. They'll come after you again if you return to the hospital and your normal life."

He has become soft on her. "You can call me Mike if you like," he says. His expression changes as a terrible thought strikes him. "Matt!" he yells. "They're going to take Matt!"

Roslyn shook her head softly. "Mike, they don't know Matt's involved. When he brought the pizza into the FBI building, he was in a great disguise. They're unlikely to recognize him."

"Pizza?" Michael asks. "Oh, that's right. He was wearing a delivery outfit."

"It worked," she says slyly.

He can feel the beginning of forever in her touch. He does not know what to think or feel now. She is willing to put her immortal life in peril for him. His mind is racing with the possibilities and the ramifications of their situation. How could he relate to someone born over two centuries before him? She is from a time where the world was much different.

The world had changed so much it seems it will be difficult for him to relate to her and vice versa. There were plusses, however, the excitement of getting to know someone who has seen more of this incredible world than anyone else alive. Someone who has literally been there and done that. What a wealth of knowledge and experience she must have lying beneath that lovely exterior.

He gazes into her unique eyes and can see the depths of eternity. A dreadful thought now crosses his mind. *It's a forever I can't give back to her. Someday I will be old and grey, and she'll still be as young and vibrant as she is now. Would she still love me then? Would she be able to stay with me when I will most likely be mistaken for her grandfather instead of her lover?* His mind races with different scenarios and possibilities.

His imagination was something that had helped make him a great doctor but is currently a source of his greatest stress. Despite his rational thoughts, his emotions are stronger. His solution is to run, to do the wild and insane thing. His anxiety and fear are subdued only by his overwhelming desire to kiss her, to touch her, to hold her.

He is beginning to act like he is possessed by passion. Not in a bad way, but in the sense that his body and sentiment seem to be in control and not his mind. He moves in to kiss her, and she meets him halfway. When their lips meet, it is a hundred times more intense than their touch. The chemistry is unquestionable! A perfect combination of emotions and sensations that completely engulfs their bodies and minds. At that moment, the rest of the world melts away, leaving only the two of them in an immortal kiss. Nothing else matters now except the passion and completeness they now feel together.

Michael never put any faith in the concept of soul mates, but, at this moment, the possibility of the notion is real. They both know, without a doubt, this is something neither can ever let go easily. Something they will both fight for, to the death, if need be. They firmly hold each other closely. She finally pulls away from him breathless.

She does not want to ruin the mood, but the fog of war is all around them.

"We have to go soon," she says, sadly breaking the mood.

"You're in no condition to move right now," Michael insists.

"I'll be fine in a couple of hours, faster if I get some blood soon." Roslyn reexamines her wound.

Michael expects to see a large gash on her arm, but what he sees amazes him. The wound has pulled itself nearly closed. It is still clearly a long cut, but is now narrow and no longer bleeding, his eyes widen in disbelief. She is still weak from her fall.

"Fortunately, my fall happened at night. During the day, I probably wouldn't have survived," she explains.

"I've never seen anything like this! It's like a miracle cure!" Michael says.

Roslyn turns her head nervously. "Yes, but with some terrible side effects. I need blood."

Michael ponders the idea and wonders, *can I give her some of my blood.*

"That's not a good idea," she tells him, reading his mind.

"You're in my mind again, aren't you?"

"Sorry, yes."

"Well, if you take my blood, will I die?"

"No. Not if I only take a small amount. But it'll weaken you, and you'll need your strength."

"Will I become a vampire."

She laughs. "No, you would have to drink my blood to become a vampire."

"Take a little," he insists.

She knows it is a bad idea, but she needs it desperately. She tries not to consider it, but is compelled to as she stares at the artery in his neck, it beckons her. Her thirst is intense. She can see the beating of his heart in the pulse in his artery and hears his heart pounding in his chest. It beats in her mind like a loud drum. She needs it, she wants it, and not just for nourishment.

"If I drink from you, it'll create a powerful bond between us. I don't know if you're ready for that," she explains.

"What kind of bond?"

"When we drink the blood of someone, their life force fills us. It gives us life and becomes part of us. No bond is made if the person dies. We can't bond to the dead. However, if the person lives after a feeding, their life force becomes apart of us connects us in a way that is difficult to explain but is intoxicating. We'll be drawn together for the rest of your life, even more so than we are already."

"I'll be fine. You need it to get well. Drink!"

She hesitates but knows she must have blood but is concerned about the bond she will form with him. It appeals to her on a level she does not fully understand. She gently puts her hand behind his head and brings his neck to her lips. She can not fight the urge any longer. She sinks her teeth into the firm skin of his muscular neck. Blood flows into her mouth like sweet nectar. She feels life filling her body like a boost of energy. She has to stop, but every fiber of her body wants more!

She can feel his body weakening. With all of her will that remains she pulls her lips from his neck. She lowers her head, slightly ashamed of taking some of his precious life energy, but she needed it. Her wound is healing much faster now, and her leg feels much better. In minutes, the wound had utterly sealed itself. She thinks her leg is now strong enough to stand on if she wanted to, but remains seated.

"Thank you," she says softly in a much stronger voice.

"You're welcome," he replies.

He can not help but notice the intense joining sensation she had mentioned begin to take hold. It is much more powerful than he had anticipated. All he wants now is to be with her, by her side. There is nothing he wants more. The connection has purified and intensified his feelings for her; he realizes now that he loves her.

She looks up at him when she feels the emotion in his mind. Deep down, she has not admitted it to herself, but she too loves him. The connection has worked it is magic, and the bond takes her. It seems too soon for it to be possible. Is it love at first sight or the bond? Part of her knew it the moment she first saw him. He pulls her lips to his, and they kiss again. The connection is undeniable and uncontainable.

She puts her arms around his neck and pulls him near; their embrace is stimulating. It is like pulling joy and ecstasy around them like a blanket they could wrap themselves in. They remove their clothes between soft, slow caresses. She reaches up as if to unlock a necklace from her neck. She is confused and stunned because there was nothing there! She pats her neckline looking for the missing locket.

"It's gone!" she exclaims.

"What's gone?"

"My locket is gone," she explains.

Michael remembers what he has done and picks up his pants off the floor. He reaches into his pocket and pulls out the necklace. "This locket?"

"Yes, where did you get it, and may I have it back?"

She holds her hand out. He places the necklace in her hand, and the lines of stress leave her face.

"Thank god! I thought it had been lost during my fall. Thank you for keeping it safe for me." She sets the pendent on the table next to them.

Her expression changes back to joy when she looks at Michael. He kisses her, and the emotional toll of the locket seems to fade. They embrace again and kiss each other in a long passionate encounter. He moves on top of her, and within moments, he is inside her. He has never felt so close to anyone; he doesn't know how it is possible. He hardly knows her. All he knows now is that nothing will keep him from her. The bond has solidified now that they are coupled in a passionate embrace. He will do anything to be with her. She is all he wants; she is all he will ever need. Everything else is second now to his desire and love for her, his immortal lover.

The door to the garage opens, and in walks Matt, a white medical case in his hand. After noticing the couple on the couch, he quickly averts his eyes.

"Geez, Mike, at least give a guy a little warning! Put a sock on the door or something."

The couple quickly pulls their clothes from the floor over themselves haphazardly. Matt tries not to stare as he walks over to them. He sets the white case down on the coffee table.

"Here's the blood. I'll be in the other room if you need me," Matt says, trying to keep his composure.

"Thanks," the couple says in unison, and Matt leaves the room.

The moment has ended, so Michael sits up on the couch setting his loose clothes back on the floor. He reaches for the case, opens it, and pulls out several IV packets of blood. He hands one of them to Roslyn; she wastes no time, she is still very thirsty. She sinks her teeth into the pack and drains it quickly. She repeats this twice more with each pint Michael hands her. She can feel her full-strength return. She lowers the final package and is clearly content.

He notices her eyes are no longer blue but now are bright red. "Holy shit! Your eyes!"

She closes her eyes and takes in a few deep breaths and relaxes then reopens them. Her eyes slowly go back to their brilliant blue. "Sorry about that. I lost it for a moment there."

"Lost it?"

"Yeah, when a vampire is consumed by their bloodlust, their eyes turn red."

He tries to calm himself, it freaked him out a little. She waits for him to settle down.

"Feeling better?" he asks gathering himself.

"Much!"

They start kissing again and go back to where they had left off.

Chapter 31

They put their clothes back on, and Michael's curiosity starts to surface.

"Can I ask you a question?" Michael asks sheepishly.

"Yes."

"Why is that locket so important to you?"

"It's a long story," she is reluctant to tell him.

Michael senses her resistance, and his mind takes a different path. The fear of death and losing her to the passage of time returns. When he is old, she will still be young and vibrant.

Is there a way to fix this, he wonders? A thought crosses his mind. He pauses. "Can I ask you another question?"

"Yes, but what you have in mind isn't a good idea," she replies as she finishes buttoning up her blouse.

Michael remembers she can read his thoughts. "So you don't want me to live forever with you?"

She sighs. "It's not a good idea. You have no idea what kind of curse turning you into a vampire could be. I don't want to put you through such a terrible experience. I love you too much for that."

"If you don't turn me, I'll get old and die. I don't ever want to leave your side. I want to be with you forever."

"I feel the same way." She pauses. "I've made that mistake before, and it was the biggest mistake of my life."

Michael ponders her words. "You turned someone before?"

She hesitates. "Yes."

"What happened?"

"It wasn't good."

Michael thinks about it for a second. "It was Vlad, wasn't it?"

"Yes," she sighs again.

"What happened?"

"It's another long story."

"I would like to hear it, if you don't mind telling it."

It is difficult for her to deny him, her love for him is complete, and she only wants to make him happy and keep him safe. But her fears will not allow her to consider turning him.

"Alright," she begins. "The reason I'm telling you this story is so you'll know why I can't turn you." She pauses to see if her words are sinking in.

"Okay."

"About 600 years ago, I met a man. His name was Vlad Dracula. He was a young prince in Wallachia, an area of the world today known as Romania. He was a very handsome man, and I felt drawn to him in a way I had never experienced before. After an unusually long courtship for the time, I fell in love with him. We wed despite my fear of having a relationship with a human. There were many problems with falling in love with a man. He did not know at the time, that I was a vampire. Back then no one knew what a vampire was. I hated keeping this secret from him, but I did not want to lose him or burden him with my problems."

Roslyn slowly reaches over to the coffee table and picks up the gold locket she had set on the table during their romantic embrace. Michael can tell it is very valuable to her. It is ancient, but, then again, so is she. She opens the locket and shows Michael the portraits inside. He looks at them with curiosity trying to play off as is if it was for the first time and marvels at the hand-painted likeness.

"I'm guessing this is you and Vlad?" he says.

The female picture is a perfect portrait of Roslyn. Vlad seems dignified with dark, straight shoulder-length hair and piercing brown eyes. He has a thick nose and a sizable mustache. His strong chin protrudes above a blue cloak with a gold clasp.

"Yes," she says softly. "It was a gift from Vlad on our wedding night."

"This locket is almost 600 years old?" he asks with astonishment! He has never seen anything that old since he went to the Egyptian exhibit at the Seattle Art Museum.

"Yes, and it's very dear to me," she explains.

She returns to her story. "Vlad was once a kind and passionate man. He was also a man of great importance to both me and his country. It was 1460 and peace had just been restored to Vlad's kingdom after the regent-governor of Hungary, John Hunyadi, had been pushed out of the land. Hunyadi had invaded Wallachia in 1447 and killed Vlad's father and older brother during the conflict.

After the war, two years of peace went by, and the people rejoiced. Just when the people thought they could finally have a life of tranquility, our world had a formidable, new threat; the Ottomans. The Ottomans had already taken over most of what was left of the Roman Empire and conquered Constantinople. The Ottomans had one goal, to spread their control over all the known world.

The Sultan of the Ottoman army was Mehmed II. Mehmed had little interest in our small country and only wanted us to pay tribute to him every year.

Vlad and the other nobles refused, saying, "We're a free country and have earned that right with our blood. We will not pay a tax to a foreign ruler."

It was not long till the Sultan grew impatient. Mehmed brought a large division of his army to begin their invasion of Wallachia, now that his victories in Bulgaria were complete.

They killed any man who stood in their path, even woman and children if they did not swear allegiance to Mehmed II. Most people feared Mehmed would take over all of Europe if he was not stopped. Vlad and his men went to face Mehmed close to the Wallachia border.

A bloody battle ensued, and Vlad and his forces were defeated. In the moments, just before the end of the skirmish Vlad was mortally wounded when a well-placed arrow struck him in the shoulder. Medics successfully removed the arrow, but an aggressive infection took over. He grew weaker by the day and knew he would probably not survive. He was brought back to Castle Dracula by his few remaining loyal men to see me before he died. They carefully laid on our bed in our chambers, and I came to him.

As I entered our chamber, I saw him lying on the bed, motionless. He had several large bandages covering his right shoulder. It seemed to be as bad as I feared. I quietly sat beside him as he slept. He awoke to my presence. He looked at me, and he smiled.

"Hello, my love," his voice was weak and shallow.

It was difficult to bear the sight of my new husband's terrible injuries and plight.

"Hello my love," I replied. I'd never seen him so frail. He'd always been a strong pillar.

"The surgeon tells me I probably won't survive much longer. He says the infection in my shoulder is getting worse, and it is beyond their help."

"Don't say that!" I said.

"Listen to me," he insisted. "The Ottoman army will be here in a matter of days. You must leave. I want you to go to Transylvania. You'll be safe there," he explained.

"I'm not going anywhere without you," I said as a blood tear slid down the side of my face.

Seeing the blood on my face alarmed Vlad, he thought I was injured. He had no idea it was normal for me to shed tears of blood. As far as he was concerned, I was just a normal human. Vlad tried unsuccessfully to sit up.

"You're bleeding. Are you ok?" he asked wincing in pain from his injury.

I wiped the tear from my face. "Yes, I'm fine, my love." I did not want to bring any more attention to my tear.

I sensed Vlad knew I was hiding something but he wanted to leave it alone. He did not have the energy or time to push the issue.

Chapter 32

"I've made arrangements for you to be taken to Transylvania. My carriage is outside waiting and will take you to safety. I have a cousin there who'll look after you."

"I won't go without you," I repeated, desperately trying to hold back my tears.

"There's no time. You must go now!'

I leaned in to embrace him one last time, as I could no longer hold back. I was absolutely devastated and distraught beyond measure. Tears flowed freely down the sides of my face, and I felt the coarse stubble from his newly forming beard rub against my cheek. He kissed my face and cheek several times, I knew he was saying goodbye.

I pulled back to kiss him but stopped when I noticed his lips were unusually red. They appeared as if they had been stained with red paint or maybe berry juice. I pulled back further and wiped my face with my hand, it was covered in blood. I pulled out my handkerchief and scrubbed my face with it. The kerchief soaked up the blood and stained it. More alarmed than ever, Vlad looked at me with dismay.

"Now, I know there's something wrong with you. It's not normal to cry tears of blood. What's going on?" he asked.

I looked into his deep, brown eyes, and I knew I could not lie to him any longer. His strong square jaw and chin were still pleasing to me. He would be dead soon, and anything I told him now would surely be taken to his grave.

"I'm not human," I told him.

He looked at me strangely. "What are you talking about?"

"I'm not human."

He did not look like he believed me. "Then what are you?" he asked after a short pause.

"I don't know what I am." I was fearful he would reject me as an abomination.

"How do you know you're not human?"

"I'm very different from a human."

"How so?"

"For one thing, I don't age."

"What!?" he questioned with astonishment. "How can this be?"

"I'm not sure. All I know is, so many years have passed since my birth that I've lost count of time. I don't remember exactly how old I am. I've probably lived nearly two millennia."

His eyes squinted. "Two millennia as in 2000 years?"

"Yes, and that's not all. I'm stronger and faster than humans. I also heal much faster than you do."

"What else is different about you?" He could tell I was still holding back.

"You know that strange bat that lives here?"

"The Ferni bat?"

"No. The brown bat."

"The one that drinks blood?" His forehead wrinkled with confusion.

"Yes. That one." I had a real hard time revealing this part to him.

"What about it?" he questioned.

"I'm like the brown bat."

"What do you mean?"

"I need to drink blood to survive," I said, fearful he would go to his grave thinking I was a monster.

Vlad seemed a little horrified. "You drink human blood?"

"Animal blood," I replied.

"So not human blood?!"

"I haven't allowed myself to taste human blood. I do constantly fight the urge to drink human blood. It's difficult to resist. Animal blood is becoming more and bland as time goes on and, the smell of human blood is becoming incredibly more tantalizing."

Vlad seemed beside himself. "This is unbelievable!" I could tell he was morbidly fascinated. "Were you always like this?"

"No. I was a normal human once. I was attacked by a man when I was a young girl, and ever since I've never been the same."

"What did this man do to you that changed you?" he asked.

For some reason, his voice seems a little stronger. "I don't know. I really don't remember much of that day. My last memory was of him attacking me, and me screaming. I passed out, and when I came to, I remember my blood-stained gown and the pain of my injuries."

Vlad pondered. "So, you have no idea how you became like this?"

I looked at him sadly. "I wish I did."

Vlad's eyes desperately looked into mine. "I don't want to die!" He tried to lean forward but did not have the strength, so I assisted him.

I looked lovingly back at him. "I don't want you to die either, but I don't know how to help you."

He lay back down on his pillows. "It's ok, my love. I know you would help me if you could."

I sat with Vlad for hours, thinking every moment would be his last. That night, Vlad astounded me when he sat up under his own strength.

"That's weird," Vlad said with astonishment. "I feel a little stronger."

"How's that possible?" I asked.

"I don't know, but I do feel a little better."

One of the male servants came in with a plate full of food. The servant set the platter down on the table next to Vlad's bed and then left the chamber. Vlad picked up a piece of pork and began to eat vigorously, for he was ravenous with hunger. He had eaten most of the pig when he stopped suddenly.

He seemed confused.

"What's wrong I asked?"

He looked at the meat as if studying it. "I don't know. There must be something wrong with this. It doesn't taste right."

"What do you mean?"

"I don't really know, but it doesn't taste like it should. Please call the servant back and have him take this away," he ordered.

I did as he requested. The servant came back, walked to the bed, and picked up the plate. Vlad suddenly perked up.

"What's that smell?" he asked.

"I don't smell anything, my lord," the servant replied.

Vlad looked in the direction of the smell, following it with his nose like a bloodhound. He then grabbed the servant's arm and pulled him closer. He sniffed the servant's limb looking at me as he did. I watched as his eyes turned ruby red and his mouth opened. I could see his white teeth gleam in the candlelight. His incisors looked like a pair of small sharp daggers and sank deep into the flesh of the servant's arm before I could react.

"Vlad!" I yelled.

The servant stood in disbelief and horror as Vlad drained him of his life-giving blood.

"Vlad stop!" I screamed.

Vlad did not stop until the servant became pale and weak. His eyes turned grey and lifeless, he then fell to the ground, dead. Vlad released the servant's arm and raised his head to the ceiling with a roar. I could see the life and strength returning to Vlad's body. He looked at me with his ruby eyes and blood dripping from his lips. I was thoroughly shocked and felt a glimmer of terror fill my heart.

How'd this happened, I wondered.

I went to wipe his lips with my handkerchief. I stopped in mid-motion when I noticed the blood stain on the kerchief. A flash of memory came to me. I could again see the red paint on his lips only a few hours ago!

It wasn't paint, it was my blood! That's how it happened. He drank my blood tears by accident! I rationalized.

Vlad tried to move his shoulder and found it was much better. He pulled at his bandages and ripped them off to reveal the horrific gash was now healing nicely.

"How'd you do it?" he asked, astonished!

"I didn't. You accidentally drank some of my tears of blood."

"Your blood?!" He thought for a moment. "The power is in your blood?" He paused again contemplatively. "And now, it's in mine too!" he said, flexing his bicep with new vigor, amazement and surprise.

Vlad shocked me when he stood with ease and laughed as he picked me up and danced with me around the room. I did not know if I should be happy or terrified. I chose to hope for the best.

Chapter 33

The next afternoon Vlad awoke. He felt weak and tired. He did not understand what was happening to him, so he woke me.

"What's wrong with me?" he asked.

I was half awake and not in the mood to talk.

"What do you mean?"

"I feel tired and weak."

"Of course you do. The sun is out."

"So?"

"The sun weakens us. It makes us tired and as weak as a normal human," I explained. "You'll feel better at sunset."

"Great!" he replied sarcastically. "You didn't bother to tell me about that!"

"You didn't ask. Just go back to sleep. You'll feel better soon."

That evening, Vlad awoke, and he felt much better but had a tremendous thirst that he could not place. I stirred when I felt him get out of our large bed. His thoughts told me he was going to hunt, but for what I was not sure. Perhaps because he did not seem to know either. I quickly got out of bed and got dressed.

"You're hungry. I'll show you where to get blood," I said, hoping he did not plan on taking another human for his next meal.

He looked at me with curiosity. I could tell he had not figured out how to use his dark gift of mind reading yet because he did not seem to know what I had in mind. I took him outside the castle walls and to a small house. It was the local butcher's home.

"I've been coming here since before we met," I said.

"How was I unaware of this?"

"I sneak out at night when you're asleep," I admitted, hoping it would not upset him. "I have an ongoing understanding with the butcher. He collects fresh blood from the livestock he slaughters on a regular basis. He was always good about keeping my bizarre purchases to himself, and never questioned me."

It was early evening, and he was used to me making unannounced visits. I knocked on his door; he already had a good idea who it was at that time of night. He opened the door and started toward me when he stopped suddenly. He recognized Vlad; he was the Prince and ruler of the land, everyone in the country knew who he was.

I could tell the butcher felt more uneasy than normal with Vlad accompanying me on my unusual errand. Despite his reservations, he led me from his house to the barn where he performed his slaughtering. He had a shelf with all sorts of sliced meats neatly wrapped in parchment.

On the bottom shelf was a ceramic jug that was very familiar to me. The blood did not stay fresh long in the jar, the butcher would slaughter the hogs during the day, and I would have to pick it up that night or it would go bad. He picked the jug of fresh blood up and handed it to me.

"Here you go," he said, apparently still wondering what I did with all the blood he'd given me over the last 22 months.

His confusion only deepened by the fact the head of the royal family was now with me.

"Thank you," I replied giving him a silver coin.

The coin's value was more than he normally received from most of his customers for an entire slaughtered pig. To him, it was strange to collect such a sum of money for a large jug of blood that was worthless to anyone else, even to him. He was not going to argue the point, and the extra money ensured his silence. He had no interest in disrupting the extra income.

We left the butcher and headed back to the castle. Vlad marveled at his new ability to move quickly and silently through the city streets. He reminded me of a child, excited from learning a new skill.

This could come in handy, I heard him think.

Once back in our chamber, I handed the jug to Vlad. He seemed a little hesitant, but his thirst was growing. He drank from the jug. After only a few seconds, he stopped and spit the remaining blood onto the floor.

"What is this?" Vlad shouted in disgust.

"It's pig's blood,"

"It's disgusting!' he protested.

"What do you mean?"

"The blood from the servant tasted sweet. This is terrible."

"Well, you'll have to acquire a taste for it."

"This blood is cold." Vlad peered at me with an abhorrent look on his face.

"Go on. Drink up," I urged. "I drink this all the time, and it's fine."

He reluctantly choked down some of the contents of the jug once again. I could tell it was all he could do not to spit it out, but he managed to swallow just over half the contents. With his thirst quenched to the point the taste was no longer palatable, he handed the jar to me. I took it and finished off the remainder of its contents. We both felt life and strength filling us!

"How can you live like this?" he asked.

"It's a choice. I choose not to kill innocent people."

"You've lived like this for two millennia?"

I nodded my head. "Now that you've tasted human blood, I'm sure it's difficult to go back to animal blood, but I know you can do it."

"I don't know how you've done it." He shook his head.

"It's not easy."

"You must have some incredible willpower," he suggested. "Human blood is almost all I can think about. If it wasn't for the army headed our direction, I don't know what I would do." Vlad's attention now turned to the threat that lingered near their border. "Now I need to return to my regiment," he said changing the subject.

"What are you talking about?"

"The Ottomans are on their way. They'll be here in days. If I'm to stop Mehmed, I must prepare for battle." He turned with determination. As he left our chamber, he yelled at the new chambermaid, "Gather my military officers!"

The maid seemed shocked to see him out of bed. "My lord, it's late. Are you sure you want the gather the men now?"

"Of course I'm sure," he shouted.

Chapter 34

Two hours later, Vlad stood at the head of a large table in his war room. I peered through the crack in the door and watched as Vlad dictated to his men. A large and detailed map laid out across it. Several small copper coins lay atop the chart in strategic locations indicating troop locations and concentrations. There were only eleven officers left after the horrific losses from the battle at the border. Some had just been promoted to take the place of those who had fallen.

All the officers were stunned to see Vlad still alive and doing so well after such a terrible injury. Many were at the battle when Vlad had fallen and watched the aftermath of the arrow that took him off his horse. Two of the men now in the room had helped Vlad to safety. They had started to pull the arrow from his shoulder right away but stopped when they realized how severe the injury was. Later they watched as an infection spread throughout his body over a matter of days. They observed as Vlad went from a robust man, to one who was about to expire.

"We suffered a great loss at the border," Vlad began. "The days of losses are now behind us. We shall never lose another battle."

"My lord, with all due respect, the Ottomans outnumber us three to one," one of his new young lieutenants reminded him.

Vlad looked at him with complete confidence. "My friends, I have a new weapon that'll send the enemy back to their homeland."

The men all stirred, and chatter fills the room. "What's this new weapon," they asked?

"You'll see my friends!"

After a little over an hour of laying out his carefully-orchestrated plan, he dismissed the officers and called for his assassins. It took a couple of hours for his seven hitmen to assemble after his summons. Once gathered in the war room, he picked up a goblet that had been sitting on the table. The dark, thick, red liquid inside did not catch their attention at first.

"Drink with me, and I will give you the power to kill our enemies," he said handing the chalice to his chief slayer.

This robust man was several years older than Vlad. He was stocky, with an admirable beard which had streaks of grey running through it. He put the drink to his nose, sniffed, and brought the goblet back down to table level. He had not taken a sip.

"What is it?" the man asked.

Vlad looked at him. "Decebal, you are my eldest and most skilled mercenary. It's wine. I made just for this occasion."

Decebal looked at the goblet again but still looked skeptical. Something about the thick red liquid did not sit well with him. "It doesn't look like wine?"

"Drink!" Vlad urged.

Decebal did not want to argue or show weakness in front of the rest of the men, so he drank.

"Pass it on. I want everyone to drink," he insisted.

Each of the men took the vessel in turn and drank. They all felt this was odd and that the drink itself had something unusual about it, but none of them said anything. After the last had drunk, Vlad addressed them.

"You now have the strength you need to help me defeat the Ottomans."

The men listened but still did not understand.

"You now are more powerful than you can imagine."

The men looked at each other with confusion.

"The drink you just consumed will make each of you stronger than ten men. You'll also be much faster and will be resistant to injury."

Mass confusion ensued.

"We'll take back our land. We'll strike fear in the hearts of the Ottomans, and we'll make Mehmed pay for what he has done!" Vlad's voice raised. "For now, I want you to rest. Tomorrow night, we'll feast on the blood of our enemies!"

Despite their bewilderment, the men cheered!

*   *   *

Later that night Vlad and I left the safety of the castle walls to walk in the moonlight through the nearby rolling hills and forest. We stood hand in hand with the cool soft breeze of the night in our faces. I can remember how magical the moment seemed to me. I could have stayed in that moment forever, but it was the calm before the storm. Had I known how different my life was about to become I would have done everything in my power to freeze time and stay there in that time and never leave.

"Helen." Vlad started, it was clear by his manner he had something very important to say.

"Yes, my love?" I replied, trying to keep a smile on my face. I knew what he was about to tell me and I did not like it.

Suddenly, he stopped walking and gently halted me. "Something tells me you already know what I'm about to tell you," he said.

"What do you mean?"

"I'm not sure, but I feel like you know what's on my mind. More clear than just an impression as in what my body language would tell you, but in a more lucid manner. Almost like you can feel what I'm thinking? I almost feel like I can tell what you're thinking as well," he said still trying to solve this mystery.

I realized he was discovering our dark gift.

"Dark gift?" he said reading my mind without realizing how he did it. "What is a 'dark gift'?"

It was clear there was no point in trying to hide it any longer. "As you're now just discovering," I explained. "The dark gift is our ability to read others' minds."

"Read minds! We can read people's thoughts!?"

"Yes."

"That's amazing! Do you know what this means? I'll be able to know what the enemy is going to do before they do it. I'll never be taken by surprise again. It'll be a decisive, military advantage!"

I looked at him with some concern. He seemed too caught up in his abilities to understand the responsibility that comes with it fully.

"Vlad, these unusual gifts should not be abused. Don't allow yourself to be consumed by the power; it'll corrupt you if you let it."

He was not concerned. "Don't worry. Trust me, I can handle it. I must go now, there's no time to lose. I'll discover how Mehmed plans to attack, and I'll be able to see his weaknesses and know exactly how to retaliate."

I was torn, the line between right and wrong was becoming blurred. He kissed me and silently ran into the night at vampire speed.

Chapter 35

Vlad returned just before dawn. It was a good thing he did; he would have been vulnerable if caught out in the open during daylight. He entered our chamber, and I waited for him to speak to me. I could tell he was in high spirits and excited about his plans.

"I know now how to defeat Mehmed and his army!"

"I can tell you want to explain it to me," I said, not as interested as he was.

He was excited, which struck me as a little morbid. I hated that he was thrilled about war, destruction, and killing.

"I do want to tell you! I silently snuck into Mehmed's camp and sat right outside his tent. He was working alone on plans for an attack. I searched his mind and saw what he will do when he comes. Mehmed is planning on a two-front campaign. He'll set his archers on the upper ridge, supporting his infantry and cavalry below. The ridge stands atop a cliff at the edge of the chosen battlefield. He plans to leave his archers unprotected. He feels the height and steepness of the cliff will keep his archers safe on the high plateau. The battlefield is so far below the ledge it would be very difficult to get up to them during the battle. His strategy will free up his foot soldiers, who would have been busy protecting the archers otherwise. Freeing up his soldiers will give him even more numbers to fight on the field."

Helen tried her best to show enthusiasm but found it difficult.

Vlad showed no sign that he noticed. "He'd be right if I wasn't aware of his plans. I'll send a group of my soldiers to the plateau well before Mehmed's men arrive. They'll wait in hiding for his archers. When they get there, I'll have my men silently take them out. Once they have completed their mission, my men will take the uniforms from the dead bowmen and put them on my bowmen as a disguise. I'll have my archers standing in wait, ready for Mehmed to give his signal to fire. Of course, he'll think they're his archers. He plans to use his infantry to draw out my infantry, so his archers can take my men out.

"I'll let him think his plan is working. Once he gives the signal to fire, my archers will take out his infantry instead. This is sure to provide us the element of surprise and drive Mehmed's men into complete chaos and confusion. Without his archers or infantry, we'll only have his cavalry left to defeat. Seeing his heavy losses, he'll likely call for a retreat. His cavalry will ride a short distance away from the battlefield and make camp for the night. They'll use the cover of darkness to give them the time they need to regroup.

"In the morning, they'll send for reinforcements. But what Mehmed doesn't know is I now have a new secret weapon. Battles normally take several days, if not weeks, to finish. At night, most battles cease because it's too dark for men to see and fight. That won't happen this time. Once night falls, I'll release my assassins upon Mehmed, and he'll be taken by surprise yet again. It'll be a slaughter," he explained with chilling glee.

I was not entirely pleased. I hated to see him take joy in the thought of killing hundreds and, perhaps, even thousands of people.

*   *   *

Three days later, the Ottoman army approached just as Vlad had seen in Mehmed's mind. Vlad's army was ready and sprang their trap, just as they had planned. Mehmed's army sustained heavy losses, crushed under Vlad's calculated blow.

After a hasty retreat, Mehmed's army regrouped under the cloak of night and set up camp. His army had to rethink their plans quickly to save the battle from complete loss. That night, Mehmed and his remaining generals stood encircling the large planning table in the war tent when they heard the cries of men in the camp!

One of Mehmed's sergeants burst into the tent. "Sultan, we are under attack!" he yelled.

General Van Helsing, Mehmed's highest ranking officer, and adopted cousin stood beside Mehmed. Van Helsing was adopted by Mehmed's uncle, during a military campaign in Germany many years earlier. Taking in young, orphaned children of war was customary back then.

Van Helsing turned to Mehmed and frantically urged, "You have to leave, my Sultan!"

The rest of the officers charged out of the tent drawing their swords! Mehmed hesitated but then ran with the General out of the back of the tent. As they fled, the two men watched as Vlad and his seven vampire assassins laid waste to the men of the camp. Mehmed's forces were entirely outmatched, not knowing what direction the attack was coming. They saw men cleaved with swords and claws. Before they could engage the attackers, the assailants vanished into the dark of the night only to repeat the attacks moments later in a new location. Repeated attacks from all directions left Mehmed's men with no chance. Vlad's forces were too fast and too strong!

Mehmed's men fell everywhere; blood stained the ground red. What few men were now left began to flee into the night as the General helped Mehmed onto his mount. The general slapped the horse on the rump, and the horse sped off into the night with Mehmed firmly attached to its back. General Van Helsing turned to see unimaginable horrors! The smell of the blood sent the vampires into a feeding frenzy! He watched as they continued their attack and began to drink the blood of the men who lay dying. Most of Mehmed's forces were either mortally wounded lying on the ground expiring or fleeing for their lives.

"Bring me Mehmed's head!" Vlad roared in a terrible voice, blood dripping from his lips.

These aren't men but demons, General Van Helsing thought. He leaped upon his horse and fled into the shadows.

The vampires searched the camp but were unable to find Mehmed; his getaway was successful. After Vlad's assassins drank their fill, they took the bodies of the dead and impaled them with long pikes. They stuck the pointed staves deep into the ground and left the bodies hanging in the air as a warning to anyone who would dare challenge Vlad and his new army. Hundreds of dead bodies were left hanging from pikes, decorating the land, a grim reminder of the carnage that had just taken place. They returned to Castle Dracula and gathered in Vlad's war room.

"Today we had a great victory! Mehmed and his army were soundly defeated. Tomorrow we start making plans to invade Hungary!" Vlad announced to the cheer of his men. "That bastard John Hunyadi killed my father and my eldest brother. We drove them out of our land but were not strong enough to fight them on their home turf. Now we'll destroy them!"

The men cheered even louder.

Chapter 36

When Vlad returned to our chambers, I sensed his plans.

"Why are you going to invade Hungry?" I asked puzzled. "The battles have been won. We can be at peace now."

Vlad explained, "That murdering bastard deserves to die!"

I was appalled. "Vlad, the men you killed tonight, were attacking this country. Although they may not have deserved to die, they brought death on to themselves. The men you kill next will be innocent. You can't kill innocent people," I pled.

Vlad had a haunting look on his face. Hunyadi murdered my family; now I will return the favor."

"This is not the right thing for us or our country. We should leave the past in the past."

"I'll never forget and never forgive that man for what he has done. He must pay."

"Don't do this."

Vlad simply laughed. "You'll be my queen when I'm king. A queen doesn't tell a king what he can and can't do," he said coldly.

It seemed like he was on top of the world, and nothing could touch him. It was like he was drunk on power.

"Vlad, please don't do this!" I begged.

Vlad ignored my pleas and continued his planning. It was clear my husband would not listen to me. A week later, Vlad and his army invaded Hungary. They killed hundreds of men, women, and children. After each battle, the impaled bodies of the dead were left hanging on long pikes over the blood-soaked land.

I traveled to the fallen country and walked among the hanging bodies. I wept for the poor, innocent souls. I could understand why Vlad hated Hunyadi but the soldiers that littered the battlefield had not killed his family. Hunyadi had killed them with is own hand. The tremendous guilt was his and his alone. The most difficult sites for me to bear were the deaths of the women and children who Vlad seemed to show no mercy. Just like Mehmed, he killed them because they refused his rule.

What have I done?!

I could not bear this responsibility. I had to stop the killing of the innocent, but how would I halt my husband. He would not listen to me, but killing him was not an option, I loved him. Despite his never-ending thirst for blood and power, I was still his wife. I was partly to blame for the countless deaths. I was responsible for giving him the thirst and the immortal power. I had to find a way to get him to see the error of his ways.

Not everyone in our country agreed with Vlad's relentless military campaigns. Some wanted peace and would do anything to stop the endless warring. A group of people called the Boyars rallied to overthrow Vlad. With his dark gift, he knew of their plans to oust him. He threw a royal banquet and invited all of the leaders and prominent figures of the Boyars. When they arrived, the Boyars were arrested and immediately impaled. They were left to hang in the public square as a message to anyone who would dare defy him.

It was not long until Vlad was itching for another fight. Vlad and his army were preparing to march off to war with Bulgaria when I confronted him.

"Please stop. Innocent blood can't be spilled," I cried. "It's one thing to kill invaders, but to seek out death is completely different."

My husband mounted his steed. "Woman, I go off to earn my crown and yours. My patience with you is wearing thin. Wait for my return."

I stood in his path with the light of the setting sun shining in my eyes. "You'll have to run me over. I'm not letting you do this."

Vlad motioned to a couple of nearby foot soldiers. The men marched to me and carefully, but firmly grabbed my arms.

"Take her to my chamber. Don't let her leave." Vlad seemed unmoved by my gesture.

The two men took me to my room and stood guard outside of my chamber door. Night soon followed, and Vlad was marching to Bulgaria. I crept out of my balcony window unnoticed using my vampire agility. I decided there was only one way to stop my husband. I hated to do it, but I had to rely on an enemy for help. I went to Mehmed, who was now back home, deep in the Ottoman empire. I crept into his chamber as he prepared for bed. He was startled by my presence when he first saw me, but my beauty seemed to help put him at ease.

"Who are you, and what are you doing here?!" Mehmed asked.

"I came to deliver you from your enemy."

"Oh," he said barely interested in what I had to say and wondered how a woman could have snuck into his chamber.

A part of him just wanted to take advantage of me; the other wanted to know just how I got in here. He approached me; I knew he had carnal thoughts on his mind. I was getting the feeling he was not taking me seriously and that my task was going to be harder than I thought.

A knock came to his door. "Who is it?" Mehmed asked stopping in his tracks.

I was relieved because I was about to hurt him for what he was about to attempt and it would be much harder to convince him to help me after that.

"It's Van Helsing," the voice replied.

"Enter."

The General opened the great door to Mehmed's chambers, dressed in a red tunic with gold embroidered designs. It was the casual wear of the time. Van Helsing noticed me immediately.

"I'm sorry, my lord, I didn't realize you had company," he said, he was about to turn and leave when Mehmed stopped him.

"It's quite alright," Mehmed answered with a creepy smile. "You were saying my beauty." He turned back to me.

I wasted no time. "I will tell you how to defeat Vlad Dracula if you are willing to make a deal with me?"

Both men's ears perched up. "What kind of deal?" Mehmed asked.

"You must agree not to harm Vlad. Not a single hair on his head."

The two men looked at each other.

Van Helsing seemed resistant. "How do you propose we defeat Vlad in a battle without harming him?"

"I'm not a military general. I will leave the logistics up to you, but you must not harm him. Can you do that?"

The men looked at each other again. "We will find a way to make it so," Medmed replied.

I could tell he was not completely honest with me. He was appeasing me to hear what I had to say.

"I don't believe you. I am very good at telling when someone is lying, Medmed." I could tell I needed to get his attention and make sure he understood me. "Do you have a wife?"

He thought about this, wondering where I was going with this comment. "Yes. Why?"

"I swear to you. If Vlad is harmed in any way, your wife will die."

Van Helsing reached for his dagger.

"I wouldn't do that if I were you," I warned.

"Nobody threatens my wife and lives. Kill her," Medmed ordered.

Van Helsing drew his dagger and lunged at me. I immediately grabbed his armed wrist and twisted it hard. His grip on the knife weakened, and I took it out of his hand and put it to his throat where he froze. He was shocked and terrified. He wondered how I could have done such a thing being a woman of my size.

I glared at him. "I should kill you, but enough blood has been spilled. I am here to end the bloodshed." I looked at Medmed. "Do we have an understanding?"

Backed in a corner, he reluctantly replied, "We have an agreement."

"I need you to say you will not harm Vlad," I demanded. I needed to hear it from his own lips and without any confusion.

He paused. "We will not harm Vlad."

I still was not thrilled with his reply but hoped my threat on his family would keep him honest. My eyes returned to Van Helsing, the knife still at his throat.

"To defeat Vlad, you must fight him only during the day. If you are unable to complete a battle during daylight, you must flee far away and fight another day. You also need to coat your weapons with silver. The purer the better."

Mehmed seemed skeptical, but I could see my words were striking a chord in general Van Helsing. I wondered if it was because of his current predicament or because of what he had seen firsthand at the battlefield had made him realize he was not up against an ordinary man.

I continued, "Vlad is currently fighting in Bulgaria. If you confront him in two days' time and advance from the southern border of Bulgaria, you'll catch him off guard. I know he plans to return to Castle Dracula at that time, with a small group of men. He'll be vulnerable because his army will remain in Bulgaria. This plan will give you the opportunity you need to capture Vlad while he is unprotected. Without their leader, his army will withdrawal. Remember, make sure you do this during the day and don't hurt him."

"Who are you?" Mehmed asked.

"I am Helen. I am Vlad's wife."

Mehmed was shocked and alarmed. He had

a perfect person to use as a hostage and did not even know it. "Guards!" Mehmed yelled.

Van Helsing had an intelligent look about him. I could tell he was not a man one could fool easily. He had not taken his eyes off me. He wondered if I too had the demon powers he had witnessed from Vlad and his assassins. How else could I have so easily disarmed him? It would have explained what I had done.

"Why are you doing this?" I asked even though I already had a good idea of the answer.

"If I take you as a hostage, you'll be excellent leverage against Vlad," Mehmed explained.

"I'm guessing there is no way I can change your mind about that?"

Mehmed just laughed.

"I was afraid of that."

Several armed guards burst into the chambers, swords were drawn. They paused when they saw the knife at Van Helsing's throat. They could tell I meant to use the weapon if pushed to that point. Mehmed hesitated, cautious not to lose his adopted cousin and most valuable military leader. Van Helsing's interest in me became even more intense. The guards were unsure what to do.

"This meeting is over. I leave you with this Mehmed, if you kill my husband, I will kill your wife and your children. After you watch them die, I will kill you."

His thoughts told me he was not confident I could kill her if I tried. My actions told him that he should take me seriously.

"I got in here on my own with no trouble, didn't I?" I said, hoping my stunt would scare him more.

Mehmed agreed but was still unmoved by my statement. Van Helsing's suspicions of me only grew stronger. A woman of my size should not be able to accomplish such feats, and his intuition was incredible.

"Mehmed, I am more than what I seem. I will end your family line if you harm my husband," I warned again.

I could tell the guards were about to make their move. I dropped the dagger and tossed Van Helsing into the guards. Mehmed did not know whether to be amazed or outraged when Van Helsing fell to the ground on top of the men. I turned and leaped from his window to the ground twenty feet below. Van Helsing was further astonished, and his concerns about me grew stronger. The general was now convinced that I too was a demon. As I left Mehmed's chambers and headed back to Castle Dracula, my heart sank.

What have I done? I've betrayed my love, my husband. Had Vlad given me no other choice? Had I pursued all other options, I wondered? For the first time in my long life, I felt entirely hopeless.

I pondered my actions, *Was Mehmed going to honor his word and take Vlad alive or was he going to take advantage of the information I gave him and use it to kill my husband? Had I done the right thing, or had I only handed the world to an even worse threat? Where would this new path take us?* I was uncertain, but what I did know was that it was a place I dreaded.

Chapter 37

For two days I sat restless, watching from the east balcony window from Castle Dracula. I waited to see if Mehmed had lived up to his end of the bargain. If he had, I would be waiting for the dreadful news of Vlad's capture, or Mehmed would betray me, and I would hear of Vlad's death.

Castle Dracula was built upon the edge of an immense precipice, which lay on the west side of the castle. In the basin of the cliff was a great river. Our sleeping chamber lay on the west side of the castle. From our chamber balcony, I could see the river churning far below. Part of me wanted to hurl myself off our balcony and fall to my death in the river below. One step and the pain of my aching heart would end.

I could not bring myself to do it, I had to wait to see if Vlad was alive. The other thing keeping me alive was if Vlad was dead, I had a sultan to kill. I'm a woman of my word and would make good on any promise I make.

Opposite the precipice and on the east side of Castle Dracula, about 500 meters from the castle wall itself, was another high stone wall protecting the area from invasion. On the inside of the wall was a small city. Beyond the city just outside the gates of the wall, was a vast grass field with vast forests on either side. From the east balcony, I had watched many sunrises over the immense field in the distance.

Time seemed to stand still as I aimlessly waited to hear the fate of my love. The following days and nights never seemed to end. A few times I thought I saw him coming home, but each time was disappointed. In the early evening on the third day, an hour before sunset, I saw something in the distance! At the far edge of the grass field, a single horse with a rider raced for the castle. I strained to see who it was. For some time, I could not make it out. Was it Vlad or was it a messenger.

Either way, I knew trouble was headed in my direction. My heart sank, and anxiety squeezed my chest like a vice. Finally, I determined who it was. It was Vlad, and he was alone! My heart sank even further, he was alive, and something terrible must have happened! I had an uneasy feeling that I already knew what that was. After some time, Vlad arrived at the city gate, and his movements suggested he was on an urgent mission! When he arrived at the castle, I heard him call to guards to double their numbers on the city walls.

He raced through the fortress; I could tell he was headed for our chamber. In the distance at the horizon, an army now rose over the far hill towards our stronghold. My heart dreaded the sight as I knew it had to be Mehmed and his army reserves.

W*hat have I done to my beloved? I wish I hadn't done this. I've killed us,* I thought.

Now the wheels had been set in motion, and the consequences of my deeds were at hand. I went to our chamber balcony to wait for Vlad.

Vlad stormed into our room. "We must leave!" he said in near hysterics. "Mehmed and his men ambushed me!" He had no idea what I had done. He noticed me on the balcony and rushed to me. His demeanor changed when he saw the look on my face.

"What's wrong?"

He attempted to probe my mind, but the setting sun prevented him from doing so. He did not need to read my mind, my betrayal was written all over my face. He did not need his abilities to know I had done something wrong.

"Why do you resemble a child who's been caught doing something they shouldn't?" He had no idea what it could be.

"Because I betrayed you, my love."

"What're you talking about?" His concern was growing stronger.

"I went to Mehmed and told him how to defeat you." The words sounded even worse coming from my lips than they had in my own mind. I had a hard time believing I had done it myself.

Vlad stood there bewildered. "What have you done?" he yelled with a terrible thunderous voice! The betrayal struck him like a ton of bricks. "Why did you do this?" A blood tear slid down his face.

I could see the fading of the setting sunlight on his angry face. He came closer to me. I could see his heart shatter as the enormity of my duplicity crashed down upon him.

"I did what had to be done," I replied remorsefully. "You wouldn't listen. You killed innocent women and children. I wanted you to have this gift to save your life, not to take lives. It was the only way to save the innocent."

He did not acknowledge my remark. "Three of my assassins, whom I consider my children, are dead now because of you!" he roared. "And now Mehmed will be beating at the city gate any second!"

He lunged at me, grabbed me by the throat with both hands. He lifted me off the ground. He still did not have his vampire strength but was a powerful man without it. He glared into my eyes, as tears of blood now flowed from his eyes.

"I loved you more than life itself."

I tried to reply but was unable to speak; his grip was too tight. The sun was inching down the edge of the horizon, the rays of the sun still shone on us.

I struggled to free myself but it was hopeless, he was much too strong for me. The city gate was closed and securely barricaded as Mehmed reached the wall. His men were now working to force open the immense doors of the city. I could hear the thunderous sound as the doors began to groan from the brute efforts of the angry army behind it.

The city guards frantically fought off the men the best they could. They dumped cauldrons of hot tar onto the men and shot flaming arrows into the crowd of angry men, but the men kept coming. The cries of the invaders echoed off the castle walls. Vlad dangled my body over the precipice with the river far below.

"I can't believe you'd do this to me," he cried.

"Please . . ." I struggled to talk.

I looked below and struggled to make out the river in the shadows of the steep crevasse. The river had cut it out of the land for thousands of years. Without warning, he released his grip, and I began to fall into the chasm. I felt like I was falling forever as I fell into the dark shadows of the abyss. Eventually, I hit the surface of the water and the world went dark.

Chapter 38

Later that evening, much to my surprise, I awoke. Somehow, I had miraculously survived the brutal fall. I guessed the setting sun, and the darkness of the chasm had given my vampire powers enough strength to save me. That did not explain how I got out of the water. Someone must have pulled me out and laid me gently down on the soft patch of grass near the river's edge where I lay still soaking wet. I had the sensation I was being watched, but had no idea where the feeling was coming from. I had several injuries that were in the process of healing. Despite my wounds, I managed to climb to the bottom edge of the precipice.

I looked up the high rock wall before me and could just make out the edge of the castle wall far above. I could see flickering lights emanating from inside the walls, which made me feel there was a raging inferno inside. The thought of the castle on fire caused my heart to sink. I gingerly scaled the cliff and finally made it to the top of the cliff. I then walked through the broken gates of the castle.

I heard the cheers of the victorious men among the roar of the raging fires. I saw the blood-spattered ground and the dead that lay scattered throughout the castle grounds. I crept among the bodies and to an even more horrifying sight. Vlad's head was perched on a pike in the middle of the square as a war trophy.

My heart broke into a million pieces. I was responsible for this. I did not want this. I desired to prevent death not cause it. I could never forgive myself. There were so many fires throughout the castle it lit the castle grounds. I tearfully walked among the horrific corpses and the isolated fires that burned bright. All was lost!

"Helen!" I heard a man's voice call from the night.

I was so distraught I ignored the words at first.

"Helen!" the man called to me again.

It took a moment, but I did recognize the voice. The man approached me from the right and emerged from the smoke. It was General Van Helsing, strutting proudly in his shiny armor. He moved closer and stood right beside me.

"Well look who it is. Just the person I was looking for!" Van Helsing said. "By the way, your advice was most helpful. He noticed the blood tears running down my face. "I had no choice but to kill your demon lover. It was a bonus to get a few of his demon cohorts."

My blood tears flowed at will.

The blood only solidified his suspicions about me. "I see I was correct. You are a demon too." He caressed my bare shoulder with the tip of his sword as if to signify my impending death.

The moment the sword touched my skin, it felt like a white-hot poker had burned me terribly despite the metal's cold temperature. I screamed and pulled away.

"It's silver plated, just as you suggested," Van Helsing said with a delighted glint in his eye. "I have to tell you; I feel awful about having to kill you too. After all, you did give us a glorious victory against a nearly unbeatable foe."

I looked up with my tear-filled eyes and saw the grim smirk on his face.

"I have to know, though," he paused. "Why did you do it?"

I could feel the rage building deep in my heart. "You promised you wouldn't kill him. Now you've forced me to do things I didn't want to."

"I never promised anything." He laughed malevolently.

The sound of my husband's killer's amusement fueled my rage.

"I'll kill both you and Mehmed, and your families. I'll make you pay for what you've done."

The general ignored my threat. "Without you, we couldn't have defeated Prince Dracula. We nearly captured him while on his way here. Three of his demon minions sacrificed themselves to allow him to escape. It didn't save him in the end; we caught up to him. After we captured Vlad, we tortured him. We wanted to know everything about you and your kind. I have to give him credit though, he was stubborn and held out to the end. I have to say I was impressed. Not many men have resisted all the way till their death.

"It doesn't matter though. My men tell me the remaining devils are with Vlad's army in Bulgaria. We'll be visiting them next. With the knowledge you've given us, we will hunt down those monsters and kill them one by one. They are a plague, and we are the cure. We came up with a name for your kind, Vampire. Do you like it?" Van Helsing announced.

"You won't find them," I replied. "They're more difficult to kill than you think." I suddenly felt defensive of my kind.

"Oh, it may take some time, but I will find them. I will kill them, all of them. Even if it takes my whole life. It's a shame to kill such a beauty like yourself but it must be done. You must die just like your demon lover." Van Helsing raised his silver sword.

His words stung my entire body, and my eyes burned with hatred. The general paused his death swing; his thoughts told me he had a hard time killing a defenseless woman, even a monster like me. Without warning, I lunged at Van Helsing with lightning speed! I violently grabbed his throat with one hand, and his wrist holding the sword in my other. I forced him to the ground and held him firmly in my grip. I could see the fear and shock in his eyes.

He had fought Vlad while the sun still shone, and his strength had not fully returned. It was the middle of the night now, and I had my full strength and was much more powerful than he realized. He had underestimated me, and he now knew it.

"Don't call him that!" I roared. "Vlad was once a good man. A better man than you. It's because of men like you he even went to war in the first place. Time to make good on my promise, you will die now."

My red eyes glared into his. Fear radiated from him like the fires surrounding us. I shook his sword loose from his grip. My thirst and rage consumed me; I bit down on the general's neck. I did not care about his life or what was right or wrong anymore. I began to drain the blood from his veins.

Vlad was right; human blood tasted like nothing I had ever experience before, it was amazing! My whole body felt electrified. It was like a potent drug, causing an instant addiction. I realized immediately, given a choice, it would be nearly impossible ever to drink anything else again.

A terrible pain shot through my leg, I released my grip on the general. I hobbled away in retreat to investigate the pain now throbbing in my right leg. I saw an arrow buried deep in my thigh and it burned with great intensity. I yanked it out, revealing the silver tip. I angrily tossed the arrow and searched for my attacker. As I glared into the darkness, I could feel the human blood coursing through my veins, giving me more strength and power than I could have ever imagined.

My senses where more keen and the world seemed different somehow. I now knew why Vlad could not go back to drinking animal blood. The blood of humans was better in every way. I continued to search in the direction from which the arrow had come. Finally, I found him, one of the general's men. He was loading a second arrow into his bow. Armed with their silver weapons, I knew staying here would mean my death, so I left General Van Helsing on the ground in his terror.

His men came to his aid after I disappeared into the night leaving the castle and its grounds for the last time. He was not dead but was very weak from blood loss. His men had stopped me short of my goal of killing him, but I wasn't finished, I'd be back.

*   *   *

That night I went to Mehmed's chambers and waited in the darkness. I pulled out my locket and opened it. Sadness filled my heart as I gazed down at the image of my true love, who I had betrayed. I had made a terrible mistake. One I vowed I would never make again. Now was the time for revenge.

Someone entered, and I assumed it would be the man I aimed to kill, but it was not him. It was his wife, and I soon remembered that I had vowed to kill her as well. I went to kill his bride and had her in my grasp helpless. All I had to do was drink her blood, but I was unable to bring myself to kill an innocent person. She had done nothing wrong, and I was about to take an innocent life as Vlad had. It was not her fault her husband had lied and did not live up to his word. I released the terrified woman; I could not take her life.

In my failed attempt, I turned my rage onto Mehmed himself, the one who deserved to die. I held the woman down in the corner of the room and told her if she moved or made a sound I would be forced to kill her. I continued to wait until Mehmed entered the room. When he did, I was on him before he realized I was there. I savored the moment and allowed him to watch me as I slowly drained him dry. After Mehmed's death, I then left his kingdom and his country, never to return. After that night, Van Helsing and his family launched a campaign against all vampires. They hunted us relentlessly and became obsessed with our destruction.

Chapter 39

Roslyn continued her story. "Several years later, in one of their attempts on my life, I killed general Van Helsing in front of his three sons just as I had promised. Vengeance was mine, but now his sons had a vendetta against me. Later, I changed my name to Roslyn to make it more difficult for them to track me. The Van Helsing men continued hunting me and my kind for generations. They traveled the world in search of Dracula's scattered assassins.

"It took several hundred years, but eventually, they successfully hunted every last one of them down and destroyed them and all of their children. The Van Helsings are fixated with the obliteration of my kind, whether they are monsters or not. As you know, they're still after me, and they won't rest until they have my head.

"The blood feud between the Van Helsings and vampires nearly ended a couple of short years ago. Decebal was the last surviving member of Vlad's assassins. Decebal almost killed William Van Helsing while hunting Agent Grey. Grey had been on his trail for several years. When Decebal made his move to kill Grey, William was there to stop him. Before he died, Decebal left his mark on William's face but was dead before he could end the feud once and for all. William is the last surviving member of his family line. Killing him would leave no one to continue the war, and it would have ended there and then."

"That's an incredible story!" Michael exclaims.

"That's why I can't change you."

"You think I'll turn out like Vlad?"

"Power corrupts everyone. I've seen good men throughout time changed for the worse by power. Power is one of the greatest evils man has ever known. Most people want it, but most people can't handle it when they have it. Once someone has it, they'll do anything to keep it."

"You turned out ok. Maybe I will too."

"Did I? The temptation to drink human blood is nearly irresistible. It's a battle I fight every day. It's a battle that wears you down. It's a battle that can't be won. I lose this battle and resolve the issue by preying upon the scum of society, the guilty. I live and relieve my hunger through the monsters who deserve to die. In time, everyone gives in to the thirst for human blood."

Matt returns to the living room. "I'm glad to see you're decent." He chuckles, he can tell the mood is serious and his grin fades.

"Thanks for the blood," Roslyn replies.

"You're very welcome." He is still a little sheepish from having seen her unclothed.

A thought comes to Roslyn's mind. "I've told you all kinds of things about me. I want to hear about you now?"

Michael's taken aback by this. "You don't want to hear about me. Besides, can't you see it all in my mind?"

"I want to hear it in your words. Besides, I can only read what's currently on your mind. Only what's on the very surface. So, your childhood memories or even what happened to you yesterday for that matter, are all out of my reach, unless you think about them," she explains.

"Wait a minute? You're a psychic?" Matt asks.

Roslyn pauses, "You could say that."

"Interesting!" Matt seems interested. "Mike, tell her the story about the stolen calculator!"

Michael looks irritated.

"The stolen calculator?" Roslyn asks.

"Thanks, Matt," Michael says sarcastically.

"Oh come on. It's funny looking back on it now," Matt affirms apologetically.

"No, it's not. It'll never be funny, and it's not a great story to start her off with."

Roslyn sweetly takes Michael's large hand in hers. "Please tell me?" she asks softly.

Her persuasive request clearly sways Michael.

"I don't want the first story I tell you to be a bad one."

She pauses. "I want to know both the good and the bad. I want to know all the parts of your life."

He does not look convinced. "Fine, but I have to warn you, it's not a happy story."

"I understand," Roslyn says clearly excited to hear his story no matter what tone it might have.

"When I was in grade school, I was the smallest kid in my grade," Michael begins.

His claim comes as a surprise to Roslyn, as he is tall now.

"One day, my fourth-grade teacher confronted the class about a stolen item. She informed the class, someone had taken her gold calculator from the top of her desk during recess and hour before. Her only request was, for it to be returned and no questions would be asked.

I remember looking about the room to see if anyone looked like he or she might have a guilty look. While scanning the class my eyes met Julie King's. I could tell by the accusing look that she somehow blamed me for the theft.

"She slowly mouthed the words, 'I know you did it.'

I dismissed her gaze and turned my attention back to the lesson the teacher had just resumed. I knew I had not taken it, so I did not care what she thought. Later, at lunch recess, I was playing by myself, as I did not have many close friends at the time. I was new to the school and was too shy to be the one to make the first move in becoming friends. I bounced a big red ball against the playground wall when a menacing group of kids ripped it away from me and tossed it aside. I turned to see the group was much bigger than I realized.

It seemed like most of the class was around me, blocking my escape. I felt a sudden wave of fear overtake me, and I could tell by the energy from the crowd they meant to harm me. The group of kids roughly pushed me back and forth between them. I recognized all of the unruly kids, they were my classmates. A few of them had been friendly to me in the past, but they all had turned on me now.

After a few moments of shoving, an opening appeared ahead of me, I had a means of escape! I moved to exit the circle when a boy I knew well blocked my path. It was Steve Nole, the meanest bully in my class. I heard a rumor, he had beat up a kid just for looking at him wrong.

I noticed Julie was delightedly standing next to him, with her arms crossed. It seemed the pair had incited this rambunctious bunch of kids against me. Steve had his fist inside his other hand cracking his knuckles as he approached. I had a feeling by the look in his eyes he was about to beat my brains in.

"Give us the calculator you stole!" Steve insisted. "We know you have it. Your brother told us you have a gold calculator."

I was not sure why he was accusing me. I had bought a calculator for school a few months ago, but I could not remember for the life of me what color it was. I had never been in a fight before. I did not know what to do.

Unexpectedly, out of what I can only describe as fear-driven instinct, I kicked Steve in the groin as hard as I could. The larger boy fell to the ground, holding himself and groaning in tremendous pain. The lucky shot only incited the mob more. They pushed and shoved me as I struggled to stay on my feet.

Kids jeered at me, called me names and yelled obscenities at me. Before I knew it, Steve had gotten back on his feet and stood before me, angry and threatening. As I raised my fists to defend myself, Steve kicked me in the groin with all his might. Pain radiated through my whole body as I fell to the ground! A few moments later, a teacher sifted through the cluster, broke them up, and sent them away.

I continued to writhe in pain rolling on the ground. When I could stand again, she took me to the office where the school secretary called my mother. When my mom arrived, she took me home to recover. Every kid I could identify was later brought to the principal's office. The principal talked to all of them, but none of them were expelled. I heard after I was sent home, that the gold calculator mysteriously showed up back on the teacher's desk.

It was difficult for me to get close to anyone after that. Ever since then, I have had an underlining fear that people could turn on me in a matter of moments. I still do not know why Julie did what she did. I talked to her years later over

Facebook, and she claimed not to remember the incident that scarred me."

"That's terrible!" Roslyn hugs Michael.

"I told you it wasn't a pretty story."

She took in a deep, long breath. "Yes, but it's part of who you are and why you're so amazing now! Every event molds you to become what you are today, and you're wonderful."

Matt rubs the side of his face. "You never told me that whole story. It sounds worse now that you tell it in its entirety."

"It's not a story I like to tell. It's difficult for me to revisit," Michael replies.

"I can see why," Matt agrees.

Roslyn hugs Michael for several minutes after. She seems more upset by the story than Michael does.

"I wish I could say that was the last time I was bullied like that."

"There were more?" Roslyn pulls away from him slightly.

"Many more. They continued until I started to grow in high school finally. Once I was as big as everyone else, the bullies started leaving me alone."

"That's a bully for you. Always picking on people smaller or weaker than them," Matt chimes.

"Thanks for sharing your story," Roslyn says.

"You're welcome," he says, grateful she seems satisfied.

"What now?" Matt asks.

"Now Mike and I leave," Roslyn states.

Matt's smile melts. "What?"

"The FBI will never let us live in peace now and they'll kill Mike and put me in a cage."

"What am I supposed to do? Mike's my best friend."

"If we stay, you won't have a best friend anymore. So, either way, you'll lose your friend, either to death or absence. Which would you prefer?"

"This sucks!"

"Yes, it does," Roslyn replies.

Michael puts his hand on Matt's shoulder in an attempt to comfort him. "I'll miss you, my friend."

A small tear forms in the corner of Matt's eye. He put his arms around Michael. "I'll miss you, too."

The two buddies share a man hug. They were already feeling a little weird about their expression of emotion and affection, so they kept it short.

"So where are you guys going?" Matt asks.

"I wish we could tell you. If the FBI thinks you know where we are, they'll torture you until you tell them. We can't put you in that kind of danger," Roslyn explains.

"Can you tell me when you're leaving?"

"Tomorrow."

Matt's heart sinks. "Is it ok if I hang out with you guys till tomorrow?"

Roslyn smiles. "Of course."

"What are we gonna do now?" Matt feels like grieving, but holds back the best he can.

Roslyn gazes lovingly at Michael for a moment. "Well, it's late, and the two of you need your rest." Her eyes return to Matt. "Michael and I are going to the master bedroom. Feel free to use the guest room, the morning is nearly here. I suspect we'll see you for brunch." She gave him a slight wink and walked with Michael to the bedroom.

Chapter 40

Late the next morning, Michael awakes to a remarkable aroma. Someone is cooking, and whatever it is, it smells incredible! He reaches for Roslyn, but her side of the bed is empty. He glances into the master bathroom, and there is no sign of her there either. He is a bit surprised by her absence sine he can see the sun shining through the window and knows she must be tired at this time of morning. He puts on some clothes and opens the bedroom door to find Matt cooking with Roslyn assisting. They are smiling and joking with each other. Roslyn looks up, still very cheery.

"Good morning my love! Matt's been telling some of your 'war' stories," she chuckles.

"Really?" Michael feels a little concerned.

"Don't worry. I left most of the juicy details out," Matt reassures him.

"It seems you've dated several women over the years."

"Oh, great!" Michael's fears begin to run wild.

"Don't worry, sweetie, after 2,500 years, I've seen worse." She is quite amused.

Michael is shocked there is so much food out on the counters, Roslyn does not need food, and there is no reason for it to be here. "Where did all of this food come from?" Michael asks, impressed with the splendor.

Roslyn nudges Matt. "Matt went out and picked up all of the ingredients! He is showing me how to cook. I've never kept human food around the house. It's kind of fun to learn something new!"

"You two seem a little chummy." Michael cocks an eyebrow.

Roslyn notices his apprehension and stops what she is doing and walks around the kitchen island that separates them. She puts her hands on each side of his face and kisses him. "Don't be like that. This is probably the last time we'll see Matt, let's make it a great day!"

Receiving a warm greeting from a gorgeous woman seems to settle him down. Michael follows Roslyn to her work area and helps prepare the meal. Once the meal is ready, they all sit down at the dining room table.

"So, what stories has Matt been telling you?" Michael inquires.

She is acting a little coy. "Well, he told me about the time the two of you met that blonde . . . Tiffany, I believe her name was!?"

Matt nods his head, while Michael's face turns pale and his eyes widened.

"You told her about Tiffany?!"

"What?" Matt shrugs his shoulders.

Roslyn sits while the two men eat. She leans towards Michael. "So, at what point did you finally realized that Tiffany was a prostitute?" Roslyn winks.

Michael sits back in his chair defensively. "Hey! How was I supposed to know? She didn't mention anything until afterward."

Matt starts to laugh. "Yeah, there was no way he was gonna get someone that hot. Being a poor, starving college student should have been your first clue."

Michael shakes his head. "I'll have you know, I've had some very attractive girlfriends."

"Yes, but how long did they last?" Matt's still laughing.

Michael shakes his head again. "That's not the point."

"Yeah, it is! That's the whole point."

"For the record," Roslyn interrupts, "money isn't the only thing women care about."

"No, but it sure does help," Matt replies.

Roslyn ignores the comment. "What other sordid affairs have you had?" Roslyn inquires now leaning on her elbows giving Michael her full attention.

Michael's lip tightens. "None that are worth talking about." Michael can not help but notice the sparkle in Roslyn's eyes. "Are you having fun?"

"Yes, I am!" she replies. "I haven't had this much fun in six hundred years. I've forgotten how refreshing it can be to flirt with a significant other!"

"Great, I'm glad you're amused," Michael chuckles.

"Hey, it's saying something when you can entertain someone who's been around as long as I have."

Michael agrees with a slight nod.

*   *   *

Later that afternoon, they decide to watch the latest "Star Wars" movie. The two gentlemen had seen in before but wanted to see it again. Matt pops popcorn on the stove, melts butter, and spreads it over the corn.

"The perfect snack for watching movies!" Matt says as he marches into the living room with his bounty. "Is it just me, or is the plot to this last movie nothing more than the combining of the original three movies?" Matt asks.

Michael turns towards him. "What do you mean?"

"The first movie, 'Episode IV', was the introduction of a young man with incredible powers that the empire wants to use for its nefarious purposes. The second movie was about the training of that young Jedi. The third movie was about the young man becoming a Jedi master, and fights and defeats a Sith Lord."

"So, you think the storylines are the same?" Roslyn asks not having seen the previous movies.

"Well yeah. This last movie, 'The Force Awakens', is a story of the discovery of a young woman with incredible powers. She begins to learn about the force and how to use her new powers. She then goes on to fight a trained Sith Lord and defeats him. It's like it's the same story, but with a young woman instead," Matt points out.

Michael thinks about it. "Huh, I never thought about it like that. You might have a valid argument. It's definitely a similar story."

"I mean it's a fantastic movie, but I wish the writers had more imagination," Matt says.

Roslyn struggles to understand their references. She has only seen a handful of movies ever in her life.

*   *   *

After the movie, they all help prepare dinner. They eat without a care in the world, like nothing was about to change. At least, that's the front they all portray. In the backs of their minds, the undeniable truth lingers, this will be their last meal together. No one wants to think about it or bring it up in conversation. It is like they are hoping if they ignore the issue, it will go away on its own. They all know it is not the case, no matter how bad they want it to be true.

After dinner, they clean up and toss out the paper plates. The sun is setting, and they all know what is coming. When night falls, it will be time to go. Matt and Michael try not to show their feelings, but they can see the hurt buried deep beneath their eyes. The sadness shadows their thoughts. They are best friends and have been since the first weeks of college. Soon, they will never see each other again.

The sun sets, and Roslyn can now hear their ponderings. She can feel the underlining emotion of those sorrowful thoughts. Part of her wants to suggest bringing Matt with them, but she knows it will not be fair to Matt.

Matt can not give up his new practice, not after all those years of hard work and study, it is all he had left now. The last rays of the sun are gone, and Roslyn feels her full strength returning.

"Mike," Roslyn calls to him.

Michael is sitting in a chair next to Matt, he looks up from his conversation. "Yes."

"It's time. We have a long drive ahead of us."

Michael turns back to Matt. A look of understanding is on both of their faces. They stand up and embrace each other briefly. They release each other and walk into the kitchen where Roslyn is leaning with her back against the counter.

"Time to pack up," she insists.

A thought comes to Michael. "What are we packing everything into?"

It is like Roslyn was waiting for that question and she guides them into the garage. She turns on the light and illuminates a dusty underused room. Matt's Audi is parked neatly in one of the two bays. The second bay has a vehicle laying under a tarp. The telltale shape makes it clear what vehicle's beneath it. The tarp has several years of dust on it. She takes the cover, and a cloud of grime fills the air. It takes several minutes for the dust to settle. Once it does an old, Volkswagen bug is revealed.

"We're leaving in a bug?" Michael's not impressed.

"Hey, this car is a classic. It's very well-made, and it's very reliable. It'll start even after years of abuse and neglect. It's also effortless and inexpensive to fix," Roslyn explains.

"I guess we're not packing anything large."

"Only the most important things," Roslyn explains. The only thing Roslyn is taking is a couple of bags of clothes and her gold locket.

Michael is caught unprepared, all of his belongings are in his home which is being closely watched by the FBI. There is little to no chance he could ever go back without being detected and detained. He has no choice but to leave everything behind. The only thing he will be taking is the clothes on his back. Anything he needs they will have to pick up on the way.

Chapter 41

Matt finally arrives at his comfortable home in Bellevue. He closes the front door and sets his keys down with a sigh; he already misses his friend. Matt purchased the house six months ago and has been very happy with his it. It is a two-story, three-bedroom residence and is brand new. It has all the modern conveniences one would find in new construction. It has beautiful, cherry hardwood floors and black granite countertops, plus all new stainless steel appliances. Even his dream home can not lift his spirits. The house feels emptier than ever before.

What do I do now, he wonders?

He turns on the light and enters his living room, where he sits down on the soft leather cushions of his couch and turns on the TV. It is very late, but he is not in the mood to go to bed just yet. Maybe a movie can distract him, but he doubts it will.

The next day, Matt is at Children's Hospital on his morning rounds. He finds it challenging at times, but he keeps an upbeat mood.

I wonder if I'll ever see him again, Matt wonders?

"Dr. Richardson, please report to the front desk . . . Dr. Richardson, you're needed at the front desk," the intercom barks!

Matt's heart races, *has Mike stopped by to see him*? *Maybe he forgot something and needs it before they leave town.* He hurries to the reception area excited to see Michael.

When he arrives, he is dismayed because it is not him. Instead, two men in black suits are waiting for him. Matt does not recognize them and wonders what they want. One thing he knows instantly is these two men are trouble. They seem to be in an unpleasant mood.

"How can I help you?" Matt tries to be professional.

"Hello, Doctor. I'm Agent Grey of the FBI, and this is my colleague William Van Helsing. Can we speak to you in private?"

Matt's face goes pale which Grey picks up on; his years of training serve him well.

This is not good, Matt thinks. "Absolutely."

Matt does not want to look guilty of anything, so he leads them down the hall to his office. Once there, they all sit down, Matt behind his desk and the two men in the lounge chairs.

Grey leans forward; he is in no mood to waste time. "Let me get straight to the point," he says sternly. "I'm only going to ask this once, where are they?"

Matt's face goes paler still. "Wh . . . Who?" Matt mumbles.

"You know who," Grey scolds.

"I don't know what you're talking about." Matt tries to keep his composure.

"Really? So, this is how you want to play it? I assure you, if you play games with us, you'll lose." Grey pauses.

Matt does not show any sign of compliance.

"Fine. Here's the thing. We've been investigating Dr. Bauer since we learned of his involvement with Roslyn. We know the two of you have been friends since college. We know you two hang out together often. If anyone knows where they are, it's you. Now tell us where they are?" Grey's getting more agitated.

"I . . . I don't know. They didn't tell me where they were going," Matt states, hands starting to tremble.

Grey peers into Matt's eyes trying to get a read on him. "You know, you're a terrible liar."

"I'm telling the truth," Matt insists.

"I'm very good at reading people," Grey explains. "I can tell you're a terrible liar." He pauses for effect, giving Matt one last chance to implicate himself. "That's why I know you're telling the truth, at least about not knowing where they are. Roslyn is too smart to have made that kind of mistake."

"Even if I did know, I'd never tell you. I would never, betray my best friend," Matt states boldly.

"Your best friend?" Grey replies coldly.

Matt was silent for a moment. He senses he may have said something wrong, although he was not sure what it was.

Grey glances at William and then back at Matt. "You should know that both Roslyn and Michael are now considered terrorists. If you have any contact with them or aid them in any way, you'll also be labeled a terrorist, and will be treated accordingly."

Matt's heart sinks even further; he can feel fear gripping his chest like a python. A bead of sweat runs down the side of his face.

Grey stands up, and pulls out his card, and hands it to Matt. "If you hear from them and don't tell us, we won't be able to help you."

Matt takes the card with a trembling hand.

"Have a nice day, Doctor," William says with a creepy look as the two men exit the office.

*   *   *

A month passes, and Matt knows he will never hear from Michael again now they have been gone so long. He misses his friend profoundly and wishes there was some way they could visit. He knows deep down there is no safe way to do this, though. The shock of having the government shake him down has worn off, but he will never forget it. His trust for the people running his country has diminished. He is eating dinner when his front door bursts open with a loud bang!

"FBI!" voices scream as a host of heavily-armed men in riot gear breach his entrance!

"Get down on the floor!" they yell, waving their assault rifles in Matt's face.

Matt complies but does not get down fast enough for their liking. A man grabs Matt and forcefully throws him on to the floor. His ears ring as his head bounces off his hardwood floor with a hard thump. Several men pounce on Matt, driving their knees into his back and painfully pinning him to the floor. He is stunned and is not sure what is going on. They violently wrench his arms behind his back and handcuff him.

"What did I do?" Matt shouts.

"Shut up!" one of the men demands as he pushes Matt's face back into the floor.

A few moments later, they force him to his feet and drag him out of his house. Several neighbors are drawn to their doors by the commotion and watch as the scene unfolds. Matt looks up at them, embarrassed and mortified as he is hastily led to the back of a black SUV. He feels like a criminal, even though he knows he has done nothing wrong. His neighbors have always liked him and wonder what he must have done to be in this situation. They can not believe they had no idea he was so dangerous.

He is roughly loaded into the back and he finds himself looking out of the rear window. The shocked looks on his neighbor's faces make him feel like a criminal as the vehicle drives away. His neighbors are relieved it is not them and even more relieved that a perilous person is now off the streets and their lives are now safer.

*   *   *

Roslyn sits next to Michael, arm in arm as they gaze over the gorgeous lake. The sun is resting lazily in the clear blue sky. The late summer gentle, breeze pleasantly caresses their faces.

"I love it here," Roslyn says as she strokes the hair over his forearm.

He loves the feel of her touch; something tells him he will never get tired of it. "Me too," Michael replies. "Coeur d'Alene is always beautiful this time of year. I wish we didn't have to keep moving."

"Me too, but we have to stay a step ahead of Grey and his minions. I'm sure Yellowstone will be amazing when we get there." Roslyn can tell he is not feeling his normal chipper self and resists the urge to probe his mind with her abilities. "What's wrong?"

"I miss Matt. This is harder than I thought."

"Your mind has been heavy since we left."

Michael gives her a look she is beginning to know all too well. "Are you probing my mind again?" He is not upset, but only curious.

"I don't have to read your mind, to see that my love."

Michael's expression changes to one of apology. "I guess that's true." He rubs his head sorrowfully.

"I know this is hard, but it's the safest way for everyone." Roslyn repositions herself behind him and starts rubbing his back and begins to massage out his worries. The gentle kneading feels fantastic. It is a terrific distraction from his emotional state.

Michael looks up at the sun. It is beginning to hang low in the sky. "I wish there was another way."

Roslyn looks up at the sky with him. "I do too."

The couple sits there enjoying the pleasant day.

Roslyn stops rubbing and takes his hand and

gently squeezes it. "Tell me the story of when you two met?"

Michael's eyebrow raises. "Didn't I already tell you how we met."

"You told me you met in college, but you didn't tell me any details."

Michael gazes at her for a moment and then goes back to the view. "Alright then, it was back in my community college days. I wanted to save some money by not going straight into the University. My very first class was the dreaded Biology 101. The class had a reputation for being one of the hardest first-year classes in the entire school. Most people passed the class, but few got an "A", and I was determined to be one of those few. Most of the students in the class avoided the front row, but I felt it gave me the best chance of learning everything I could. The only other person sitting in the front row was Matt, but at the time I had no idea who he was.

Matt's attention was on the teacher when my movement next to him caught his attention. He turned his head and leaned over, "Only "A" students sit in the front row," he said.

I laughed. My distracting chuckle did not amuse the professor and he momentarily paused the class to show his disapproval. The instructor taught for nearly an hour when the class bell rang and the class quickly burst into action, students stuffing their books into their perspective bags.

"Don't forget to read chapter two and answer the chapter questions for the next class," the professor announced.

Matt turned to me when he finished closing his bag. "I am thinking of starting a study group after school. Would you be interested?

The suggestion did appeal to me. "Sure, why not."

"Great, what's your number," he asked as he pulled out his phone.

I gave him my number, and he promptly thanked me. We started walking for the door side by side as we did.

"What degree are you studying for?" Matt adjusted the strap on his backpack.

"I'm studying to become a doctor," I replied.

Matt perked up to this. "Really?"

"Yes. Why?"

"That's what I'm doing! Do you know what you're going to specialize in?"

I felt the connection building between us already. "I'm not sure yet, I'm thinking about becoming a surgeon."

"Oh. You need a steady hand for that," Matt

said as if I did not know.

I stopped walking and held out my hand; it was steady.

Matt examined my hand looking for movement. "That's not bad. That should work."

We walked through the door and headed down the hall. Just when I thought I had seen him for the last time that day, Matt nudged me.

"Look, it's Arlene Smith!" Matt pointed down the hall.

I looked up to see a stunning, tall brunette walking towards us. Her hair was shiny and seemed to almost glow. She had long gorgeous legs and a short skirt to show them off. There was a large jock at her side talking up her ear.

"Who is she?" I asked.

"Arlene? She is only the most beautiful girl in the school."

"I can see why." I noticed the jock was doting over her like he was trying to claim her for himself.

"Is that her boyfriend?" I pointed at the jock.

Matt followed the path of my finger. "No that's Tim. He wishes. She flirts a lot but hasn't settled down with anyone yet. I plan to make her my girlfriend," Matt said half joking.

I gave him a look, "Really."

The corner of his mouth sank. "No. I'm sure she would never give me the time of day, but she's my dream girl."

Suddenly we heard something hit and then skip across the floor. I had no idea what it was. I was looking at Matt at the time. The object came to a rest at my feet as Matt and I suddenly stopped to investigate. I reached down and picked up the object, not sure from where it had come from. It was a cell phone, and I looked at it to figure out if I could determine whose it was.

"May I have my phone back please," a soft female voice asked as I analyzed the phone.

I looked up from the phone to see Arlene patiently holding out her hand. Her gorgeous smile seemed to light up the hall. I felt like a deer caught in headlights. She was not in the mood to wait for me to regain my bearing, so she reached for the phone and gently took it from my hand. Her soft skin slid against mine as she did.

"Thanks," she said as she tilted her head and gave me a quick peck on the cheek, then continued down the hall.

Tim gave me a quick, dirty look. A few moments later Matt playfully bumped into me.

"You just kissed Arlene Smith!"

"Not really. She kissed me." I looked over my shoulder as she walked away. It appeared as though she had already forgotten me.

"You lucky dog."

"She only kissed me on the cheek," I replied.

"I would kill just for that."

"It was no big deal."

"Did you see the look on Tim's face?"

"Yeah."

"He was so mad."

"Great, that's all I need, a jock who has it out for me running around." The corners of my mouth shrugged.

"You're as big as he is, you could definitely take him. Especially if I have your back," Matt insisted.

"You'd have my back?"

"Of course I would. Mostly because I would love to impress Arlene."

"I'm not sure if that would impress her," I said.

"I wish that phone had fallen at my feet. I would have turned and kissed her on the lips."

I looked back at Matt for a moment. "I'm not sure that would've gone over well. I'm pretty sure Tim would have punched you in the face."

"It would be worth it." Matt had a huge grin on face. I'm pretty sure he was fantasizing about the moment their lips would have met.

"So, when did you want to start this study group?" I asked changing the subject.

Matt shook out of his short daydream. "I was thinking about Thursday since the test is Friday. What do you think?"

"Thursday will work fine."

"5 PM, my place?" Matt started to text me his address assuming that would work for me.

"Sounds good," I replied.

"Ok, see you then." Matt turned and headed down the adjacent hall, and I headed for my next class.

Chapter 42

On Thursday afternoon, I knocked on the door to apartment two of the Ravenna apartments in the "U" district. The "U" district was the area closely surrounding the university. I had my book-bag slung over my shoulder and a pizza box in my hands. The door opened, and Matt smiled and greeted me.

"Come on in!" Matt said cheerfully, he was happy to see I had brought food. He was starving and did not have much to offer me in his fridge at the moment.

I was not sure if he was happier to see me or the pizza. "Thanks." I set the pizza on the dining table.

His place was nothing more than a studio apartment and was small. He did not need much, he lived alone, and city rents were high-priced. He was a starving college student, after all, so he needed to save as much money as he could, where ever he could.

The best thing about his place was it was not far from school, and it was all his. As long as he paid his rent anyway. He did not have much furniture. There was a dining table with three chairs, a small black futon in the small open area, and a frameless mattress and box spring covered in blankets sat in the back by the bathroom. The entire apartment couldn't have been more than 600 square feet. It was not much, but it was cozy. I set my bag on the floor and opened it. Matt's book was on the table, and he pulled up a seat and sat down at the table.

"Make yourself at home." Matt gestured to one of the free seats.

"Don't mind if I do."

Matt opened the pizza box; he was much too hungry to wait for me to did it. "This smells good!" Matt said. "And you added pineapple!"

"Is that bad?"

"No, I love pineapple on pizza!"

"I know, right! It just isn't pizza without the pineapple," I said.

Matt bit off a piece. "Oh, that is so good! If you keep this up, you'll be up for the position of best friend," Matt said sarcastically. At that time he had no idea how right he was.

We studied until it was late, and when I thought my mind would explode, I finally went home. I hoped I would retain the copious amounts of information I had just attempted to download in my brain. I wondered if I was pushing my mind too hard. I had a feeling I would soon find out.

*   *   *

The next day in class came the test and I could not have been more nervous. Matt and I had studied hard, but that was no guarantee of any success. It was my first college exam, and I was not sure what to expect. The test was laid in front of us by the professor, and it did not disappoint my expectations.

The first question on the test was challenging. It felt like a trick question. It seemed unclear, as depending on how you interpreted the inquiry it could change the answer. Fortunately, most of the remaining problems were a bit more cut and dry, but that first one threw me for a loop.

After I finished, I handed in my test and left the classroom and could not wait for the next day for my results. After classes ended for the day, Matt and I got together to discuss what we thought of the test.

"What did you think if that first question?" I asked.

"It was a trick question. I hear professor Dalton always puts one on his test to try and mess with students. He doesn't like anyone to get a perfect score."

"Well, I hope I did well. How did you feel you did?"

"I think I did well. Not sure how well but I passed for sure," Matt replied.

I told him I thought I had passed too.

"Do you have any plans for the weekend?" Matt asked.

"Not really, no."

"Would you like to hang out? Maybe play some pool?" I had played pool on several occasions and loved it. It seemed Matt and I had many common interests. I was beginning to like this guy.

"Sure! Sounds like fun," I said.

"OK, I know this great place. It's called the Dub Pub in Kirkland."

"I'll meet you there," I answered.

"Excellent!"

Later I met Matt at the bar. We had a great time playing pool and meeting women. It was clear from the very beginning we made a great team. We had chemistry you don't find often. In time, we developed a routine of studying and letting off steam after each test by going out. It was how we managed to keep our sanity through our rigorous college schedule.

It was not long before we were the best of friends. We spent most of our spare time together, helping each other in and out of class. We would often take the same courses and would save even more money by only purchasing one copy of the class textbook. We shared books, and when we moved to the University level, we shared a dorm room. In grad school, we shared an apartment. We continued to live together until he bought his new house. It was hard not seeing him at home every day, but we still hung out at work when we had the chance."

"I can see why it's hard." Roslyn's heart goes out to him.

Michael pulls out his phone.

"Is that the burner phone or whatever you called it?"

Michael looks at her lovingly. "Yes, it's a burner phone. It's a pay as you go phone and doesn't have any fancy features like a GPS. I made sure to purchase it with cash, and I'll get a new one in a couple of weeks. Hopefully, this will make it harder to track us." Michael checks his messages but looks disappointed.

"What's wrong?"

"I haven't heard from Matt in a couple of weeks now. I'm beginning to get worried."

"I'm sure he's fine," Roslyn replies.

"It's not like him not to say at least 'hi' for more than a couple of days."

"I'm sure he's just busy."

Michael gives her a dubious look. "He's never that busy."

Chapter 43

Several days later, Matt is in a small concrete detention room in the downtown Seattle FBI building. It is dark and has a thin concrete slab protruding from the wall at knee level for a bed. A small thin mattress pad and a threadbare blanket lie on the slab. The room is almost completely empty, other than himself, the bed and a small toilet. From the looks of it, Matt does not get the impression he is in a jail cell, but something more terrifying.

The conditions in the room are reminiscent of something he has only seen in movies in concentration camps. Matt lies on the mattress struggling to stay warm. The small blanket is not large enough to completely cover him unless he is in a fetal position. The windowless room is cold, and a single light hangs from the center of the ceiling dimly illuminating the room. A menacing metal door guards the entrance of the room.

Matt can not remember how long he has been here. It is difficult to keep track of the hours and days when there is no way for him to determine the passage of time. He does not have a watch, and there are no windows in the room to show if it is day or night. He still has his street clothes on, which consists of a navy t-shirt and blue jeans. His shoes, socks, wallet, watch, and all his personal items have been taken from him. He still can not believe this is happening to him.

What have I done to deserve this? He wonders.

The door to his cell opens, and two girthy men come in and jerk him up off the hard, concrete bed. They are both much stronger than Matt and easily drag him into an adjacent interrogation room. They sit him at a table, cuff him to his metal seat, and leave him alone. He feels like he has sat there for several hours when the door to the room finally opens, and Agent Grey enters.

"How are you doing Doctor?"

"How do you think?" Matt snarls.

"I'm sorry you've had to go through all this, but it's a matter of national security."

"National security, my ass," Matt says, clearly pissed off.

Grey pauses for a moment. "I'm here to help you, Doctor." He tilts his head in a friendly manner. "You want my help, don't you?" He pauses.

Matt looks unconvinced.

"But I need your help first."

"I'll never help you, asshole!" Matt replies defiantly.

"You need to help yourself. Do you see anyone here helping you?" Matt is silent.

"We need you to send a message to Michael," Grey continues.

"What kind of message?"

"Tell him the truth. That the FBI is holding you."

"Why would I do that?" Matt asks.

"If you don't, you'll spend the rest of your life rotting in that tiny cell," Grey explains.

Matt lowers his head and stares at his feet trying to figure out what Grey is up to and whether he should send a message or not. If he could tell Michael what was going on maybe he could alert the media or get a politician who needed to win some points with the public to help. He would not do it though if he thought for one second that it would get his friends in trouble. Grey is getting impatient with Matt's delayed response.

"Perhaps you need more time to think about this." Grey motions for the guards to take him away.

Matt awakes to a sudden noise but is not sure if it was real or imagined. He has been alone in his cell for what seems like at least a couple of weeks, from his recollection. It is hard to tell because he has lost track of time. There is no calendar to keep track of the days that have slipped away. His only indication of the amount of time passing is his regularly scheduled small, simple meals. He has been hungry for as long as he has been there. Hunger has become his only constant companion.

Hopelessness has set in, and his only peace comes from the thought his friends are safe miles away. His only escape from his cell is in his imagination. He often allows himself the luxury of dreaming himself far away. He often brings Michael, Roslyn, and, of course, a beautiful woman or possibly even two for himself. It is a fantasy, why can't he have two girls? He likes the idea of being on a deserted sunny beach far away from his captivity; it is a pleasant fiction. It almost seems real at times; his psyche is so broken down.

The door to his room suddenly opens, bringing him back to his hell on earth. He is never happy to mentally return to his cell after spending hours on his beach. As always, the FBI men don't say a word, they pick him up and carry him back to the dreadful interrogation room. His body has grown week from lack of use and food. Matt knows their routine by now.

He goes through the motions in his mind.

Now, they cuff me to the chair, he tells himself. *Now, they leave the room, and I'll wait for an hour or two for the dumb ass to show his face. Maybe I have time to go back to the beach.*

He is shocked when a few moments later, the door opens.

This is odd, he thinks. They n*ormally make me wait for hours. They must be in a hurry*.

It is Grey, just much earlier than expected. The Agent pulls out a chair and sits down and folds his hands on the table. He sits there for a few moments looking Matt over as if he is analyzing him for some reason. The agent taps one of his fingers on the back of his hand in the folded cluster. Matt does not look directly at him. He just keeps staring at the table. He can feel Grey's eyes crawling over him, it is a very unpleasant feeling.

Grey takes in a deep breath, and finally, he speaks. "It seems," he takes a frustrated pause, "that your friends don't care about you. It has been several days since you sent them your message, and they haven't responded. It is clear they're going to leave you here to rot."

Matt does not budge, does not acknowledge the agent in any way. Matt does not want his friends to come. He does not want them captured by these terrible people.

"Your usefulness here has come to an end. You're being executed in three days," Grey is lying, but Matt does not know that.

This caught Matt's attention though. He looks up into Grey's face. "F . . . for what crime?" Matt can barely speak he is so weak, his own voice sounds shrill to him. Having no one to talk to in his cell his voice has rarely been used.

"You're being transferred to a federal prison where you'll be put to death by lethal injection."

Matt has lost his strength to fight. He can only merely sit there, helplessly pondering his death sentence. He can not believe he is here. He is a well-respected doctor. He has worked hard and done his best to be a law-abiding citizen. He even paid his taxes. Now, he is on death row, without having had a trial or his day in court. His rights have been stripped away. Dogs have more rights than he does right now. He has done nothing wrong, and this terrible man on a power trip somehow seems to have the right to do this to him.

What has the world come to, he ponders.

Chapter 44

The next day Matt is handcuffed and taken from his cell by two uniformed officers. These guys are not the same officers he has dealt with in the past. The sight of someone new gives him hope.

Maybe these guys are different. Maybe they don't know what's going on here. "H . . Help me," he pleads.

The officers ignore his pleas.

"H . . . Help me. I'm an American citizen. I have rights." he implores them.

"Quiet!" One of the officers orders.

He can see it is hopeless. He finds no assistance with these two men. They appear to be no different than the others and do not seem to care what is going on. His spirits fall even further. He is helpless to do anything to help himself. He is brought to an elevator, and they hastily walk him in. One of the officers hits the button for the parking garage, and the elevator begins to slowly move. Once in the garage, the doors open, and the gloom of the fluorescent lights of the underground garage is all around him. It seems so depressing to him, which surprises him in his predicament. He does not think it was possible to sink any further.

Meanwhile, Grey is carefully setting up his real-life chessboard. He is barking orders over a radio, while he watches the monitors at his command station. William's watching over his shoulder.

"Team one, are you set?" Grey asks.

"Team one, foot patrol set on parking garage exit," a man's voice answers.

"Team two, are you set?"

"Team two, chase vehicle one set at location bravo," the other answers.

"Team three, are you set?" Grey questions.

"Team three, chase vehicle two set at location Delta."

Grey is starting to feel comfortable with his board when William gets his attention.

"Grey, camera three just went out," William says with some concern.

"What?"

"That's the parking garage level," William added. "Do we have anyone down there?"

"Other than our two guards, no," Grey replies. Grey raises the mic to his mouth. "I need a team in the parking garage, now!"

The two guards continue to lead Matt, half dragging him, until they reach an unmarked black patrol vehicle in the garage. One of the officers holds him as the other opens the back passenger door. The officer holding Matt suddenly starts to shake violently. He let out a faint, incoherent sound and falls to the ground, still reeling. The other officer turns to see what is happening when a small pronged device strikes him in the leg, and he, too, starts to shake violently. He also falls to the ground convulsing, and both are out cold.

"Are you ok, Matt," a familiar voice asks.

The prisoner turns to see Michael holding a TASER he has just deployed into one of the officers. Roslyn is with him and is sporting a dark backpack. She too is carrying a TASER she has used on the other officer. Matt is happy to see his friends. They received the email notification of his incarceration and are here to free him.

"Boy, am I glad to see you two," Matt says in his frail voice.

"Ok, boys, let's save the heart felt reunion for a better time. We have to get out of here, and right now." Roslyn picks up the unconscious officer's keys from his waistband and tosses them to Michael. "It won't be long till they notice the video feed to this area is out." Roslyn quickly removes a shirt from one of the unconscious officers and takes his hat and assists Michael in putting them on.

Roslyn then ushers Matt into the backseat and closes the door. Michael moves the two officers just enough to be able to pull the car out without running them over. He then jumps into the driver's seat, puts the keys in the ignition and starts the patrol vehicle. He pops the trunk, and Roslyn hops in, closing the lid behind her.

Michael pulls the car out of the stall and heads for the exit. He draws a pair of sunglasses off the sun visor and puts them on.

"What's going on down there?" Grey screams into the mic.

The officer at the exit gate responds. "We don't have eyes on the vehicle yet sir. Wait, here they come now. Everything seems fine."

"Are you sure?" Grey starts to calm down a little.

"Yes, sir. I see officer Keener in the patrol vehicle right now."

The patrol vehicle approaches the gate, and Michael waves to the guard, who waves back and opens the gate. No sooner have they exited the parking garage, three officers bolt out of the parking garage elevator. The pursuing officers see the two unconscious men on the floor of the parking garage.

One of the officers raises his radio to his mouth. "They're getting away, close the gate!"

The guard at the gate complies, but it was too late, they are out!

Grey hears the announcement. "Do we have eyes on them?!" he barks into the radio.

"Yes, team one has marked the vehicle," a voice says over the radio.

"Team two has marked the vehicle," a second voice said.

"Team three is on the move! The GPS tracker signal is strong, we know exactly where they are," a young agent says over the radio proudly.

"I want a GPS tracker pad right now!" Grey screams.

"I guess there was a hole in our trap," William states.

Grey glares at him for a moment. It is hard for him not to take his comment as an attack on his competence. The young man with them has anticipated Grey's request and hands him a small electronic pad. Grey's a little surprised that this rookie is on top of things. He takes the device from the young agent's hand.

"Let's go!" Grey orders.

William and Grey run towards the stairs, they are not going to wait for the elevator. The pair race down the stairs nearly tripping, they are moving so quickly. They fly through the doors to the garage and bolt for their government-issued SUV. The engine fires up with a loud roar! The tires squeal as they make haste with no time to waste. The gate to the garage can not open fast enough, it seems to take forever.

Grey turns on his flashing lights and is out the driveway like a racehorse out of the chute! He speeds down the streets, following the blinking dot on his new GPS tracking pad, William holds the pad so Grey can see it clearly as Grey drives.

"Team two, where are you at?" Grey speaks into the radio.

"We're on Pine, headed west following the target vehicle."

"Don't lose them; the suspects are in one of our patrol vehicles!" Grey explains. "Where're they headed now?" They just turned south on 1st Ave. They're headed for highway 99."

William analyzes the direction of the blinking dot's travel for a moment and confirms their location. "It looks like they're going to try to get on the highway!" he replies.

Grey pulls the mic to his radio back to his mouth. "Dispatch, get a unit on every on-ramp to 99. I want every on-ramp between Lenora and Yesler, closed down now!"

Dispatch complies, and the order goes out.

Michael is driving like a man possessed, he is desperate to get out of the city. Matt pulls the release lever for the seat next to him. It folds forward, and Roslyn tosses her backpack forward and climbs out of the trunk and pushes the seat back into place.

"Did you hear that? They've closed off all the on-ramps to 99!" Matt states a little frazzled and doing his best to aid Roslyn to her seat.

"Yeah, I heard!" Michael replies. The radio in their car squawks loudly. "They won't stay on this channel long, they have to know we're listening."

"What are we going to do now?" Matt asks a little frantic.

"Change of plans," Michael says as they approach the on-ramp.

They can see a squad car just now moving to block the entrance. He turns the wheel hard and turns down a side street headed east.

"How do they know where we are going?" Matt asks.

"They're tracking us!" Roslyn states.

"And they're following us!" Matt's looking out of the rear window.

"What?" Michael exclaims.

"That's an unmarked patrol vehicle behind us, or my name's not Matt."

Michael looks through the rear mirror; a white van is closely following. The men inside definitely look like they are cops. Michael turns the car, and the white van turns with them.

"You see! They're following us," Matt yells.

Roslyn opens her backpack and pulls out a smaller bag.

"What's that?" Matt asks.

"This is our tail buster."

"What the heck is a tail buster."

"This will get rid of our tail," Roslyn explains.

Matt still looks confused.

She does not have time to explain this further. "You'll see."

She opens the smaller bag and pulls out a thin rope with spiked stars that resemble a jumbo set of jumping jacks fastened to it in four-inch intervals. The stars have long sharp ends and are sure to shred any tire that have the misfortune of running over it. She opens the rear driver's side window and sticks her torso out of the window.

She tosses the line of spiked stars towards the front driver's side tire of the trailing patrol vehicle. The rope spreads out, and the stars hit the ground and bounce up and wrap around the front tire. The spikes puncture the tire in several places instantly flattening it. The van pulls hard to the left and strikes a street light!

"Holy crap!" Matt says. "What was that and why did you have it on you?"

Roslyn is pleased with herself. "It was an idea I cooked up years ago. I figured if I was ever chased in my car that I would use it to get away. It always pays to be prepared."

Matt looks at her curiously. "I guess so."

"Nice work!" Michael says. "We have to find a new getaway vehicle." Michael turns down another street to keep their movements unpredictable. "We have to get back to my car."

"Where is your car?" Matt asks.

"It's a few blocks from the FBI building!"

"What? Where we just busted out of?" Matt asks, disturbed by the thought.

"Yeah," Michael says.

"We can't go back there, that's suicide," Matt replies, terrified of being caught and put back in his cage.

"If you have a better plan, I'm open to suggestions." Michael turns down yet another street.

"That may not be a terrible idea," Roslyn states. "That's what raccoons do to lose hunters and their dogs, they backtrack. It's the last thing they'll expect."

"News flash, we aren't raccoons!" Matt blurts out more terrified than ever. "And we're being tracked!"

"Yes, but right now, every officer in the area is moving to the perimeter of the city. If we head for the center, it'll give us time to consider our next move," Roslyn explains.

"If we do that, we'll be trapped in the city," Matt points out.

"We're already trapped. They are closing every exit in the city, as we speak. There's no way out right now. We need to regroup and find another way out," Roslyn explains.

Michael wrestles with the wheel again and heads back to towards the FBI building. A few moments later, a huge, black SUV with lights flashing, speeds around the corner and pulls in behind their vehicle.

Matt looks out the back window. "Shit! We have company!" Matt can see Grey behind the wheel with a determined look.

Michael glances into the rearview mirror with a grimace. He turns down another street and stomps on the accelerator hard. The SUV turns with them and continues to gain on them, undaunted. Michael sees an appealing alley and turns again at such speed the they slide around the corner, and its rear end strikes a garbage can, crumpling it. The following SUV turns the corner right after, and both cars speed down the narrow alley.

The passage ends abruptly, and Michael turns the wheel as they round another corner. The pursuing SUV speeds up and strikes the rear of their car while still in their turn. Their stolen car spins around as the tires scream. Seconds later the car crashes into the side of a brick building. The right rear bumper and side of the vehicle crumbles and the rear window shatters into a thousand pieces as the they come to a stop.

Michael turns the wheel and slams it into reverse and tries to pull away from the sturdy structure. Grey stomps on the gas as they meet head to head. Grey pushes them into the buildings concrete staircase trapping them like rats. The two automobiles come to a sudden crashing halt still facing each other, their front ends crumple.

Michael's vehicle is pinned between the SUV and the stairway that protrudes from a corner of the building. Michael shifts into first and floors the gas pedal. The tires squeal and smoke as they inch forward. Michaels's automobile moves forward pushing Grey's vehicle. Grey presses on the gas and his SUV strains back, forcing Michael's vehicle back into the corner so hard the fender and bumper crumple further.

"We're trapped," Matt yells.

"Let's get out of here and head for Pike Place market," Roslyn yells.

The doors to the car spring open, and the threesome bolt out of the vehicle. Michael assists Matt, who is having trouble breaking into a full run. Matt's adrenaline surges and he finds new strength as the friends scamper down the alley.

Chapter 45

"Shit!" William yells as he watches the fleeing felons race down the passageway.

Grey puts the SUV in reverse and adeptly pulls his car out of the corner. The metal groans as the vehicles release each other from their entanglement. He slams on the gas and sends the SUV lurching in pursuit. Michael continues to aid Matt as they dash down the alley. Roslyn tries to help as well but is unable to do much. The last afternoon sun drains her vampire strength. The SUV gains on them rapidly. Michael does not think they will get to the end of the alley in time as they race for the outlet.

"Run them down!" William yells.

"Goodbye Roslyn," Grey bellows as he pushes the gas pedal to the floor!

They are near the opening. Grey's SUV looms over the trio as the SUV speeds towards a crushing death blow! As they exit the outlet, Roslyn and Michael leap to the side trying their best to drag Matt with them. Matt's strength is completely depleted and he is unable to make the leap. He falls to the ground as the speeding SUV tramples his legs. Roslyn and Michael spring back to their feet unharmed. After the would-be assassin races by, the pair goes back to Matt's side. They try to lift him when he screams in pain.

"My leg is broken! Leave me! Go, get out of here!" Matt yells.

Grey slams on the brakes and turns the SUV violently! The couple continues to attempt to get Matt to his feet, but his leg is badly broken and no longer functions. His other limb is badly bruised and moving him is hopeless.

"Leave! Now! Before it's too late!" Matt begs.

The SUV's tires squeal, and the death machine heads right towards them! Michael and Roslyn have no choice but to leave their friend behind. They scurry down another alley as fast as their legs will carry them. Another police vehicle slides around the corner and blocks their escape route. They turn down an adjacent open street, racing as fast as they can.

Their hearts pound, their muscles ache, but there is no stopping now! Grey's SUV turns the corner with high speed and continues the pursuit into the street. Now in the open, the distance is too long. They will never make it to the end of the road in time. Michael and Roslyn move out of the street and rush down the sidewalk hoping it would provide some protection, but the SUV jumps the curb, striking Michael! He is knocked off his feet and hits the windshield of the SUV, shattering it.

The impact sends Michael hurtling through the air and into the side of a building where his body smashes into the structure and falls to the concrete walkway. He comes to a violent and sudden stop with a loud thud. The SUV barely slows down as it continues down the sidewalk chasing Roslyn. Just before it strikes her, she turns quickly into another alley, barely escaping!

She rolls across the passageway on her back and knees as the SUV pulls back on the street, dogging a few cars and pedestrians in the process. A speeding truck barrels down the alley where Roslyn is kneeling, when the driver notices Roslyn! He slams on his brakes and his tires screech. His car slows and ultimately stops just in time!

"Are you crazy?" the man screams from the cab of the truck through his open window.

Roslyn has no time to debate the issue with the driver and immediately gets back to her feet and runs to Michael. She can see he is right where he had fallen and has not moved. When she reaches him, he isn't moving. She turns him slightly, only to see the grim sight of blood covering his face. It looks bad, really bad. His eyes are closed, and he looks like death has taken him.

"Mike!" she screams, but there is no response.

She listens for the sound of breathing and checks for a pulse. She can feel a faint heartbeat; he is barely alive. The menacing SUV finally turns itself around and heads right for the couple.

"End this!" William insists.

Grey forces the accelerator down once again, more determined than ever. The menacing vehicle speeds directly for Roslyn and the injured man.

"Mike, we have to move!" Roslyn begins to sob, blood tears streaming down her cheeks.

He makes no movement and death is taking him. She stares at the oncoming SUV and then down at Michael.

"We have to get out of here, my love!" she begs, but still, he makes no sign of life.

She gazes lovingly at his face. She has resolved herself to their fate.

"If we die, we die together," she says softly, focusing only on his face and ignoring the oncoming vehicle of death. "Goodbye, my love," she whispers, moving her face next to his.

If he dies, she does not wish to continue any longer. The murderous vehicle will only deliver them back together on the other side of death. The SUV jumps the curb and is nearly on them when a massive white truck smashes into it's side. The SUV careens into the brick building only a foot or two from the duo, with a deafening, thunderous crash! The occupants of the SUV are rendered unconscious by the forceful impact that cripples their vehicle and stops it suddenly.

Roslyn looks up, surprised to be alive and untouched. Someone gets out of the driver's side of the large white truck and walks around to Roslyn. As soon as she sees him, she recognizes him immediately!

"Lucius!" she yells. "I thought they'd killed you!"

"It takes more than a Van Helsing to kill me," the tall Scandinavian says in his deep voice.

He towers over Roslyn, his shoulder-length blond hair shining in the sun.

She notices he is holding a rifle. "What's that for?"

He looks up into the sky. "We have one more bug to get rid of."

He aims the rifle at the police helicopter that hovers a few hundred feet above. He fires a round, striking it in the windscreen. The pilot does not hesitate to vacate the area. He lowers his rifle and tosses it in the bed of his truck.

He turns to Roslyn. "Now, let's get out of here." He holds out his hand.

"I'm not leaving without Michael," she insists.

His face wrinkles a little. "What do you want with a mortal. We don't have time to bring a snack along," he replies.

"He's not a snack!" she protests.

"He's not going to make it. He's in bad shape."

"I don't care. I'm taking him with me."

Knowing there is no time to argue with her, he sighs, "Very well."

Even without his vampire strength, he easily hoists the hefty man off the ground and onto his massive shoulder. He holds out his other hand and pulls Roslyn to her feet.

"Come on," he insists.

"Wait! We have to get Matt!" she pleads.

"There's no time!" he raises his voice.

He is done arguing and is not going to give her a choice. He takes hold of her wrist and leads her down the road, through a narrow alley, and down several small streets. They turn again into an abandoned building.

"Where're you taking us?" she asks.

"I'm taking you home."

Once inside he leads her into a vacant side room. Lucius opens a hidden panel in the floor that leads to an old staircase. They hurry down the steps and close the door behind them. They descended twenty feet underground where the narrow stairs open to an abandoned underground street-like passageway. Rustic buildings constructed into the walls line both sides of the ancient drive. The passage opens to a labyrinth of passageways that lead down old stone and brick walkways with even more old builds on either side of the street.

The old structures that line the walls seem to be built into the stone walls and appear heavily worn from use and time. Some are made of old wood, some of brick, and still others of stone and mortar. It feels like a hodgepodge of various construction and architectural styles, all blended in harmonious chaos.

"What is this place?" She asks with wonder.

"This is the old Seattle underground."

It is a strange sight to behold. The new city

had been erected right above the old one, and the ancient city was abandoned with time. Lucius leads her to a small structure that seems to be in better repair than most of the other structures. It almost looks like someone lives there. He escorts her inside and he lays Michael down on a dusty couch in a room that has some resemblance to a living room. He then sits in a nearby chair that groans under his massive weight. Roslyn goes to Michael's side.

Lucius finally feels safe now. "He's in bad shape. I can hear his heart fading. He doesn't have long." Lucius seems almost too calm for their situation.

Roslyn runs her fingers through Michael's hair with blood tears building in her eyes.

"You should finish him off. His blood will strengthen you. You'll need your strength for what lies ahead," Lucius states.

"And what's ahead?"

"A war is coming. We need to prepare. We need to build a new kingdom and an army. This place is perfect for my plans." He waves his hand, to indicate the whole underground and sitting in his chair like it was a throne.

"What are you talking about?"

"Do you think it's a coincidence that you found yourself drawn to Seattle?"

"I came to Seattle because the sun is less intense here," she replies.

He grins. "That's what you may think. The truth is that I summoned you here."

Puzzled, she questions him, "How? For what purpose?"

He is pleased to finally tell her his plans he has been working on for over a year now. He wishes to share his genius. "I have the power to summon all of my children. You are the strongest and the last. I've summoned you here so you can take your place at my side . . . as my queen." He speaks as though it is a great honor.

"As you are well aware by now, the older we get, the more powerful we become. I need a formidable queen by my side to help me build the new vampire kingdom and my army. You're nearly as old as I. You are the perfect choice to be my queen. Together we will make a new army of vampires to fight the humans who would destroy us."

Roslyn turns back to Michael.

Lucius continues undaunted. "Recently, I was nearly killed by Van Helsing and his FBI bastards. Although they have actively hunted my children, I've never seen them as a great danger to myself until now. Now I see them for the threat that they are, and together we will put an end to this menace once and for all!"

Roslyn does not seem impressed. "And if I say no?" she asks turning back to Lucius.

"You don't have a choice. If you don't join me, the hunters will find you and destroy you. Just as they nearly did today. If you refuse, you will no longer be under my protection. Do you think it's a coincidence you've made it this far? I have always been there to protect you. Most of the time you had no idea I was there. Sometimes I had no choice but to reveal myself to save you. Who do you think pulled you out of the river? You would have drowned if I hadn't."

Roslyn knows exactly what he is saying. He had managed to be in the right place at the right time on several occasions. She does not want to admit owing her life to him, but she can not deny it.

Lucius turns his gaze from her back to Michael. "Looks like your friend is done."

Roslyn looks back at Michael. "What . . NO!"

"After ending so many lives, I know the sound of a heart that's about to stop beating. It's unmistakable. Can't you hear it?" he asks lifting his head and closing his eyes as if to listen more carefully.

Roslyn's much too upset to concentrate on anything, let alone the faint noise of Michael's heart. She finally gathers her thoughts and focuses on the beat. She can hear the terrible sound of his heart entering its final ending rhythm.

"He only has moments," Lucius states.

Roslyn's heart sinks, fear squeezes her chest.

"No . . . I will not lose you! I can't lose you!"

She knows there is only one thing to do to save him; her fear is gone. All she can think about is saving Michael. Roslyn finally gives in to her desperation. She does not care about the consequence anymore. She bites her lip hard, and blood oozes from the wound in her lip.

Lucius looks down curiosity. "What are you doing?"

Roslyn moves her lips to Michael's and kisses him. Michael does not budge and exhibits no sign of life. She fills his mouth with her blood and continues to kiss him. She softly massages his mouth as if to pump the blood into him.

Lucius laughs. "It's too late my Queen. He is done."

Roslyn ignores the Scandinavian and kisses Michael again and massages his lips and mouth for several minutes, hoping somehow her blood will save him.

Lucius dislikes the sight of his new queen locking lips with a mortal, and he stands. "I'll be around if you need me. I'll leave you to it. I tire of this futile gesture."

He then walks out of the building and closes the door behind him. Several more minutes pass, and still no sign of life from Michael. Finally, Roslyn stops, it is no use. She lowers her head.

"I'm sorry, my love," she whispers.

Red tears begin to stream down the sides of her beautiful face. She gently holds his hand in hers. She has no desire to move, no desire to breathe, no desire to continue. Her will to live has ended. She sits for what seems like hours, unable to move under the incredible weight of her deep despair. Time stands still in her moment of agony.

Suddenly Michael's hand twitches in hers, Roslyn perks up.

Had she imagined it?

She gazes at his face with hope, only to see there is no sign of life or any movement. Her optimism begins to fade again, then his lips twitch!

He did move; she rejoices with continued hope.

He groans softly.

Roslyn anxiously leans over him. "I'm here, my love! Come back to me!" she pleads.

Michael suddenly takes in a deep gasping breath! She lean over his face; she wants him to clearly see her.

"Mike!" she cries.

Michael's eyes gradually open . . . they glisten ruby red!

The End?

About the Author

Joe Black is an Author, Magician, and Hypnotist who lives in Washington State. He has performed as a professional entertainer since 1996. Joe created his own entertainment company and is the CEO of Black Magic Entertainment. He honorably served for six years in the Marine Corps.
He has written several books to include:
"The Spirit Among Us"
"Pat the Panther"
"Premonitions"
"Turmoil"
His website is BlackMagicEntertainent.com

Intro:

Deep in the Seattle underground lies a frightful, harrowing secret. An immortal creature with incredible power and abilities lurks in the shadows. This creature of unnatural origins plucks its victims off Seattle's crime-ridden streets, feasting on the ambrosial blood of evildoers. The government has plans for this gifted creature of the night. To turn it into an ultimate, unstoppable weapon they will use against enemies of the government both foreign and domestic.

Once in the hands of the government, this great and appalling weapon will give the government the power to probe the minds of anyone it chooses. They want to discover everyone's deepest darkest secrets. This new power to violate the minds of people is sure to only further corrupt an already corrupt entity. Aided by a family hell-bent on destroying vampires forever, the newly formed alliance has hunted down and eradicated all the creatures of darkness, but one. This sole remaining being is the alliance's last chance to create this powerful weapon, but the vampire has plans of its own!

18399331R00222

Made in the USA
San Bernardino, CA
20 December 2018